Tell
Me

Tell
Me

stories

Joe Baumann

Curbstone Books / Northwestern University Press
Evanston, Illinois

Curbstone Books
Northwestern University Press
www.nupress.northwestern.edu

This is a work of fiction. Names, characters, places, and incidents either are the
product of the author's imagination or are used fictitiously, and any resemblance
to actual persons, living or dead, business establishments, events, or locales is
entirely coincidental.

Printed in the United States of America

10   9   8   7   6   5   4   3   2   1

Library of Congress Cataloging-in-Publication Data

Names: Baumann, Joe, 1985– author.
Title: Tell me : stories / Joe Baumann.
Description: Evanston, Illinois : Curbstone Books/Northwestern University
    Press, 2024.
Identifiers: LCCN 2024002011 | ISBN 9780810147300 (paperback) | ISBN
    9780810147317 (ebook)
Subjects: LCGFT: Short stories.
Classification: LCC PS3602.A96276 B38 2024 | DDC 813.6—dc23
LC record available at https://lccn.loc.gov/2024002011

For teachers everywhere, but especially mine.

CONTENTS

The Vanisher

The bandana made Hyland disappear.

Disappear wasn't quite the right word. It wasn't like a finger snap, the sound there for a second and then gone. His body didn't slurp out of the world into a translucent nothingness. Instead, Hyland turned into a vague, blurry thing, and if he stood still long enough, he and his clothes would blend in with his surroundings, body taking on the color of the signs buzzing behind him about Bud Light Lime and two-for-one cosmos. But the bandana didn't affect the things he touched, so someone taking a break from the greenhouse of the dance floor and looking in his direction would see what appeared to be a pint glass full of Fat Tire floating chest high.

He'd felt silly the first time he put on the bandana, proffered by his roommate Nolan while he tried to convince Hyland to go clubbing at Booth. They stood in their shared bathroom that smelled like artificial lemon. While Nolan smeared his hair with pomade, Hyland practiced standing still, letting his form blend in with the cheap towels strung messily on the rack bolted to the back of the door. Nolan was whistling and nodding, looking back at Hyland in the mirror.

"See?" he said. "You'll be fine."

The bandana was a gift meant to assuage Hyland's nerves about stepping foot in Booth, where half-naked men, all more muscular and smooth than Hyland could ever dream of being, danced and flirted in a glossy slalom, taking breaks to glug down Washington apple shots and citrus martinis. A way, Nolan said, for Hyland to make himself comfortable, invisible enough to take in the scenery until he was ready to merge into the throng.

"And if I don't want to merge?"

"Maybe meet someone then."

"And if I don't do that either?"

Nolan rinsed the excess pomade from his fingers. "You will find someone. You found Beth, didn't you?"

"She was different."

"How was she different?"

"Well, she found me, first of all."

"Okay," Nolan said. "Someone else will find you."

"Not if I'm invisible."

Nolan shook his head. Hyland smiled. He did like his teeth, if nothing else. Certainly more than the biceps he couldn't get to grow no matter how many curls and pull-ups he sweated out at the gym. When Nolan rushed out of the bathroom to put on his shoes and answer a text that had announced itself with its electronic chirp, Hyland lifted his shirt and pinched at the small layer of fat covering the abdominals he knew the clubbers at Booth would be scrunching and flexing and showing off while electronica blasted from oversize speakers.

His hand was shaky as he held it out to be stamped by the bouncer, a cement block of a man with frosted tips and a T-shirt so tight it must have been cutting off his circulation. The bouncer smirked, gave Hyland a once over, counting the imperfections and deciding whether they outweighed the pros of letting him in. He curled his lip like a snarling dog and, by some miracle or mathematical error, put Hyland in the plus column, waving him and Nolan through. They bought their drinks, screaming into the ear of the shirtless bartender with shoulders like balled fists and abs like a tic-tac-toe board. He nodded and winked at Hyland when he ordered his beer.

Nolan disappeared into the throng after Hyland cinched the bandana on his head in the graffiti-laden bathroom that smelled of latex and piss. Someone whistled in the stall next to the sinks, booted feet stomping to the music. Hyland then pushed himself into the darkest corner of the club he could find and watched. When he finished his beer, he didn't venture across the dance floor until Nolan appeared.

"You're really good at standing still," he said. "I almost didn't see you."

Standing beside Nolan was a tall, clean-shaven man. Unlike Nolan, the man was still fully clothed, though his tank top did reveal dripping blue veins laid over muscled arms, the flared wings of strong lats peeking through the fabric. The man wasn't smiling, exactly, but he didn't look unhappy to have been hauled over either.

"This is Ethan," Nolan said. "Take off the bandana."

Hyland said nothing and didn't move except to pretend there was still enough beer for a last, languorous swig from his pint glass, his body shimmering back into focus for a moment before fading away when Hyland stopped moving.

"Come on," Nolan said.

Hyland sighed and plucked off the bandana.

"Hi," Ethan said, extending a hand. His teeth glowed in the neon lights, and his grip was strong, fingers smooth and warm.

Nolan led them around the edge of the dance floor, where Hyland swore he could see sweat flying like the spit off a sprinkler. Where one dancer ended and another began was a blurry uncertainty of skin.

The bartender laid out three shots before them. Ethan turned to Hyland and offered a silent toast. They took their shots and Ethan frowned, sticking out his tongue and waggling his head like an eighteen-year-old who has just slurped down his first hit of Popov.

"I'm new at this," Ethan said, waving a hand around him.

"Me too," Hyland said.

"You guys chat," Nolan said, snapping his finger at the bartender and pantomiming pouring two beers. He spun toward the throng.

"Your friend is interesting," Ethan said.

"He's like the Energizer Bunny. And he's not new at this."

"We all start somewhere, I guess."

While Nolan's short frame bobbed in the flood of dancing torsos and arms, Hyland gave Ethan another quick scan. His hair was cropped short, shiny with sweat like every other surface in Booth, and he had a sharp jaw, jutted forward with a shadow of underbite that looked good on him. Hyland wasn't sure what to do with his hands, so he palmed the bandana, which he'd shoved into his back pocket. It felt like a ball bearing pressing against his skin.

"Cheers," Hyland said, picking up his glass. "To being new at this."

Ethan connected their pints. "To being new."

———

They drank two more beers each. Nolan dashed from the dance floor and waved down the bartender for another round of shots, this time something fiery and cinnamon that burned going down. Hyland coughed and shook his head. Then Ethan announced that he had to work the next morning. He shook Hyland's hand again, his hard grip pinching at Hyland's bones.

"Tell me something," Nolan said when Ethan was gone. "What's wrong with you?"

"What?"

"How could you let him just leave?"

"What was I supposed to do? Tackle him? Hold him hostage in the bathroom? Tie him up with this?" Hyland wriggled the bandana at Nolan.

"Or you could have just given him your phone number."

"Oh."

Nolan rolled his eyes. "So it's a good thing I did before I even introduced you."

"What?"

"I knew you'd mess it up, so I gave him your number."

"Before we even met."

"Yes."

"And he also gave me his. To give to you. You want it?"

⸻

Hyland disappeared again, back into the corner. He felt the heat of his cell phone in his pocket as he watched Nolan, whose eyes had gone glossy with drink, his forehead slippery with sweat as he danced and pawed at a tree of a man whose chest was swirled with hair. Nolan had taken Hyland's phone, plucking it from Hyland's hands like he was snatching an apple from a bin, and programmed in Ethan's number.

"You should send him a text," Nolan had said. His body was wiry and jouncing to the beat of the music while they leaned against the bar.

"Now?"

"God, did Beth do everything in your relationship? Did she buy the condoms, too?"

Hyland coughed and scowled.

"Sorry. That was uncalled for."

"You're right." Hyland then unspooled the bandana, and despite Nolan's objections, he stuffed himself in the corner while Nolan, who promised they would leave in thirty minutes, returned to the fray.

Noland was, if nothing else, a promise keeper, and in exactly thirty minutes, Hyland watched him detach himself from his most recent dance partner, who wore a pink mesh shirt that displayed a hairless, fatless body, and come pouncing over to the corner.

Without a word he snatched at Hyland, yanking off the bandana. Hyland felt the swoop of coloration, his vanishing act whirling away like a thrown baton.

"There you are. Let's get out of here, huh?"

Drunk Nolan always tried to seduce Hyland, his tongue loosening itself like a rotted board, eyes fluttering and cartoonish in size. They had an understanding: Hyland would tolerate these alcohol-spiked flirtations, waving them off as driven by too much tequila and gin; in the morning, after a handful of ibuprofen and a greasy takeout burger, Nolan would assure Hyland that he wanted only to be roommates and friends, even if nonsober Nolan was interested in seeing what was hidden behind Hyland's belt buckle.

Nolan stumbled into their apartment, flicking off his shoes with sanguine ease but tripping along the wall; Hyland, following, was sober enough to keep his words crisp, vision straight, and steps regular while Nolan charged toward the kitchen to raid the fridge, plucking the door open and grabbing the soggy box of leftover crab rangoon from lunch, shoving a wonton into his mouth with crumbly abandon. He took a slug of orange juice, pulp gathering at the corner of his lips like an infection, then let out a vodka-tinged belch. He waggled the Styrofoam container toward Hyland, where the last rangoon rattled. Hyland shook his head and marched to the bathroom to brush his teeth and glug down a glass of water.

When he emerged, Nolan was lying on the couch; he regularly fell asleep there, streaming uninteresting tennis matches on the television, the announcers' Eastern European accents strangling Hyland's understanding of their commentary. The court was bright pink, and two women howled as they slapped the ball across the net. Without a word, Hyland slunk into his bedroom. As he was about to shut the door, Nolan yelled out: "Send him a text! Use a sexy emoji!"

Hyland stared at his phone. He squinted, fingers hovering over the digital keyboard's squashed letters, and started typing. He deleted each word he wrote. Then he darkened the screen and set the phone on his nightstand next to his alarm clock and box of tissues. He flicked off the reading lamp. Shrouded in darkness, he felt the heaviness of his comforter, the give of his mattress under his spine, the puff of pillow as it cupped his neck.

He and Ethan hadn't touched except for the goodbye hand-shake, but Hyland felt a strange linkage, a hooking in his stomach, as if the two had hugged, gripping at each other's lower backs, chins pressed on clavicles. He imagined the sensation was nothing like holding Beth, who was birdy, all bones and sharp points. He tried to picture the hard strength of Ethan's body, the tautness of his lips, how much power would flow through a kiss delivered by his mouth. Hyland felt the stirring warmth of an erection.

He leaned down over the side of the bed where he'd let his jeans pool in a cobra of fabric and pulled out the bandana; Nolan had not demanded it back. He unfurled it, smoothed out the wrinkles, folded it, and cinched it around his forehead, the knot a square against the back of his skull. Then Hyland laid down and let it work its magic.

The vanishing felt like a buzzing, as if his body was turning into champagne. His toes tingled, and a dotting, like ants were crawling along his skin, crept up past his knees, crotch, hips, belly button. He interrupted his disappearance to peel away his boxers, slingshotting them toward the closed closet door. It began again, and Hyland watched as his features—ankles, kneecaps, groin, elbows—melted into the white fabric of his bed.

The only men Hyland had ever seen naked were his high school basketball teammates, when they pulled down their mesh shorts in the locker room that smelled like old feta cheese; unlike Nolan, he'd never actually slept with another man, so he could only invent the pressure of muscle, the bristle of stubble against his lips and throat, the feel of hip bones and thick pecs. He'd watched porn, of course, but scenes of anal sex scalded him, a trench of discomfort settling in his stomach like a peach pit when he tried to imag-ine the pleasure on-screen. When he'd whispered a confession to

Beth about his sexual orientation, the word *bi* had lodged tight and heavy in his throat. She'd stared at him and chewed her lip, a drawn-out *okay* streaming from her like a yawn. He knew his admission had been the beginning of the end, despite what she said a month later when she took his hands in hers and told him, words pouring out like an automated message in an airport about a gate change, that she didn't think their relationship would lead to the kind of long-term future she was after. She insisted it had nothing to do with what he'd admitted to her, but he could hear the falseness in her voice, the lie rampant and soggy like rotting vegetation. He had wanted to disappear then, poof his way out of existence so she'd be left staring agog at the space he'd occupied.

She'd asked, "Are you sure you're not gay?"

And then, "Is this why we had sex only sometimes?"

She'd left, crying.

Hyland was torn between trying once more to formulate some suave message to Ethan and remaining still, allowing his body to fall into a state of full invisibility. Nolan hadn't said so, but Hyland was convinced that if he remained quiet and unmoving long enough, if he took a deep breath and stilled his lungs and controlled the thump of his heart, he could make his translucency permanent. He could stalk through the world as a shimmering blur like heat rising off asphalt, could curl himself into living rooms and kitchens and marketing offices and television studios and bars, hover into the sexy spaces that made his head lurch and his vision blur. He could find Ethan, flutter to him without fear of appraising eyes and lay down beside him, press one see-through hand to his chest and one to his crotch and feel the sort of touch he'd never known: the electric response of a hardened body as it reacted to the invisible spray of his fingertips.

A twisting shiver shook Hyland's shoulders and he blipped back, a momentary flash of peach on his white sheets. He took a deep breath and settled himself again, bit back the image of his cell phone screen, him typing away, winky, squirty emojis plastered in a message to Ethan. As his body started to fill up with empty light, he heard a whir from his nightstand, his phone crooning for his attention, and he felt a new sharp brightness cutting down his spine like a drizzle of warm water. His mouth went sour, an acidic slough gathering behind his teeth and in his gums. The glimmering feeling in his gut was overpowering, like the queasy, pleasant wave that comes during a drop on a roller coaster.

The phone vibrated again. Hyland rolled his eyes just so, enough to see that he'd received a text message.

Sweat bloomed across his forehead, gathering beneath the bandana. He felt the shiver again, like he was suffering delirium tremens. Through the crack under the door, he could hear the tennis commentators howling about a great forehand down the line to save a match point, their wondering aloud "Could this turn things around?" It was overwhelming, the power and confusion of the world. Hyland felt his body melt further, his whole self becoming scattered and indistinct like a pile of marbles squelched apart.

What does it mean to be invisible? he thought. To disappear, to become unreadable. To be as incorrigible as a bank vault, as confusing as a jigsaw puzzle without a picture.

He remembered the befuddled look on Beth's face when he'd spluttered it out. *Bi.* Then, forcing the frog clogging his throat to evacuate, the whole tumbly, institutional phrase: *bisexual.*

Hyland shuddered again. Though invisible, he felt beads of sweat gathering at his forehead, his crotch, the base of his spine.

He pulled off the bandana and felt the lurching weight of his body again. Hyland turned to grab his phone. He unlocked it, opened the text messages from Ethan. And then Hyland began to read.

Veneration

The church made of ice did not melt despite the air so hot it smelled like breath exhaled from a mouth of never-brushed teeth. Children loosed in the park to traumatize one another on the monkey bars and cargo nets were the first to see it, their eyes glazing down the long hill as they kicked high on the swings, whose rubber seats burned the undersides of their thighs. They stared and pointed, then screeched for their harried caregivers, who allowed themselves to be yanked down the path that drizzled into the valley marking the middle of the park, where a pair of tattered and abused baseball fields sprouted weeds along the baselines. The dugouts were home to tetanus, used condoms, empty beer cans.

When the first mother saw what her son was gawking at, while yanking her arm so hard she thought her shoulder would pop out of its socket, she felt the blood leave her head, the perspiration at her hairline evaporating like a fine mist. The church was nothing like the Sistine Chapel or St. Peter's Basilica, wide and squat instead, but it was a gorgeous blue like the untrammeled waters of the Indian Ocean. Every surface was glistening and cold, puffs of air turning to clouded condensation as the ice steamed. The columns of the narrow atrium, the apse, the visible arch of the chancel, the balustrades, all sparkled and gleamed and were cut as if chiseled from marble by the finest rasps and rifflers held in the steady hand of Michelangelo himself. The points were sharp as teeth, etched edges vibrant, every pock and pimple detailed and defined.

Mothers and fathers gathered with their children, staring. One man, wearing a pair of green mesh shorts that licked past his knees, his cotton T-shirt blanched with sweat even though all he'd been doing was pushing his adopted son on the swings, was the first to shove out of the crowd and approach the church. His name was Paul, a freelance writer who spent his hot mornings dragging his boy to the park while his husband, Andrew, a tax attorney, commuted an hour to a sterile downtown office building with humming fluorescent lights and acidic pink hand soap. He wrote in the evenings, hidden away in an office in his attic. Paul felt the cool blast of the church's facade from thirty feet away, as if a commercial air duct honking out freezing air was pointed directly at his face. He felt his stubble stand at attention; a tremor rippled his shoulders. He twisted his head and looked back at the assembled crowd, which included a trio of mothers who spent their park forays batting eyes at him and flicking their fingers toward his well-formed biceps while they laughed at his bad puns. They urged him forward with a flutter of hands and insensate murmuring.

Paul was not religious, not since seventh grade, when the nun who taught theology proclaimed that homosexuality would get you sent straight to hell. He'd found dogma and ritual ashy and gruesome, the pompous proclamations of the saved and self-righteous stinky and ruinous, echoing with an emptiness he associated with vampirism. As he approached the church he wasn't sure what he expected. Perhaps that when he stepped onto the sleek hockey rink of ice that made up the atrium floor his flip-flops would freeze, all their temperature sucked out so his toes felt the spiky beginnings of frostbite. But when his plastic thongs kissed the ice, nothing happened. He simply placed one foot, then the other, onto the ice, and stood still. The cold made him shiver, and he felt the sheen of sweat drizzled over his forearms begin evaporate, taking a part of him in the process.

When he tried to open his mouth to speak, Paul found he'd lost the words. Along with the heat leaving his body, language had flown the coop, and although his lips moved, sucking and puckering and gnawing like dying vermin, he couldn't turn the words he could see in his mind into sound. He let out a small groan, something akin to a sex noise, which felt right, because even though his capacity to speak had poofed away, he was filled with a warm pleasure that sucked at his gut as if Andrew were running his tongue along the crease where Paul's hip met his inner thigh. He felt fifteen pounds lighter, and stronger, and fulfilled.

"What is it?" someone from the crowd yelled.

But sound was fading fast as Paul stepped closer to the doors of the church, heavy and wooden (but still blue) like they were built of oak or fir, aged and weather-beaten and covered by ice shaped like pointed ironwork, the ancient, rusted sort that seethes and moans when wrenched open. With each step his sense of ecstasy increased, but so did a drizzling away: first his hearing, the din of the park and the nearby residential street with its horn bleats and tire thumps and whirring garage doors all dialing down as if he were plugging his ears. Then his vision, first fading to blurry, then foggy, and finally black. A tingle ran up and down his arms, a numbness crawling along his flesh as his fingers stopped sensing the cold. His legs kept moving, but his entire body felt like a shadow. When he opened the church door—it groaned, clanking and cantankerous, but Paul couldn't hear it—he didn't pause once, didn't look back for even a second, before disappearing inside, letting the iced hinge suck shut the door behind him. His son, stranded at the cusp of the gawking crowd, cried out a gunky, nasally sob.

Paul did not come out. His trio of fangirl mothers pattered on the edge of the baseball fields and cawed about what should be done. Should someone call 911? The news? Follow him in? A bottle blonde named Andi, whose body kept its shape from Pilates and Zumba four days a week to offset the cheap Riesling she drank by the bottle at her monthly book club, led the charge, stomping toward the church and experiencing the same euphoric loss of sense. As her mommy friends watched, she tumbled into the church after Paul and didn't emerge. Over the coming days, more and more would enter and not come back.

The police were called, and the news vans followed shortly, nudging themselves behind a cavalry of cop cars and ambulances and fire trucks blinkering their lights in the cutting, warm sun. A man from the Parks and Recreation Department whose eyes remained permanently googly and confused as to the reason for his presence appeared as well, his green uniform eking out sweat from his armpits. He stood around, watching firefighters and police officers scratch at their chins and bellies as they wondered what ought to be done. Unlike the police chief and fire captain, no one asked him for an interview, and none of the bewildered, excited children pointed and giggled at him or approached him shyly for a hug or autograph.

So he took the initiative and walked up to the church, not from the front but the side where there was no door. He felt the same insensate drainage, so he couldn't communicate to those who ignored him ignoring the caution tape the cops had strung up around the perimeter. He placed one hand along the exterior wall, a stained-glass rendition of one of the Stations of the Cross, capturing the moment of Christ's death. Icy droplets of blood spun out of the tiny Jesus figure's hands, winking in the sun; a gash cut into his lean trunk. When the officer pressed his fingertips to the bumped, cold surface, he felt an intense warmth coursing through him, as if he were absorbing the purest rays of the sun.

The man was found hours later, wandering in the woods behind the church. By then, the caution tape had been torn away, belligerent onlookers demanding the right to see and touch the venerable church; evangelical preachers had already published blog posts and YouTube videos and streaming sermons about the Rapture, the end of days, the return of Christ. A dozen of the faithful pushed their way into the church, vanishing in the same blind euphoria as Paul and Andi had. The Parks and Rec officer, agog and delirious, was scooped up by a pair of beat cops assigned to patrol the park's perimeter. He was taken to the hospital and diagnosed with severe dehydration, as if he'd been wandering a desert. Doctors shined penlights into his unresponsive pupils, pushed otoscopes toward his ear canals, knocked his knees with rubber mallets. His legs sprung up and down but the rest of his body was a calm lake's surface.

CNN, MSNBC, BBC, and Fox News hosted coverage as local feeds linked to their national syndicates. Television screens were smattered with images of the church as it glistened in the afternoon sun, spangling as if covered in glitter. Guffawing news anchors lilted their voices with surprise and awe as videos ran of random bodies sliding through the church doors. Interviews were played on loop, loved ones stunned and speechless, their voices trailing off, sentences broken like hunks of concrete. Their eyes glanced toward the closed doors of the church while fanatics stood in the background, heads bowed, arms raised, bodies swaying to some unsung hymn. One commentator raised an eyebrow, mouth curled and creasing his pancake makeup, stating that the small Missouri town was expected to see massive swaths of the faithful swarming in; he would later be berated on Twitter for calling the phenomenon "a fool's trek to a yokel Mecca."

Crowds came in cranky buses, sleek vans, barrages of sedans and pickup trucks. They flooded the Holiday and Red Roof Inns, backed up the drive-thru lines at McDonalds and Raising Cane's, clogged the self-checkout at Schnucks. People of all stripes: a choir

decked in their Sunday regalia, purple robes dampened by perspiration; women in bonnets and men in skinny black ties and
too-large white shirts bulging over beer bellies that sagged across
beaten leather belts; chorales of blue-haired women with tattered
Bibles in hand, eyes narrowed and fingers curled in prayer. The
police were abused by the mammoth crowd when they tried to
impede access to the church.

"You cannot stand between the faithful and their God!" one
white-bearded man with a bullhorn shrieked into a stoic officer's
face. Spittle rattled through his gummy lips. The officer blinked
and adjusted his weight, feet scuffling in the hot dirt. People snuck
past, and when they stepped onto the ice, the police had no choice
but to let them disappear, their eyesight draining away, hearing
going daffy, language evaporating like the cold steam billowing
from the church's roof. No one expected law enforcement to make
such sacrifices; if the ignoble sheep wanted to throw themselves at
the mercy of the church, one talking head said on HLN, who are
we to stop them?

The summer softball league was canceled; too many tents, filled
with migrant worshippers too cheap to pay for the Super 8, had
clogged the outfields. The smell of urine and fecal matter and
unwashed skin pinched the hot sky, baking the park with olfactory
displeasure. Children from day camps frowned and crowed about
the stench and the strangers, scowling down the roll of the hill from
the playground, where they continued to swing and slide despite
the throng. Frizzy camp counselors in T-shirts with rolled sleeves
kept careful watch after one boy reported that a grizzled man tried
to coax him away from the wood-chipped playground. The story
spread, and parents demanded the camps move their program-
ming indoors, to the local elementary school gym, where prying
sickos couldn't prey on their offspring. The counselors assented,
giving thanks for air conditioning and the water fountain.

And then, six weeks after the church appeared, one youthful onlooker, bussed in all the way from Virginia with his youth

group, frowned and pointed toward the edge of the church's corbel, which ran along the roof like a thick stony gutter. The corner closest to the road looked—well, was it—was that—it couldn't be melting, could it?

A puddle, small and indistinct on the glassy surface that surrounded the church, had, in fact, formed, and when onlookers squinted, they could make out the minute dribble of water as it slipped from the icy edge.

"How can this be?"

"What does it mean?"

"What do we do?"

Waves of panic slipped and slid through the crowd like a sickness. Preachers started prayer chants, eyes rolled back and hands splayed palms toward the sky, invoking the Holy Spirit. Bodies swayed, beating back the tremble of tears with their solemn humming and song.

But the church continued to drip.

The news vans wrestled for prime real estate near the church, cameras wedged between bodies, reporters half shouting into their microphones while the church wept behind them. More interviews, battering preachers and laypeople with questions like "What do you think will happen if the church melts?" and "What kind of sign is this?" and "What will you do when the church is gone?" Pulpit masters and congregants alike squirmed and smiled and tried to keep their cool as the frosty house of worship started to go lumpy, a sad, hopeless snowman barely clinging to its shape during the first heavy thaw.

The loved ones of those who had vanished inside the church returned to the scene, fresh from mourning their losses. They clasped hands in their shared grief, blinking through Ray-Bans, eyes squinted as if they could force the church's melting to speed up. Fifty-odd spouses, significant others, siblings, children, and parents had formed a support group via Facebook and text message, gathering by the dozen in one another's homes and dilapidated apartments, sharing casseroles and no-bake pies. Andi's husband and Andrew had grown close because their lovers were the first to disappear; one night they met at a bar inside a nearby Howard Johnson's and split three scorpion bowls and told each other stories about their respective spouses and Andrew vomited electric pink muck all over his bathroom and then cried because Paul was the tidier of the two and Andrew had no idea where to find a bottle of spray cleaner in the cabinetry beneath the sink.

They watched and waited, willing their spouses to appear. The church drooped, and finally a large cry rang out, pain from the believers and hope from the mourners: the ceiling of the entryway collapsed, the door shattering outward with a loud crack. People began screaming, but pandemonium was stanched by their awe at the glimmering destruction. The white-bearded preacher, who had grown lank and tan from his time in the sun and lack of proper nutrition, cowed into his bullhorn that the Rapture had arrived. He spread his hands toward the heavens, expecting dark clouds and perhaps a rain of blood, or for the bodies of the saved to begin their ascent. But the pure sheet of sky remained unbroken except for the white pearl of the sun.

The church fell quickly, and hope turned to horror for the mourners; instead of a slow drip, a rain of melt revealed the stumped bodies of their loved ones, the church disintegrating in slicing sheets like a building imploded by a wrecking ball. The nave collapsed like it was being slurped down a toilet; had the flat ceiling been pinched up into a transept, its point would have speared into the ground like a falling missile. The apse fell in on itself; balustrades crumbled in hearty chunks. Andrew felt spikes of queasy fear rushing through him like snakes snarling along his digestive track, tongues flicking at his intestinal walls.

Soon all that was left was a steaming, melting heap of jagged ice like the sluiced-off edges of the McBride Glacier.

No one moved; who knew whether the power of the church remained? The Parks and Recreation officer was still blind and deaf; his GoFundMe account had exceeded its goal. No officers wished to risk contact with the melty swamp of the decimated church, and none of the faithful threw themselves toward the destruction; the preachers were silent. Andrew and the other loved ones stared, breathless.

They remained that way, in cold silence, until the church had gone to soup. A clutch in every stomach, a wondering whether the lost would become found. As the ice melted away, suffusing through the grass and dripping toward the baseball infields to turn the dirt to muddy cakes, the crowd stared in unison, unblinking and short of breath, turning into a scene of stone, waiting for the next miracle.

The Night of Missing Children

After Lewis closed and locked the door, Calum hugged him from behind. Both resisted the urge to throw the door open and call for Thomas to come back, and they stood long enough that the motion-detecting porch light shut off. Thomas, the darkness outside seemed to say, had truly gone.

"Come," Calum said finally, his voice soft as he peeled himself from Lewis. "Let's have a drink."

They kept pricey, dusty bottles of dark liquor atop the hutch in the dining room, which was home mostly to canisters of coins, ticket stubs, receipts that they tossed down at the end of each workday, emptying their pockets of stray dollar bills, the occasional facial tissue, cherry lozenges when the dry weather made their throats crack. They knew Thomas pilfered the dough sometimes, but as far as they could tell, he hadn't taken up smoking or other hard drugs, and if he drank beer with his friends, he did so safely.

At least so far. Who knew what would happen tonight.

Calum pulled down a bottle of Blanton's Original while Lewis opened one of the cabinets and extracted a pair of rocks glasses. They didn't raise a toast because neither could think of a thing to be happy about. All they found themselves able to do was hope that Thomas came back in the morning.

For a long time, they wouldn't have expected otherwise, but then their neighbors, Lynn and Donovan, were shocked when their daughter Cindy didn't return three years ago. Sometimes, they could hear Lynn's sobbing through an open window while they ate brunch on their back deck. Once, Thomas sat with wide eyes, his mouth full of french toast. Syrup started leaking from between his lips before Calum cleared his throat, which seemed to snap him out of it. Thomas looked from Lewis to Calum and swallowed, his tongue licking at the corners of his mouth, then said, "Why wouldn't she come back?"

His voice was thin and cracking, not out of fear, Lewis thought, but thanks to the ravages of adolescence. Thomas had shot up six inches that summer and had whirled through the kitchen on an hourly basis, staring into the pantry while he shoved chips and cookies and granola bars and Pop-Tarts in his mouth. He peeled slices of cheese from their deli bag, folding them up and gnashing them in single bites. He heated Hot Pockets up three at a time. He was still skinny, had the body of a cross-country runner even though he hated exercise unless he was on a tennis court or in a sand volleyball pit. He never stayed out late, even when his best friends turned sixteen before him and could drive him wherever he might want to go; he always returned before midnight, as though to do otherwise would turn him into a pumpkin or a mouse.

"But that's the thing," Calum had said when Lewis pointed out their son's good behavior. "It's always the good ones you have to worry about."

They sat down on the living room sofa and turned on the television, all blue light and noise, and soon enough Calum leaned forward, plucked up the remote, and turned off the TV. They both finished their first drink fast, and Calum, standing, said: "Fuck it. I'll just bring the bottle."

They stretched out, Lewis crammed between the couch cushions and Calum's body, which was warm and rigid. He had to snake an arm past Calum's head to pick up his glass; if he held it in his hand, he'd drink too fast. But then he wondered whether there was such a thing on a night like this. He decided, quickly, that there wasn't and gulped down the bourbon, his eyes tearing at the sear as he tried to stop himself from coughing.

"Sexy," Calum said, managing somehow to pour Lewis another drink without having to sit up or spilling anything on the floor or himself or Lewis's outstretched arm.

The room was full of sour silence. Normally, Lewis and Calum could sit in this contented emptiness for hours, so long that Thomas tended to come marching out of his bedroom, frowning, wanting to know whether something was wrong. Had someone had a stroke? Were they both dead? Were they high? Had they passed out? What's wrong with you two? The last, usually, he said with a laugh, high and celestial and sweet.

Lewis was tempted to talk about his own missing night, but he knew he shouldn't. That would mean he expected Calum to talk about his own, and one of the understood rules was that the things one did on that night were private. If you wanted to share what you did, fine. But you never asked.

Not that Lewis had many secrets. While his classmates were busy with drugs, booze, and probably gobs of awkward sex, maybe some graffiti and petty theft—though, in general, by the time his missing night had come around, it had become understood that the only destructive kind of behavior that was generally accepted was of the self-destructive sort—Lewis simply wandered. He caught sight of a gaggle of girls he knew, and he followed them for a bit, thinking he might finally speak with the cheerleader he harbored a crush on. But then those girls met up with half a dozen football players, including the quarterback, on whom Lewis also had a crush. He peeled away before anyone noticed him and spent most of the night sitting by himself on one of the swings at a nearby park. He was back at his front door before dawn, and he slipped inside, careful not to wake his parents, whom he knew were relieved and thrilled to find him already munching on a bowl of sugary cereal when they appeared in the kitchen seeking coffee and eggs.

He let Calum fill his drink again. Lewis knew that he'd have trouble when he finally tried to stand up; already his vision was spangly at the edges, his tongue feeling loose. Rather than say anything, he pecked at the back of Calum's neck. The skin was smooth and tight, and he felt an urge to lick it.

"Oh," Calum said. His neck vibrated as he spoke. "Okay."

Their mouths were both sticky with booze, Calum's breath woody and tart and a bit smoky. Their bodies were tangly, and twice they nearly fell off the couch. When Lewis started to unbuckle Calum's belt, Calum said, "Maybe not here."

"But who's going to see?" Lewis said.

Calum looked up at the ceiling, eyes rolling around until they settled back on Lewis's face. He smiled, laughed, and shoved his hands down Lewis's underwear, his fingers cold. Lewis let out a small gasp.

"Whoops," Calum said.

⸻

Their relief was brief but necessary. Lewis pressed his ear to Calum's chest and said, "Your heartbeat's slower than mine."

Calum grabbed Lewis's wrist, fingers pressed on the delicate inner side. "I'd say they're similar."

"You don't need to lie," Lewis said. "I know I'm nervous."

"So am I."

They pulled on their clothing and made sandwiches. Lewis kept glancing out the kitchen window, wondering whether he was seeing bodies moving through the dark of their neighborhood. Calum spread mustard on wheat bread and then stacked strips of deli turkey and roast beef. He found day-old bacon for crunch, then laid down slices of cheese.

"If you had to guess," Lewis said. "What do you think he's doing right now?"

"You know we shouldn't think about it. Eat."

"Come on. Tell me. Just hypothetically."

"You'll stress yourself out," Calum said. He bit into his sand-wich. Lewis watched him chew.

"I think I'll stress out more if I think but don't speak."

Calum swallowed and blinked at him. "Then speak."

But Lewis found himself suddenly unable to speak. When he tried to envision the trouble Thomas might be getting into, all he could see was himself, sixteen and alone, legs whisking through the air as he swayed forward and back on that swing, the rusted chain groaning under his weight. He'd spent hours staring up at the night sky, which was full of plump clouds moving fast and hard, and bright stars that jangled and slalomed as he swung. His neck had gone sore, his hands twitchy and cramped from gripping the chains.

He let out a sigh. "I guess I have no idea what he's doing."

Calum seemed satisfied by this answer. He nodded and took a bite of his sandwich, then gestured toward Lewis. "Eat."

"I don't know if I'm hungry."

"You're always hungry," Calum said. "Don't be one of those weirdos in movies who suddenly lose their appetite."

Calum was right, of course. Lewis was starving. He bit into his sandwich, relishing the vinegar sting of the mustard and the salt of the bacon. He nodded. Calum nodded back. The refrigerator hummed, and for a moment he thought everything would be okay.

Lewis knew that they should just go to bed. They were drunk, they were sleepy from sex, they were bloated with sandwich meat and bread. But Calum, after finishing his last bite, threw himself back down on the couch and poured another round. Then he stared at Lewis, his eyes puffy like he hadn't slept in days, which was entirely possible. Lewis, until today, hadn't let himself think too much about Thomas's missing night, and he'd managed to while away the nights in dreamless sleep, the kind that slips by in bare blinks, hours erased as if they never happened. He knew Calum wasn't having that kind of luck because he was always yawning and groaning in the morning, slurping down too much coffee.

Lewis sat down next to him.

"Now what?" Lewis said.

Calum shrugged and sipped. Lewis let the bourbon hit his lips but he didn't drink.

"Don't pretend," Calum said. "If you don't want to drink, don't."

"How could you tell?"

"I can always tell."

Lewis let that sit fat in the air.

"I was a loser," he said.

"Was?"

Lewis socked Calum light in the shoulder, which elicited a smile.

"On my night. I didn't do anything interesting."

"Neither did I." Calum's face was a map of shadows, one eye and cheekbone hidden in the gloom of night, the other lit up by the side table lamp.

"I find that hard to believe."

"Believe it or not."

Calum grew up in a house not dissimilar to their current one, though much nicer, larger, a two-story with bright columns like bleached teeth, a decorative second-story balcony inaccessible from the inside, a kidney-shaped pool in the backyard with expensive lawn chairs and topiary. Lewis tried to imagine Calum wandering his neighborhood all by himself, refusing to get in trouble. Rich kids were supposed to have easy access to drugs, a cavalier attitude about sex. Wouldn't he hop in someone's car, go careening off at high speed to some party, snort cocaine or pop E while drinking needlessly expensive keg beer before finding someone to bed down with? Lewis couldn't picture Calum alone, shuffling down a sidewalk, finding his way to a park bench or a curb, leaning back and staring up at the night sky. But he liked the idea that they'd both spent their nights doing nothing at all.

"You weren't a loser in high school," Lewis said.

"No," Calum said. "But I was lonely."

Lewis set his hand over Calum's and nodded. This, at least, he understood.

The bottle was half-empty, but Calum had done most of the drinking; he was passed out on the couch, letting out wet, rhythmic breaths with the steady cadence of a grandfather clock. Lewis extricated himself from Calum's prone form and returned the bottle to its place among its peers. He rinsed their rocks glasses, peering into the living room as he turned on the faucet; Calum didn't stir. Lewis drew himself some water and drank two helpings, swishing the second through his teeth because his mouth had gone dry.

Outside was deeply dark. Lewis checked the pulsing green of the microwave's digital clock: nearly two. Returning his attention to the window, he leaned over the sink to peer through the glass, which stubbornly reflected a wavering, puffy version of his face. He stared for a long time before accepting he would see nothing of interest.

Lewis knew he should go to bed; his alarm was set for five thirty so he could get to the junior high school, where he tried to get students interested in anatomy and physiology and the body systems, regularly failing miserably. He should pull Calum up, help him stumble down the hall and into their bedroom, where he would have to remove Calum's socks and his jeans and peel off his shirt, his limbs noodly, his body loose and goofy from too much alcohol.

Lewis knew that Calum would groan and beg for extra sleep in the morning, and that Lewis would thus be left to greet Thomas on his own. Or, worse, to face Thomas's absence on his own.

Instead, he decided to sneak outside. Checking once more that Calum was KO'd on the sofa—his breathing was still regular and wet, and, if nothing else, louder and soggier than before—Lewis unlocked the front door, the metal click a booming noise like a bomb had just exploded. He sucked in a breath and turned the knob, expecting a rush of clamorous sound. But all that swooped in was the late-night breeze, cool and moist, and the tiniest sounds of bugs.

He pulled the door shut behind him. The motion-detecting porch light snapped on, and Lewis felt like a cat burglar invading his own property. He glanced back through the sidelight; he couldn't see Calum, but there were enough lamps on inside still that the additional outdoor glow shouldn't be enough to wake him. Lewis tried to steady himself. As he sat down on the lip of the porch—a simple concrete slab, ten feet long and half as wide, the only decoration a quartet of simple columns holding up the roof awning—he realized he was trembling. He set his hands down on the concrete and leaned back to listen to the darkness.

Their house was situated deep in a labyrinthine subdivision, a branching maze of cul-de-sacs and four-way stops; the only way to stumble upon their property was purposefully, the streets with tree-themed names curling and looping and shooting off one another a dozen times. Mulberry Trail was hidden several left and right turns from the main thoroughfare, and Lewis couldn't imagine, as he sat with his eyes closed, that any of the children out in the night would find their way to his street. He could picture Thomas, an itinerary already constructed in his head—perhaps preplanned with his friends—of where to go, what to do, his route out of the tumble of their suburban enclave sharpened and sure.

Lewis stood. He decided, despite the hour, to take a walk. He knew the streets by instinct after six years in the neighborhood, and there was no worry of getting lost, even if he chose to march down a street that led further into the maze of manicured lawns and two-car garages. When they first moved in, ten-year-old Thomas wanted to explore, so Lewis and Calum and their son had spent many weekend afternoons wandering. At each intersection, Thomas would blurt out "Left!" or "Right!" or "Forward!" and they would follow his instruction. Not once did Thomas grow frightened or express any concerns over being lost, even when Lewis felt the bite of nerve because he had no idea where they were. He wrestled with himself on these trips, a part of him desperate to map their route, another part equally hopeful that they would end up completely lost, forced to maneuver their way through a totally foreign landscape. But no matter how random their turns were, they always made their way back home, eventually.

He walked for a long time, his bare feet blistered and stinging against the sidewalk. More than once he stepped on stray pebbles and twigs, but he bit down on his lip so as to not shriek out. He kept moving, the streets that were familiar in the daytime suddenly obscure and foreign in the dark, picture windows and columns and mailboxes and driveways and landscaping all warped by darkness and shadow and the heaviness of night.

As if pulled by an indistinct magnetism, he eventually found himself back on his street. On the lowest, longest horizon, the first signs of daylight were breaking through, Easter-egg colors just beginning to gleam at the lowest edges of the black. Lewis passed houses he'd been inside before, during block parties or barbecues or the Super Bowl. People had come knocking when he and Calum and Thomas pulled up in their car, followed by the moving truck that disgorged their couches and Calum's heaping boxes of books. They brought wine and pies, and then later, when Lewis's mother died, they brought casseroles, leaving them on the porch, ringing the bell and scurrying away, their condolences squashed at the bottom of stationery that explained how long to reheat the dishes in the oven. He knew his neighbors' names, waved hello when he left for work in the morning and saw them dragging out their trash cans or recycling bins or bending down to pick up the newspaper.

A voice calling out his name broke the silence. Lewis juddered and looked around, his eyes suddenly unaccustomed to the dark. He heard his name a second time and was finally able to locate the source: his next-door neighbor Lynn. She was sitting on her front porch wearing a plush terry-cloth robe. He squinted through the dark and made out that she was holding a coffee mug with both hands. She looked snug and comfortable, like she was in a Folgers commercial and the sun was about to blinker over her shoulder as she sighed away all her worries.

"You shouldn't be out," she said.

"Neither should you," he said.

"Come. Sit."

Lynn was going gray at the roots and wrinkled at the eyes. He saw her bounding through the neighborhood sometimes in Lycra, working up a swelter that stained her clothes. Burning off all her sorrow, he thought sometimes.

"School night," she said. "Won't you be tired in the morning?"

"Everyone will be tired in the morning."

"That'd make a good song title."

"What about you?"

Lynn sipped her coffee. "I always stay up this late."

"Always?" Lewis said.

The darkness was lifting fast. Lewis tried to remember the last time he'd watched a sunrise. Yes, his job teaching thirteen-year-olds the basics of physical and biological science required he wake up early, but he spent the transitory hours between dark and light showering, brushing his hair, making Thomas breakfast, filling his satchel with graded papers, maneuvering through traffic en route to the junior high school. He never got to savor the morphing of night into day.

"Ever since Cindy," Lynn said. "Every time I hear a noise at night, I'm convinced it's her, coming back. Donovan sleeps in the guest room now because of it."

Lewis couldn't quite make out her face—the porch light was off, and the fast-arriving day wasn't quite solid enough to give her features shape; her lips were still indistinct smudges in the dark. But he could hear how far away she was, and he could imagine her eyes, unfocused, thrust back in time.

"But if you mean out here, like this. Well." Lynn sipped her coffee. "Every missing night. And every Wednesday. Just in case. Hers was a Wednesday."

"Right."

"You're worried about Thomas."

It wasn't a question.

Lynn pulled in a breath through her nostrils. It sounded difficult, like she was congested by spring allergies. "He'll come back. Most of them do. Cindy was an exception."

"But you can never know, can you?"

"No, I guess you can't."

"I'm sorry."

"For what?"

"That she left and didn't come back."

Lynn sighed, and through the dark, one of her hands reached out and fell onto Lewis's shoulder. Her fingers squeezed at the muscle as though she was digging, trying to reach into him and stroke the knob of bone. Despite the discomfort, Lewis didn't lean away or tell her to stop. He let her probe for a long moment before her hand stopped, fingers shaped in a claw around his arm.

"I know she'll be back someday."

"How can you know?"

She shrugged, and he felt the motion down through her fingers. "I have to. If I don't, then what else is there?"

"Why do you think we do it?" Lewis said. "The missing night. Why have it at all?"

Lynn was silent for a long moment. "I think we all need to get things out of our system eventually. Why not when we're sixteen?"

"You think there's enough built up by then?"

She shrugged.

"What did you do?" Lewis asked it before he could stop himself, and he wanted to pull the words back in. Lynn laughed.

"Things," she said. "Things both worth talking about and not worth it at all." When Lewis said nothing, she stood, releasing his arm. "I should get inside." She let out a yawn and stretched. Real light was starting to seep through the darkness, leaking between the houses on the other side of the street in mealy, low bands.

"I'm sure you'll see Thomas soon," she said, and then, before Lewis could say anything in response, turned and walked into her house, shutting the door carefully behind her.

Lewis stood. An early-rising songbird trilled. Far in the distance, on the edges of the neighborhood, he could hear the first noises of cars, the earliest risers heading off to work or coming home. He wondered when he would see the first child slouching back. Lewis looked down both ends of the street and saw no one. Finally, he started the walk toward his own house.

Morning light winked off the windows. Lewis realized he hadn't taken his phone with him, and he felt a squeeze of guilt that he'd left Calum drunk and dazed, alone. Lewis hurried to open the door, but it was locked. He didn't remember locking it and he was without his keys. His stomach flopped like he'd been dropped from a high height. He banged on the door.

Lewis stood for what felt like an eternity, waiting. More light popped through the trees. He heard a garage door rumble open a few houses down. Lewis kept listening for the sound of Thomas approaching, and he turned away from the locked door, craning to look down the street, but his vision was blocked by the dogwoods in his and Lynn's yards, their bright white-purple blossoms in full burst. In the pale, earliest light, they almost glowed.

Then the sound of the lock turning. The door opening. Lewis hoped that, instead of Calum, it would be Thomas at the door, that he had somehow miraculously beaten Lewis home. He would gather his son up and thank him for coming back, wouldn't ask any questions about where he'd been or what he'd done. Lewis would simply be grateful for everything inside, the life waiting for him, the things he would tell himself would always and forever be enough.

Vernix

The neonatal nurses couldn't remove the vernix from Evan's skin. They tried hot water, scrubbing with their hands through the squeaky latex of their gloves; they soaked washcloths, scratching them against his pink baby body, at first with a delicacy reserved for afternoon tea and then increased gusto when the cheesy substance wouldn't budge. They bathed him like a grease-caked pan in need of soaking, smearing him with antibacterial soap and then hydrogen peroxide and even squirts from a tube of iodine borrowed from the surgical ward, all to no avail.

His mother rolled the word *vernix* around in her mouth, foreign and snooty like the kinds of wine she never bought—Beaujolais, Syrah, Malbec. She was in a cloudy state, having been jammed in the arm with an IV immediately after Evan finally squirmed out because her uterus had followed suit, prolapsing and squelching out with the placenta that wouldn't detach, and in order to relax her enough to reposition her fundus inside her, Marione's doctor had called for a drug too many syllables long for her to follow in the haze of post-pushing. She was sweaty and hollow, her grip on her husband's hand limp like a cooked noodle. When the nurses passed Evan to her, she took in his waxy visage only momentarily, then pressed him to her chest. The vernix clung to his skin and didn't smear against her hands or sternum or breasts at all, as if it were nestled deep into Evan, a protective coating or a candy shell.

***

They never called it *vernix* after that. When he could talk, Evan referred to it as *the goo*; his parents simply didn't speak of it, like he had impetigo or eczema, one of those conditions that blares out on the surface but adults make no mention of, like kids with lisps or Down syndrome. When Evan was old enough to be teased for it, the vernix became *this white junk*, a dismissive exhalation he used to diffuse the pointing fingers, the stares, the snickers, the outright laughter, the girlish screams when he came too close to his classmates. And once he knew curse words, it became *this sick fucking joke the world is playing on me*. Evan didn't believe in God, although Marione and Carl went to church on Sundays. By the time he was fourteen, they'd stopped waking him up or giving him ties for his birthdays or demanding he go to confirmation class, and although Marione lamented her son's lack of faith, she felt her own tremors of disbelief when she stared at him across the dinner table and saw the sorrow pooling in his eyes, their downward cast revealing the hate burrowed deep inside him. She wondered the age-old question—*how could any god do this to my boy?*

They'd considered homeschool, if for no other reason than to protect Evan from the rampant bullying and teasing the vernix would cause. Marione had seen it coming; the little sleep she could muster in that first year of his infanthood was plagued by nightmares of her teary-eyed son and the mounting insults that would batter him. As he grew, the dreams multiplied like replicating cells. Preschool was all right; though the boys and girls tottering around gawked at him, they were quickly distracted by finger paints and wooden blocks they built into towers and then destroyed. In kindergarten, the laughter began, followed by the horrible nicknames in elementary (Slimer, Rotface, the Stinky Cheese). But contrary to what she'd expected, Evan didn't cry. He didn't slam the door behind him after school, throw his books across the living room in a rage, stomp into his bedroom; his anger was quiet, simmering instead of boiling. He did lament the vernix, cursing it under his breath, constantly asking that his parents take him for yet another consultation with a dermatologist or a surgeon (the former had always gawked at his skin and shrugged, offering the same super-powered acne medications that never did a thing; the latter, after tugging at the vernix and then scheduling biopsies, always came back with the same prognosis that the vernix was far too attached to the dermis for removal to be safe). Evan privately lambasted his skin, but in public he embraced his nicknames.

He played sports, excelling at soccer. Defenders, convinced Evan was contagious and sticky, gave him just enough room to dribble the ball past with ease when he came barging down the field in the striker's position, lumbering toward the goalie. They winced at the waxy blobs stuttering across Evan's face just long enough for him to send the ball thumping against the rear of the net, his teammates hooting and chanting, "The Stinky Cheese! The Stinky Cheese!" over and over between pulls of water and slices of orange. They raised their hands in celebratory fist pumps but never clapped his back or piled around him in a raucous circle like the other forwards when they netted the ball. They wouldn't even touch his sweat-slick uniform. He considered wrestling and all the championships he could win by default when opponents gawked and shook their heads and refused to initiate contact, but he didn't like the exposure of the singlets.

Although they sang of the Stinky Cheese, no one wanted the Stinky Cheese. While his teammates scored dates to homecoming and prom with cheerleaders and girls from the pom squad, Evan found himself slumped on creaky folding chairs during slow-dance numbers, watching football players paw at the asses of their dates. Girls with hair twilled into braided buns reached their corsage-draped hands around tuxedo-clad necks. The only skin-to-skin contact Evan ever mustered came in his dreams—sharp, sparking things in which his pairings were indiscriminate, girls and boys jumping in and out at random, their bodies slim and muscular and naked, radiant and welcoming. He woke up dizzied and dry-mouthed, a haze of confusion pattering his forehead when he was wrenched from illusions of giving blowjobs to movie stars.

The summer after his junior year, which included leading his school to a state championship in which he scored six goals in three games, Marione and Carl took him and two of his favorite teammates on a quiet vacation to the Lake of the Ozarks. Brian and Dean were the only ones who called him by name and didn't shy away from invitations to come over to his house on Friday nights for dinner and video games on the big screen in the basement. They rented a too-large house built of redwood and glass that lolled out over the water like a dog's tongue lapping toward hydration. Evan's parents spent their hours lazing on the back deck with a sweating bottle of white wine between them, ordering pizza and Chinese food and twice managing to burn burgers and hot dogs that the boys slathered in mustard and relish and ate anyway.

On the third night, when Evan and his friends wandered into a keg party two houses down, he met Marcus.

The lake was a black pearl, its onyx surface reflecting the lights from the house's back porch and the streaky bonfire in a firepit built out of fresh bricks and beach sand. Teenagers were huddled in insular, unbreakable circles that Evan didn't bother trying to penetrate. He kept to the shadows; in the dark, the splotches of vernix were less visible or could be taken for simple tricks of the low light as the fire flickered and licked at the sky. His friends brought him a cup filled with dire, nasty beer, and he only took one sip. Brian and Dean hovered with Evan until he sighed and set them free to flirt and play drinking games. He watched them seamlessly throw themselves into the throng of strangers as if they'd known these mysterious people all their lives, and he wondered how anyone could so easily strum up the power to become a part of a group of unknowns.

After surreptitiously pouring his beer into a row of azaleas, Evan slipped down toward the house's dock, where two plastic chaise lounges pointed out toward the water. It wasn't until he was about to sit that he realized one of them was already occupied. A duo of tan, squat-leaned thighs were splayed out, covered by pink board shorts etched with stenciled green flowers, a white cord knotted just below an outie belly button. The owner of the legs twisted at Evan's approach and looked up at him. A boyish face, angular nose, eyes set light on a narrow skull. Wide philtrum and teeth that, even in the dark, Evan could tell were perfect and white and straight.

"Sorry," Evan croaked. "I didn't know anyone was down here."

"That's okay. Seat's not claimed." A hand, palm up, gestured toward the chaise.

Not knowing what else to do, Evan sat.

"Marcus," the boy said, extending his hand. His grip was tight and strong, hands callused below the fingers, and he didn't flinch when he grabbed Evan's and crunched his waxy vernix skin. Evan watched, waiting for some response, but Marcus just leaned back, stretching out on the chaise and resting his hands on his thighs. He reposed as if soaking up sun, shirtless, his torso lean and muscled like a basketball player's, nipples tight and tiny, the size of dimes, and he shut his eyes and sighed, saying nothing else, as if Evan had vanished.

The detritus of party noise cascaded down toward them—boys chanting as their peers attempted keg stands; girls screeching at one another in greeting and drunken rage; at one point, the tizzied howl of the entire party hooting at someone slipping and busting ass on the concrete patio; an argument over the rules of beer pong. Through it all, Marcus remained silent, and Evan wondered whether he was asleep. He felt an itch crawling over him as he stared at the lake, silent and unmoving except for the No Wake Allowed sign buoyed twenty yards out. Along the far shore, over-sized homes blazed with lights like parked UFOs.

"So tell me. What's your story?"

When Marcus spoke, the break in silence was such a whiplash that Evan flinched, his entire body twitching as though he were freezing, even though the night was tumid, with the kind of heat that carried a carrion stench with it, the perspiration and spit of every living creature seeming to gather in a knitted, pressing cloud.

"Sorry?" Evan felt like a frog, voice croaky and slow.

"You from here?"

"No."

"You know any of them?" Marcus fluttered a hand back toward the party.

"Not really. I'm staying two doors down."

"Ah."

"You?"

"I'm from over there." Another flutter of tan fingertips, nails scalloped and strong and beating with keratin, Marcus's hand gesturing toward the other side of the lake. "I'm a townie."

"A townie?"

"I live here year round."

"Oh."

Marcus jerked a thumb over his shoulder, pointed like a heron. "They're not so nice to townies. Your kind, I mean."

"I have a kind?"

Marcus peered through the darkness. Evan felt a curdling roil in his midsection. He prepared himself for the shuddering disgust that clapped over strangers when they first noticed the vernix drizzled across his cheeks and elbows. He didn't breathe while Marcus stared. Then something changed in Marcus's eyes, like a squall dissipating. Marcus smiled.

"Nah, you're okay, I think." He slapped his thighs. "Want to go for a swim?"

Evan looked down at himself. "I'm wearing jeans."

"Those are removable, you know."

"But I—"

"Afraid to be naked in the water?"

"I have underwear on."

"Well, that's just silly. Come on, then."

Before Evan could object, Marcus stood, unstrung his swimsuit in a whiplash-quick motion, and tugged it past his prominent hip bones. Evan forced himself to look away when the fabric pooled on the planks of the deck, then couldn't help but glance as Marcus's tanned body trundled toward the dock end and overturned in a smooth dive into the water.

A moment later, Evan heard a "Well?"

Something wired through his spine, a warm toad hopping along his back, and so Evan stood and started to undress. He paused for a moment when he was in nothing but his underwear, the warm night air skirting across the backs of his knees, licking up at his thighs. He'd stripped in the locker room after soccer games and practices, seen plenty of his teammates in their skivvies and even less.

But this, Evan could see and smell and taste in the back of his mouth, was different.

He pulled the fabric away, kicking everything under the chaise. Without giving himself a chance to reconsider, he threw himself down to the end of the dock and plunged in, feet first. The water was like that left over in a tub, with skin and dirt and seepage stewing. He exhaled through his nose and wallowed beneath the surface, feeling the burn in his lungs. Evan opened his eyes, letting them pinch with the sting of lake water, and tried to glance toward where Marcus's naked body bobbled, legs whirling, but all he could see was a smudgy shadow, like a barracuda darting through the gloom. When he finally broke the surface, Evan was quick to examine his skin. Slaked with the dim ambient moonlight and the glistening wetness, the vernix shimmered, silver like the back of a blister pack. He ran his fingers over the familiar tangle of tendrils. They felt like drinking straws.

Where Marcus had been stoic and still on the dock, his body took on a frenetic boyhood in the water. He pedaled his legs and bobbed, grinning toward Evan, and without a word, sent a trio of hearty splashes in his direction. Evan sputtered and splashed back, clapping his hand against the surface and sending dark spumes toward Marcus. Soon they were laughing and pushing waves at each other in a churning fury, the darkness boiling into a whirlwind around them. Before Evan knew it, Marcus was right in front of him. He could feel the gravity of their bodies pulling them toward each other as the water vacuumed and shifted around them.

A final wave hit Evan, and then Marcus was still, the only motion the sucking of his legs displacing water as he treaded in place. Through the dark, Evan watched Marcus stare at him, and he felt as though his skin had been lit up, like the vernix was high-lighter set ablaze in the black light of night.

"You glow," Marcus said.

"No I don't."

"Yes, you do." A hand peeled out of the water and set itself on Evan's shoulder. It felt like a dinner plate, freshly washed.

"It's not very bright."

"Doesn't need to be."

They churned in the water like that, Marcus's hand pressed on Evan's arm, his fingers warm and strong, the calluses on the pads of his palm itching at Evan's skin. Their ankles knocked once, and Evan felt himself flush, suddenly aware of their nakedness, their closeness, their breathing. The sounds from the party on the shore dipped away. Somewhere nearby, a fish flopped against the surface of the water.

His teeth, Evan realized, were chattering.

"Cold?" Marcus said. He slipped the word out in a whisper. Evan was able to see the curl of his mouth, the flash of teeth, the warm roll of Marcus's tongue.

"I'm okay."

Marcus released his grip on Evan's shoulder, and the spot felt evacuated, like an abscess. Evan dipped into the water so it lapped toward his lips, and he sputtered just so. Marcus did the same. Their bodies whirled, and under the surface, their fingertips grazed one another. In the quiet of the dark lake, Evan felt like he and Marcus were the only two in the world, the black water stretching on for eternity.

Suddenly, noise on the dock—a cluster of partygoers drunkenly stumbling down the tongue of wood toward its edge, tripping past the chaise lounges and heaped clothes. Evan felt like a railroad spike had been jammed through him, but Marcus's eyes were lidded and cool.

The kids on the dock were laughing and singing the lyrics to the Journey song that was blasting from the shore. Evan could make out the whispers of their bodies—four boys and two girls, the latter clinging to each other like they were falling through the sky. One of the boys drank the remainder of whatever was in his plastic cup, which he crumpled and tossed toward the lake. None of them, in their laughter and tumbling gait, had seen Marcus and Evan.

"This way," Marcus whispered, cutting through the water with a simple breaststroke, heading off to the right of the intruders.

Their bodies sliced through the water in silence. While the kids laughed—the boys dared one another to leap into the lake naked—Evan and Marcus reached a neighboring dock and stationed themselves beneath it, clinging to the wet wood of a post buried in the lake's sanded bottom. Evan could smell the rot, like an unclean aquarium. Something old, lost, ignored. Marcus's breathing was shallow and raspy, his hand splayed like a starfish on the post. Evan watched as the boys on the dock unbuckled their belts, letting their cargo shorts fall to their ankles while the girls with them snorted and laughed. One of the boys twisted away from the others, peeling at his socks, and leaned over the side of the dock like a crane so he was staring straight at Evan and

Marcus but didn't register their bodies in the dank underside of the dock.

Marcus's touch came suddenly, a hand dipping into the water and pressing against the small of Evan's back, where a particularly knotted clump of vernix marked the hard flare of his sacrum. He said nothing, forced himself not to react to the feel of Marcus's fingertips except to let his eyes slide from the kids on the dock toward Marcus.

"Huh," Marcus said, blinking at Evan. Then he gave his attention back to the partiers on the dock. The four boys were stripped down to their boxers.

"Ten bucks," one of them said.

"Twenty."

"Twenty bucks just to flash your junk and jump in the lake? No way."

"Then you do it. Ten bucks."

"Okay."

Before long came a splash that sent small ripples of water toward Evan and Marcus. Evan felt invaded, the pulse of liquid like an earthquake turning the world beneath his feet upside down, sending everything off-center. He hoped, momentarily, that the boy who had dived into the lake wouldn't breach the surface, that some watery monster would recognize the sin he'd committed and snatch him by the feet, use its powerful jaws to drag him down to be chewed up and shat out into the weedy bottom. Three more splashes followed, then laughter floated through the air, throaty noise with manufactured depth. The boys' shapes were tangled and bobbing against the surface of the water fifteen feet away, and Evan felt his breath catch when he imagined them discovering him and Marcus huddled beneath the dock.

Marcus's hand was still pressed against Evan's back, a burning, sizzling pan of fingers spread against his skin. The fingertips were tracing the line of vernix that cut across him at his hip. The sensation was blurring, an intoxicant that threatened to make his vision go spangly, as if he'd held his breath for too long. He glanced at Marcus, who was still staring down the boys in the water nearby.

"Hey, you fucks," one of the girls shouted, rattling an empty beer can. "I'm thirsty."

"Come on, Melissa," one of the boys crooned from the water. "The water's fine. You should hop in too."

"With your mangy dick flopping in the water? No thanks. I don't want AIDS."

The rest of the gaggle guffawed and lowed like a cluster of cows. The boys made for the shore, bodies slicing like silverfish through the dark surface. They looked like monsters as they hauled themselves up into the scutch grass poking toward the bank, skin dripping with rivulets of water like little bays of tears. Clutching at their groins and giggling, they dashed up to the dock and wriggled into their clothes while the girls hooted and chided the swimmers' sudden embarrassment. The group was effervescent, purling out bubbly chuckles while fabric slid up wet thighs and belts clanked like bells.

When they were gone, Marcus pulled his hand from Evan's back. "Come on," he said.

They swam back toward their clothes, Marcus in the lead, cutting across the surface of the water in a slow crawl, his skin lit and taut in the shine of moonlight. He had the body of a lacrosse or tennis player, narrow in the trunk and thick on the bottom, shoulders rounded and twitching but not huge, back crenellated like the surface of the moon. Evan watched as Marcus threw himself up onto the lip of the deck, latissimi dorsi muscles stretching like little bird wings. But then, when Marcus had one foot on the dock edge, a pool of water sinking into the cherry-red wood, he turned, blinked at Evan, and let himself slip back into the water, bobbing up directly in front of Evan.

The kiss was a warm shock, bludgeoning and spreading through Evan like hot oil. Marcus's lips were wet and rubbery, shocked cold despite the warmth of the water and the summer night air. His breath was sweet, as if he'd just chewed mint leaves. The kiss lasted only a moment, but neither of them wrenched away with violent terror, revulsion, or regret. They parted, looking each other in the eyes, and then kissed again, this time deeper, teeth clicking together like champagne flutes during a toast. Their mouths opened; Evan felt the warm, salty press of Marcus's tongue. He could feel all of it—the glimmering bumps of taste buds; a strip of flat flesh, burnt from something hot; and the smooth, veined underside. It felt like running his hand along sanded and varnished wood.

When they began to sink, the water gurgling up toward their mouths, they separated again, dipping under the water and rising with paired, chimed laughter. Marcus smiled and turned to the dock again and hauled himself out. Evan watched him march toward their piled wet clothes, his hands spreading water out in large ripples like the billowing folds of a cancan dress, his legs kicking to keep him afloat.

"Are you coming?" Marcus asked. His voice sounded far away, strained, so Evan cut through the water and lifted himself toward the dock.

As he unfurled his wet body on the end of the dock, the vernix, curled around his body like potato vines, began to shimmer. But this was not a combination of water and moonlight; something bright from inside of Evan was glowing across his skin. The wax grew brighter and brighter, taking on first the lumens of a cigarette lighter, then a torch, then a bulb, then a spotlight. It grew and grew—stadium-light strength, eventually, so strong he himself was blinded by the shine emanating from his naked skin. He was sure the partygoers on the grass thirty yards away must be staring at him, their games of circle of death and canoe races interrupted, their attention diverted from keg stands and Jell-O shots, the funk of teenage body spray and vomit cut apart by the slicing light coming from Evan. His whole self tingled with it.

And then, just as quickly, the light faded, vanishing into a pinprick along his chest and collapsing like a black hole. The party raged on, shrieks of laughter and celebration coursing through the air. Evan looked down at himself and had to paw at his stomach and arms; the vernix was gone, slaked away without a trace, the lines of his body smooth and clear. He looked up, ready to call out to Marcus, but then Evan felt a plunge in his throat as if he'd swallowed his tongue. The dock was empty. The chaise lounges were lonely and uninhabited, the only pile of clothes snaked under the wood his own.

The Time You Give and
the Time You Take

My twin brother, Dave, was one of the first people approved to go through the wormhole that settled over Los Angeles in 2005, which burst into the sky like a flower shoving out of soil. The fact that he was a twin was a bonus, apparently, to the researchers who wanted to understand the wormhole, a twisting purplish bruise hanging in the foggy downtown. When he told my parents that he'd been accepted onto the crew, my mother sobbed into her bowl of spaghetti and my father pressed himself away from the table, leaning his chair back on two legs, the wood whining. He shook his head while he dabbed meat sauce from his lips and mustache, as if to say, *Look what you've done, kid*. My father was the only other person in the world besides me who could see that my brother was a fuckup, unmoved by Dave's wry smile that on me always looked like a sign of insanity but on his face managed to put other people at ease, like they were petting a puppy or receiving a shoulder rub.

We were mirror-image twins; the ruddy splash of birthmark on my left cheek streaked across Dave's right; the mole on the end of my right pinky finger bloomed on his left. The fertilized egg that was going to make us one person split in half more than a week after conception. As children, our mother would remind us of our connection when we were scared at night or during thunderstorms. When sirens blared and we crammed into the small closet under the basement stairs, a cramped room that smelled of mold and old plastic toys, my father grunted and complained while our mother nudged us. "Hug each other," she'd say. We were five years old, obedient string beans. I would clutch Dave, and he would grip me back, our skins sticky with fear, and I would close my eyes and imagine us mucking around in yellow yolk, arms crossed at the elbows, doing a gloopy dance.

My mother, father, and I watched on their small tube-backed television as the squat, arrowhead-shaped spacecraft crawled up into the air toward the swirling gash in the sky; clouds twisted into spirals as they drew near the wormhole and were eventually sucked through, disappearing without a sound, though I imagined a slurp like water shooting down a freshly unclogged drain. The streets of downtown LA were filled with people who looked like sprinkles thanks to the news cameras' towering helicopter height. Some were science enthusiasts, enamored of the potential gateway to other worlds; others were members of religious groups convinced the wormhole was evidence of the end of days. All of their faces were upturned, a sea of various shades of peach and brown, noses tiny smudges on the ocean of faces.

The silvery white pod containing my brother and nine other people—one intrepid astronaut, a physicist, an aeronautical engineer, and six others who were no more extraordinary than Dave—ascended like a polished pearl floating up to the surface of a sooty bathtub. When the craft had closed in on the wormhole, it shot forward, spitting inside and disappearing. My parents sobbed, my mother barely breathing. I made dinner that night and crushed up a sleeping pill in my mother's water so she would rest, something she hadn't done since my brother announced his departure.

No other aircraft wanted to get close to it, and the wormhole neither expanded nor retracted. Nothing came out of it until the globular pod reappeared exactly ten years after it went through. People had effectively given up on those ten explorers ever returning, and only every now and then did a sleepy reporter pop up on the late-night news to announce that there was no activity or progress in unlocking the wormhole's mysteries. Sometimes, *60 Minutes* or one of the nightly national news stations would run an episode on the families of those who went through the wormhole, pallid reports that no one really cared about. They aired on Friday nights, everything about them lifeless: the backdrops were always the pinkish-beige of drab, cheap hotel room curtains, the reporters unremarkable and unknown. The guests sat wrinkled and dark eyed and somehow damp looking, their suits ill fitting and dresses unflattering. I never participated, erasing the voicemails from agents and producers desperate to get me on camera. I was busy with my own life's transformations: in the ten years that Dave was gone, both of our parents died and I had moved to Oakland, come out, and met my boyfriend Rand.

I had seen Rand Murphy on television many times before the night I met him at a quiet pub called the Streampunk, a small mahogany-lined room with a horseshoe bar and six or seven high-top tables, each illuminated by a green, glass desk lamp that gave the place the dizzying, dull quality of dreams. The bartender wore all black, her ropy hair swaying down past her waist as she glided across the holey Teknor Apex mats to fill my beer. When she set the glass down, I leaned in and asked if the guy sitting by himself at the end of the bar was Rand Murphy.

She smiled. "He comes in here a lot because no one recognizes him, probably because they'd never expect him here."

He wore an Oakland A's hat pulled tight over his short black hair, and he was leaning over his beer, his huge baseball player's shoulders hunched up as if protecting the glass from some unseen rain. I watched him for a few minutes; he was staring up at the single television, a bright flat-screen TV fastened above the alcove leading to the restroom, the fluorescent, shining colors of flashing basketball players clashing with the room's humble dim. He sipped his wheat-colored beer every thirty seconds or so, and I mirrored his drinking, looking up when he turned to glance in my direction, giving my attention to the USC game on the TV screen.

I played basketball in high school—not as well as Dave, as was the case with everything athletic; we were both lanky, but he had the attacking attitude of a linebacker that made him seem twenty pounds heavier—and followed USC religiously. Dave had abandoned ship and cheered for whichever team became the clear favorite every year, mocking my devotion to the Trojans; they never made any headway in the NCAA tournament, but I cheered them on and watched as many of their games as I could, imagining myself on the floor of the Galen Center surrounded by cheering fans whose clamorous screams sounded like rushing water from my spot on the court.

At some point, Rand materialized next to me, pulling out the nearest barstool. I turned, and he was smiling, his dimples cavernous, jawline sharp and covered in a spiky, day-old beard. On television he looked muscular, with a broad back and a Titan's legs, but up close he was gargantuan, an impossible rawness of power radiating from his skin like a force field. I suddenly felt very small, slippery and round as a tadpole.

He slid onto the barstool and turned toward me. "I'm Rand," he said, smiling. His teeth were perfect-model white, and his lips were glossy and kissable. Even more kissable because he didn't seem to assume I knew exactly who he was.

"Daniel," I said, raising my glass to hide the tremble in my hands. He raised his back, and smiled wider.

I never asked him how he knew, how he could tell that my furtive stares were more than those of the gaping, awestruck fan. How he could tell that, had he invited me to take my clothes off, I'd have shucked my khakis in a heartbeat, sent my boat shoes crashing through the top-shelf liquor bottles and mirrored wall behind them.

Three years later, when Dave showed up, he knocked on Rand Murphy's door, which was also mine.

Until Dave's departure, I had felt no sense of my aging; having a twin made that process undetectable, because not only did I see myself every day when I looked in the mirror while I brushed my teeth or wrangled my uncooperative hair or popped in my contact lenses, I also had Dave—my exact self running around, a living reflection. We shared a room growing up, straight until college, our beds one opposite the other. When we were children, we would roll onto our sides and talk to each other until our mother rapped on the door and berated us for not sleeping. Even through the dark I could see my own face, its slow, day-by-day transformation from childhood to puberty to adulthood invisible. Although I'm thirty-three now, I still get carded by bored teenagers at the grocery store when I buy a bottle of wine with my cereal and lunch meat. People often think that, because I'm with Rand, who is still a spry twenty-eight, we're the same age. And while our half-decade gap doesn't seem like much when I think about the wide swath of years between many celebrity pairings, I'm at the point in my nonyouth where I do wonder what thirty-three looks and sounds and feels like. Should I drink more tea? Load up on kale and spinach? Read the *New York Times* and understand the stock market?

I recognized Dave's knock, the same he'd used we went trick-or-treating or harassed our neighbors during school fundraisers: one long rap, a pause, two short taps, and one final heavy thud. I had expected him to get in touch eventually, but he hadn't called or written or any such thing upon his return two weeks prior. I wasn't surprised that he'd found his way to me; for all his flightiness and buoyancy, I would never accuse my brother of being unresourceful. Once, when we were twelve, we begged our father for a dog, and he told us that if we could build it a doghouse, he'd get us one. Dave trekked back and forth from our yard to an abandoned construction site six blocks over, stacks of unmatched lumber stretched over his arms, and put together a ramshackle thing I wouldn't wish upon the most vicious dog in the world. Our father shrugged, relenting.

And so I opened the door with a manufactured enthusiasm, a flourish of welcome-back.

And for the first time I saw not the me I'd seen in the mirror that morning or the day before, but the me of nearly ten years ago, when Dave disappeared into the sky.

⸺

Dave and I stared at each other. Seeing himself ten years advanced was scrambling his brain just as much as seeing a living, breathing replica of myself from a generation earlier was playing games with my own. His mouth lay slack like uncoiled rope, eyes stretched wide like Edvard Munch's wobbly screamer. If Dave had aged at all, the difference was immaterial and unnoticeable: his forehead was still swept clean; a thick fence of hair rose against his skull. His jawline was intact, and the broad shoulders—the biggest thing that differentiated us as we grew, as Dave fell in love with the gym and weights and I did not—strong and swagger-filled as ever.

"Holy shit," I said.

"Wow," he said.

I stepped aside to let him into the house.

"How did you find me?"

Dave looked around, as though seeing vaulted ceilings and an open floor plan for the first time. "I was working for the government, Dan. It wasn't hard to track you down." He wandered through the foyer on a self-guided tour, and I trailed after him.

"I'm sure you have questions," I said.

"I'm sure I do, but damn, this house. The kitchen is bigger than Mom and Dad's whole place."

I felt a tightness in my stomach, and I wondered whether Dave knew all that had passed. He was never a mourner. When our grandmother died when we were ten, I was tormented by nightmares and the blackness of her absence. All Dave had wondered was who would send us dollar bills on our birthday; while I cried in the car on the way to the funeral, Dave fidgeted at the tie cinching his collar shut.

I asked if he knew how long he'd been gone.

"Well, yeah." He stared at me. "Ten years is a long time."

We lapsed into another prolonged appraisal. I tried to imagine what Dave was thinking of me: since meeting Rand I had worked my way into better shape, my chest tighter and more defined than it ever had been, and my legs weren't as stringy and sallow. But my hairline had started to recede, and Rand had found a few grays in the scraggly cowlick behind the crown of my head. Crow's feet nipped at my eyes. As I looked my brother over I wondered which of us would have it worse: Dave, who could see what his future had in store for him, always having a ten-year preview of himself, or me, who would constantly have to be reminded of what was gone.

———

I took Dave out for a beer after he dropped his things in one of the two guest bedrooms ("Such choices!" Dave said, slapping his hands together and rubbing them like he'd just come in from the cold), and took a shower. I led him to the Streampunk, and I pulled out the very barstool I'd been sitting on when I first met Rand.

"So," I said when the beers had been delivered. "You're obviously welcome to stay with us for however long you need to figure out what you want to do."

"Well." Dave sipped his beer and smacked his lips. "I hope you'll let me stay longer than that because I've already got it figured out."

"Oh?"

"I want to open a bar. Kind of like this one, actually."

"You do."

"Yeah. I've always wanted to own this sort of place. And my payment from the good ol' US of A is plenty to invest."

"Do you even know anything about running a business?" Dave had majored in English, barely passing—and sometimes not—his courses because he loved to read but hated to write. I wasn't convinced that he actually knew how to do math, even the easy stuff before algebra and the inclusion of letters.

He shrugged. "That's where you come in."

"Dave, I already have a job. A well-paying job that takes up a lot of my time."

"Yeah," he said, "but this way you can be with your kid brother every day."

"We're twins, Dave."

Dave smiled. "By the look of things, not anymore."

We took turns asking questions, volleying answers and inquiries back and forth like we were playing tennis.

"Was I really gone ten years?"

"Yep. Ten years. What did they tell you when you came back?"

"Not much. So you and some baseball player, huh?"

"Yeah. How long did it feel like to you?"

"A flash, then we were back. In and out. Like that one movie. Tell me, how long have you been with this guy?"

"A long time. Three years. We met here, actually. You serious about this bar thing?"

"Hell yeah, I am. So, are you gay, or what?"

"Or what, I guess. Mom and Dad are dead. You know that?"

"Yeah, I know. Cancer, right?"

"Dad was cancer. Mom was a stroke. She went first."

"That's a shame," Dave said, flicking up a finger toward the bartender to pour us more drinks.

I took a deep breath. "Why do you say that?"

"Well, Dad was always worried about being alone."

"He didn't last much longer than Mom."

"I guess that's good."

"He was in pain, mostly. Emotionally speaking."

"And physically?"

"That too, yeah."

Dave leaned against the bar, propping his head up with his fist. "You seem angry at me."

"Well, you did kind of leave for ten years."

"That's not my fault. First of all, I didn't know we'd be gone that long."

"You still left. You had to assume. How could you possibly know you'd ever come back?"

"And second of all, it was no time for me, which, I would like to note, is a very strange feeling."

"Kinda brought that upon yourself though, didn't you?"

Dave shrugged. "I did it for scientific inquiry."

"And that was it? Just in and out. Nothing on the other side."

"Really, Dan, I mean it. Going through a wormhole? It was a fucking thing, let me tell you. Scrambled brain and all."

I stared at him.

"You really think I wouldn't tell you if there was something on the other side?"

I picked up my newly delivered beer, took a deep sip, and shrugged. "I dunno."

"Come on."

All I could do was drink.

———

We drove to the cemetery where Mom and Dad were buried. On the way Dave pried at me, demanding I paint a picture of what they'd been like in their final days. I told him that the two deaths were as different as could be, Mom's a sudden knifing, like ripping out a perfectly healthy tooth. She had been cooking a bolognese one rainy afternoon, our father sitting at the kitchen table playing solitaire while she browned salsiccia. As he started shuffling for a second game, a queer, quizzical look came over my mother's face, like she was trying to solve a complex math problem in her head. She held a wooden spoon like an extended appendage, then dropped it on the floor, spattering the white linoleum with flecks of grease.

She collapsed without saying another word, dead before the paramedics tracked their muddy footprints through the house. The wheels of the stretcher that carried her out, body zipped up in a bag while my father looked on from the corner, still clutching the phone, left dual tracks along the living room carpet that I could never entirely get out; even after going over them three times with a steam cleaner, I could still make out the paired lines leading to the door like a running lane on a track.

Although our father also went quickly, his death was not unexpected. I told Dave to imagine himself driving down a road and seeing that there is a dead end far ahead. You have plenty of notice, all the time you might need to slow down, stop, and turn around, but the steering column and brakes are jammed, so the only thing you can do is find some kind of peace, steady yourself against the seat, and tighten your seatbelt. I told him how our father had melted into a skeletal, pale version of himself, the tumor in his pancreas spreading its wild growth to his bones and lymph nodes, swelling his armpits with searing pain. Dave was staring at the trees swaying over gravestones as we ambled along through the cemetery. I imagined him trying to picture our parents' tombstones, what would be etched there, whether fresh flowers were laid upon their graves.

The grass was dewy and the faint smell of honeysuckle and lilacs clung to the air. Dave started humming, looking into the sky, a single blue dome like a crystalline lake.

"I can't believe you managed so well," he said.

I wanted to tell him that I hadn't. That I had contacted the church our parents attended for decades. I walked rows of caskets, choosing the right color, style, price. I filled out life insurance forms and spent hours on the phone with realtors to sell the house, retained a lawyer to settle the estate, pestered credit card companies and the bank to close lines of credit and checking accounts. Liquidating their money market account took months, plenty of lost sleep, and truncheons of stress knobbing into my muscles. I sorted through my parents' basement, choosing which keepsakes I would haul into my own life and which to donate to the Salvation Army. I chose the memories that mattered, and I did it all alone.

———

Rand came home for the weekend. Dave oohed and aahed that he was meeting a professional baseball player despite the fact that Dave had no clue who Rand was. We stood in the kitchen, Rand and I on one side of the marble-topped island and Dave on the other, holding tumblers of Bunnahabhain 25, the oaky bottle standing like an obelisk between us. Because Rand wouldn't talk of his fame as a player, I did for him: a third baseman, four years into his career, a power hitter with great fielding finesse, a leading defenseman who was also in the top ten in the American League in RBIs and home runs.

"Do your teammates know you're gay?" Dave said.

"Really, Dave?"

"Or bi or whatever. Sorry. I'm just wondering. When I, you know, went away, there were no out athletes. I'm curious. What?" He stared at me. "I want to know the times I'm living in now. Should I not be asking? Do people not ask these kinds of things?"

"It's fine," Rand said in his rich voice, not quite deep like James Earl Jones but masculine and easy, waltzing the fine line between alpha and sensitive with the deftness of a dancer. "They know, yes. And most of them don't care at all."

"Most of them?"

"Dave."

Rand shrugged, letting one finger press against my arm.

"There are a few guys who are clearly freaked out, like they think I'm ogling them in the shower."

"Which he's not," I added before I could stop myself. I felt my face growing hot. This was a conversation Rand and I had never had; in our years together we had never spoken of our lives as out men, especially his, on television so many nights of the year. Partly this was my fault: I never knew how to broach the subject. I'd barely been able to do it for myself, drunkenly announcing on Facebook one night that I was attracted to both men and women. People had flooded me with support before I could bury or retract what I'd written, but life moved along as if nothing had changed. Now, though, I felt a pressing, chest-heaving shame: Dave, knowing my boyfriend for less than an hour, had recognized important questions that had never occurred to me.

We ate dinner at a low-lit Italian restaurant. Dave insisted on paying. I thought the place must be out of his price range, but I had no sense of what his price range was. He kept hinting at his "sizable" income from the wormhole trip, but Dave never dropped a solid number, and I didn't press because that was so clearly what he wanted me to do. Dave and Rand did most of the talking, pausing only to chew hunks of lasagna and tagliatelle; my longest utterances were to our petite waitress, whose voice was softer than the candles lighting the tables in their red, enclosing sconces and who clearly had no idea who Rand was. While Dave and Rand laughed at each other's jokes—their chuckling too hearty and gregarious for a restaurant that wouldn't let you in the door in anything less than slacks and a tie—I drained three sizable glasses of Sangiovese, the bulbous light on the table turning watery. My steak knife scraped against my plate with abandon while I sawed my pollo ubriaco. I kept picturing Dave floating in space, not the black, star-sprinkled expanse one sees in pictures and movies but something intangible and pink, a swirling, psychedelic purgatory, all floating and silence, my brother bouncing along, his lovable, shit-eating grin plastered across his face like an ad in *Good Housekeeping*.

Getting into bed that night, Rand, pulling off his undershirt, said, "Your brother seems like a nice guy."

"He's young," I said. I knew my voice was slippery, my tongue lacquered with alcohol.

"Do you think it's weird for him? Having, you know, ten years just gone?"

"He seems to be adjusting okay." I slipped into the bed and waggled my toes against the crisp sheets.

"You alright?" Rand curved onto his side to face me, his bicep flattening against his ribs like a sandbag. I looked him over, admiring his caterpillar eyebrows that crinkled the skin of his forehead when he raised them in concern. He looked like a stuffed animal. Rand reached toward me with one arm, poking at my chest. "I'm talking to you."

I tried not to smile. "Yeah, I'm okay. It's just weird."

"You never talked about him much," Rand said. "I have to say I found that a bit strange. No offense."

"He's more open than I am."

"I got that."

"You two would probably be more compatible than us," I said.

"Nah." Rand reached out with one finger and traced the edges of my birthmark, running a ridged fingernail toward the pinch of my cheek and nose. "This thing looks much better on you." He scooted closer, the smell of his piney aftershave still clinging to his pores.

—

Dave spent his days lying on the couch in sweatpants and ratty old T-shirts he'd overpaid for at pop-punk shows in the early 2000s, his bare feet propped on the arm as he sloughed through the two hundred channels Rand insisted we subscribe to, shrugging whenever I asked what he had planned for the day. He said he was taking his time with things.

"It's a slow process, Dan," he said whenever I mentioned his dream bar.

"Could you please call me Daniel? I don't go by Dan anymore."

"Since when?"

"Since about seven years ago. After both of our parents died. Neither of which you were around for."

—

When I admitted why I looked familiar to him, Rand slapped the table, shaking our water glasses and frosted beer mugs. We sat in a half-empty pizza joint on our second date on a chilly Friday night, the windows crowded with condensation that spotted and blurred the pedestrians darting down the sidewalk. I'd caved and told him my brother was one of the people who'd gone through the wormhole.

"I knew I'd seen your face on television before. Well, your face from years ago. How long have they been gone?"

"Little under seven years. Seven years next week, actually."

"Do you do anything to celebrate? I guess that's not the right word."

"Not really."

"Think they'll ever come back?"

I looked over Rand's shoulder and felt a strange shame for having suggested this place, which reeked of childishness: white and red tiles everywhere, a cartoonish Italian chef tossing dough in the air painted on a far wall, his exaggerated clown nose hovering over a bristly mustache shaped like a comb. His hat flopped to one side, and his bell-bottoms cupped over the tops of his black shoes. Every surface was sticky like flypaper, and the lighting shone with a fluorescent hardness, but it was exactly the kind of place, like the Streampunk, where someone like Rand would never be expected and thus wasn't noticed.

"I actually don't think about Dave that much anymore," I said. "I guess I've kind of accepted that he's gone."

"Why did he go in the first place?"

"I don't know. He was kind of a failure. Didn't finish college."

"Me either."

"Yeah, but you signed a lucrative baseball contract. My brother didn't finish his senior seminar project."

"I probably wouldn't have finished an English paper either." He smiled, face creasing in all the right places.

———

Suddenly, Dave started aging. I like to tell myself I'm a young thirty-three, but even I can feel in my bones that I'm not as spry as I was ten years ago, when Dave left. My muscles tighten with soreness faster, I have to run more miles to account for my decreasing metabolism. I can't drink more than three beers without feeling their drying effect in my mouth the next morning. I strain and yawn after ten at night.

Dave woke up complaining of headaches and hangovers but after not drinking; bags crowded under his eyes like he hadn't pulled in eight hours of sleep, and his hair started climbing back against his scalp as if marching away, a dime-size bald spot erupting overnight.

"I've had checkups," Dave said one afternoon. "They can't figure out what's wrong with us."

"Us?"

"It's happening to the others, too. We keep in touch."

"Naturally."

"How did you deal with this?"

"With what?"

"Getting older."

"Well," I said, "I had a lot more time to do it than you seem to."

Watching him age was like a slower, nonfatal version of the moment in *Raiders of the Lost Ark* when the ark is opened and all of the Nazis go gooey, crumbling to death in seconds while their muscle and skin and hair peel away, sloughed off like winter coats. Dave's hair didn't shrivel to white and his skin didn't boil, eyeballs popping out and tongue standing stiff like a diving board, but he did droop. He couldn't exercise with enough intensity to stop himself from wilting, his muscles still well formed but sliding down all over, like he was some blurring, melting version of himself.

———

Dave's decline slammed to a stop when, one morning, he and I again looked exactly alike. He barged into the master bathroom while I was brushing my teeth. I was wearing only a towel.

"Jesus, Dave."

He, too, was shirtless, his hips and groin covered by a sweat-stained pair of mesh shorts.

"Why won't it stop?" he said, looking me up and down. I flicked a spray of shaving cream from the corner of my mouth.

"It doesn't ever stop, Dave."

"I'm as old as you now."

"It would appear so."

"I look just like you."

"What else is new?" I set down the razor and stared at him. For the time being our only difference was his shorts and my towel, his slightly grizzled face and my half-smooth, half-lathered one. I searched his eyes and saw his bewilderment, his unhappiness: he'd been given a chance to step forward in time without aging, but now his body had decided to make the leap to catch up. That was not all: he had been remolded, musculature and mass rearranged into a near replica of my own. Not all of Dave's hard work in the gym in his younger years had been wiped away, but enough: we'd been made equals.

"Help."

"What do you want me to do?"

He thought for a moment, then to my surprise, said, "Tell me about Mom and Dad."

I set down my razor. "What do you want to know?"

He shook his head. "I don't want to know. I want to remember."

I felt a sudden sorrowful, irrational responsibility for Dave's unhappiness, like seeing an ASPCA ad filled with droopy-eared animals for the first time. He glanced at himself in the mirror and must have seen what I saw when I looked at him, something he couldn't find in me: the deflation, the emptiness left behind when all of the time he had been given was suddenly yanked back from him. I tried to imagine losing what he had lost, those ten years, the vast blank space that would ache behind his sinuses for the rest of his life, stolen in the time it takes to snap one's fingers. I reached out and set a hand on Dave's shoulder. His skin was still smooth, the muscle perhaps not softball size anymore but still muscle, the same hard surface I felt when I massaged my own shoulders, the round shape Rand feels when we hold each other at night.

I thought: Dave doesn't have someone like that. No one to hold onto when the world is spinning away.

Dave took a deep breath. "I don't know what to do, Dan."

I didn't tell him to call me Daniel. That was now, Dan was then. And Dave didn't need now. Now had invaded, flooding in, chasing and engulfing him like a swarm of bees. But he also didn't need then. Then, as his reflection in the mirror announced with unflinching brutality, was gone.

I chose instead to pull him close, to let our mirrored bodies touch. His skin was cold, and he was shaking. I felt my warmth soak into him. I pressed my chin against the soft part of him between his neck and shoulder and I squeezed tight, my hair brushing against his, holding him hard in the hope that I could somehow give back a small cut of the time that had been taken away.

Lockstep

The morning after the funeral, Denny finds all the doors padlocked from the inside, the heavy, ribbed type with strips of red rubber around the bottom so they don't ding up anything. Each lock is looped through an identical hinge that has been bolted at chest height across the frame, dark steel that is cold to the touch.

He tugs on the locks, but none of them gives. He runs a finger around each keyhole. Denny could break a window, he supposes, but the sound of shattering glass has always made him nauseous. Plus, Mikey had just replaced all the windows—they were ancient, leaky, killing the heating and cooling bills—and the idea of destroying them makes his guts hurt, as if he's swallowed something jagged.

Worry nudges its snout into his chest, so Denny takes several deep breaths. He goes into the bathroom and stares at himself in the mirror, surprised by how refreshed he looks; he went to bed at ten last night and woke after nine. Eleven hours of dreamless, uninterrupted sleep that he hadn't expected, prepared as he was for horrible nightmares, for his body to jolt him awake, for him to reach out his hands and feel at the empty bed. But then again, all of that had already happened in the week that led up to the funeral, when Denny found himself suffocating beneath all the requisite phone calls and arrangements. He'd forgotten, in all that weight pushing at him from different directions, to call the university. When he finally remembered, he felt lucky to still have his job. The English Department chair, for whom he worked as a program administrator's assistant, told him to take a few more weeks off.

He decides he is still asleep. Denny thumps his head with the heel of his hand, but all he gets is a throbbing temple. He pinches his triceps and feels a bruise bloom, but he's still standing rather than stirring to life in his bed, body twisted in the unwashed sheets. So Denny decides to go back to bed. His stomach is suffering an itchy ache, something spicy and vaguely molten, equal parts hunger and heartburn. Eventually, when the hurt in his stomach turns to hunger, Denny throws his pillows against the wall and heaves himself out of bed, annoyed that something as basic and simple as nourishment has the gall to rear its head.

While he fries an egg and a turkey sausage patty, his eyes keep sliding toward the lock on the kitchen door; it glimmers, clean and fresh and new. He can look out at the back patio but can't go into the sunshine that beams down on the salvia plants that Mikey arranged in a blaze of reds and purples. The grass could use trimming, a chore Mikey loved but Denny hates, but what's he to do about it now?

He burns the turkey patty. He eats it anyway, the meat crackling between his teeth. Chewing it is like gnawing on a strip of leather. The eggs are rubbery and bland; he has forgotten salt or pepper, and the yolk has congealed into a pasty, crumbly mass. Mikey was the better cook. He was better at just about everything, except maybe paperwork, which Denny did pro bono for Mikey's contracting and landscaping business. He'd had to call all of the current clients and explain what happened. He offered to help them find new builders and electricians, but they all said, "Oh, no, of course not. Don't worry about it," even though he could hear the annoyance in their tight breaths.

Denny decides to try opening a window. He and Mikey loved fresh breezes. Some nights, when the weather was mild, they would pull open their bedroom window and turn off the air-conditioning and let the sounds of suburban sprawl—cars humping over the road, birds throating out morning songs, katydids and cicadas sawing up their wavy noises—wash over them as they tried to sleep or read or have sex. In the morning, they would stand at the screen and look outside, Mikey's hand on Denny's hip.

But the windows won't open.

Denny thinks maybe he's just exhausted. He tries all three bedroom windows again, shoving aside the thick bamboo-slatted blinds. None open. Denny squints at the frames: they're painted shut, carefully, the white thick but elegant. He works the latches, tries poking at the paint with a butter knife he grabs from the kitchen, but nothing doing: the windows refuse to open. The same in the living room. The same above the sink. The same in the guest bathroom, where one has to be cognizant of who might be in the neighbor's side yard while taking a piss. He returns to the front door and shakes the padlock.

He hears his phone ring and remembers that he is meant to get brunch with his cousin Calista. She insisted at the end of the funeral, cornering him in the vestibule of the funeral home with its dizzy green walls and too many calla lilies. He was buzzy with grief and allergies and couldn't come up with a reason to say no. Denny knew that his family didn't want him to be alone; his mother and father came over right after he called to tell them about the accident and his sister came a few hours later. They wouldn't leave his orbit until he let out a howl of frustration and asked—please—for some time alone. His mother blinked, tearing up, but then Denny's father led her out of the house, and they stayed away until the next morning. His sister, Jenny, had done the same, but she'd texted him that night, *If you let me come back tomorrow, I'll bring wine.*

When he answers, Calista says, "I'm outside."

Denny forks apart the front window blinds and sees her cherry-red Camaro growling in the driveway. She waves through the windshield.

"I see you," he says.

"Well? Hurry up. I need coffee and mimosas and biscuits and gravy."

"I can't come."

"Denny."

"No, really."

"I know you're hurting. But don't do this. It's not healthy."

He watches her pop open the driver's-side door, the engine quieting. She's all brown hair and sunglasses. She lifts her Ray-Bans and catches sight of him staring from the living room. Her eyes are shadowed a neon blue, like a popsicle. Denny and Calista grew up together; their families had bought houses in the same neighborhood, and although the intention was for Jenny and Calista to become best friends, the moment Denny got his first video game system—a Nintendo 64—Calista plopped down cross-legged on the floor next to him. She picked up an unused controller, fitting it into her hands like a pro, and said, "What are we playing?"

He watches her pop out her left hip, drumming her free hand on the hood of the Camaro.

"I really can't come out."

"Denny. Talk to me. Tell me what you need."

"There are locks."

"You have keys. It's your house."

"You don't understand," he says.

"Of course I don't understand. I can't imagine what you're going through."

"That isn't what I mean."

"Then what do you mean?"

"Hang on," he says, hanging up. He lifts a finger toward the window, signaling *one second*, and then goes to the front door. He snaps a photo of the lock and texts it to her.

"What is this?"

"It's a lock."

"I know that. Why did you send me this?"

"It's on my door."

"Just take it off."

"I can't."

"This isn't funny, Denny."

"No jokes. They're everywhere."

"Denny."

"I didn't do it."

"This isn't going to help."

"I didn't do it."

"Literally locking yourself in."

"I swear."

"It's childish, really."

"But I didn't."

"I can't help you if you won't help yourself."

"I'm not trying to keep myself locked away in here," he says, but he feels the squirming roots of a lie. Maybe he does want to stay here, vaulted in his house, a tomb that contains the world as it last was when Mikey still moved through it.

"There's got to be a key somewhere."

Denny doesn't say anything. Eventually, Calista exhales an angry breath and turns on her heels.

"Call me when you want to come out, okay?" she says. She hangs up before he can say anything. Denny can't decide whether he wants to say "I want to come out now" or "I never want to leave again."

———

Calista doesn't leave right away. Denny watches her watching him through the window, and eventually he shrugs and lies down on the living room sofa, throwing an arm over his eyes. He listens to her tires crunch over the concrete, the chassis giving out the briefest moan as the car galumphs into the road. With his eyes closed, he can almost feel the tilt of the planet as it spins its daily revolution, and he wishes there was a brake he could yank, some simple lever he could tug to bring everything to a halt.

Eventually, he makes a pair of loose, cold quesadillas. Denny chews slowly, standing at the kitchen sink, letting crumbs and shreds of cheddar collect in the basin. Halfway through eating, Denny can't swallow anymore. The cheese and tortilla are a hardened lump, lodged deep in his thorax, aching between his ribs. He drinks a glass of water, but instead of smoothed out he feels like he is drowning.

He checks his email. Someone, probably his boss, must have spread word about Mikey, because his inbox is full of notes of condolence. Denny deletes them, one at a time, barely reading. He offers no thank-yous in reply; he wants silence to do the talking for him, though he has no idea what he wants it to say.

On Monday, someone comes to the door, to deliver flowers. Denny is lying on the sofa, the blinds open, and the man can see him. When Denny doesn't get up, he rings the doorbell again. Denny tries to gesture for the man to leave the flowers on the welcome mat, but he's sure he just looks like he's having a seizure. The man glares at him through the window, but then eventually shrugs, sets the vase down, and leaves. A spray of chrysanthemums, Denny can see, if he twists his neck just so.

He watches the mailman stuff his box full of envelopes, bills and junk and maybe a copy of the *New Yorker*. Mikey liked the cartoons and entered the free caption contest all the time. He never won, but Denny always enjoyed his entries more than the ones printed in the magazine.

Calista calls twice. He doesn't answer. She texts him, *Please just let me know you're alive.*

Definitely dead, he replies. She tries to call a third time, but he sends her straight to voicemail.

I can't do talking, he writes.

The phone stays silent after that. He expects his parents to call, or Jenny, but they do not. Denny can't decide if he's relieved or upset. He assumes Calista has passed along her concerns, maybe even mentioned the locks. He receives a text from one of the adjuncts who teaches freshman comp, extending her sympathies.

He doesn't text her back. Maybe later.

Later seems to be the ideal time for everything. He'll worry about the flowers later. He'll get the mail later. Later, later, later. When his groin goes tight with the need to urinate, he thinks *I'll pee later. I'll drink water later. I'll do some jumping jacks later. I'll read a book later. I'll settle my upset stomach, my seared throat, later.*

On Wednesday, his sister finally calls.

"Hi," he says.

"Calista's worried about you."

"You're not?"

"Should I be?"

"You remember you went to Mikey's funeral last weekend, right?"

"Do you need groceries? Are you exercising? The endorphins help."

"I can't do any of that."

"Can't or won't?"

"There are locks."

"Calista mentioned that. What did you do?"

Denny wanders while he talks. The locks are still bright and steely. He squishes his fingers over the keyholes until his skin pulses with dull pain.

"I didn't do anything," he says. "They're just there."

"Are you feeling suicidal?"

"Do you just straight up ask that to all of your patients?"

"The ones who lock themselves in their houses, yes."

"I didn't lock myself in."

Jenny lets out a ragged sigh that sounds like static. He's always thought of his sister as a thunderstorm, full of black rain and electricity. Denny can never picture her sitting next to someone having a mental breakdown or suffering post-traumatic stress disorder and offering cool, calm advice. Maybe, he thinks, she uses so much of her patience and kindness with strangers that the well has dried after working hours.

"Tell me you're eating at least," she says.

"Some. It hurts to swallow."

"And sleep?"

"Plenty of that."

"There's such a thing as too much. When will you go back to work?"

He doesn't bother explaining that he couldn't go to work if he wanted to.

"You need stability," Jenny says. "Routine. Work is good for that."

"So spreadsheets and scheduling appointments for students is the way to heal?"

"Denny."

He doesn't know what to say. Denny touches his throat, which feels full of pebbles. He lets out a raw sound and tells his sister he has to go. She objects, but she can't stop him from hanging up. No one could, not even if they wanted to.

—

Jenny sends him links to websites about grief, sophomoric stuff that makes him feel ashamed of her, a trained psychiatrist, whose best solution to her brother's aching loss is listicles that look like they were made by amateurs using GeoCities or WordPress. They speak in clunky, stupid language about the five stages. As if things can be distilled with such simplicity. Check this box, move on from bargaining to depression, and you're that much closer to being over it!

Each morning he touches every lock. Sometimes the metal is warm, others a hard chill. Denny twists himself to see the chrysanthemums, whose decline sends a jar of fresh sadness through his chest. He wants to stop them from shivering away into bare stalks. Sorrow flares up hard, a horrible stab in his gut like he's been filleted.

Mikey is all around him. Their dresser is a mash-up of their clothes, boxers and socks and undershirts stuffed together. Denny puts on Mikey's pants, which are loose, and a T-shirt, wispy on him, Mikey's body swollen up from years of hauling two-by-fours and raising joists and balancing on tilty, tar-papered roofs. The clothes smell of sun-sweat and spicy aftershave. Denny wants to chew on the shirt collars just to taste something of Mikey's skin. The bathroom is full of his shampoo bottles and body wash. Denny is tempted to depress the atomizer on Mikey's cologne, fill the room with the peppery winter smell, but he knows there's only so much of it left, like the limited wishes of a genie's bottle.

Friday is shiny and wet, a sun shower that makes the sidewalk and driveway glisten. The grass, unkempt and overgrown, is a green slick. He imagines himself sliding across it. He met Mikey in college when one of Denny's friends bought a Slip 'N Slide as a joke, the banana yellow scrolled across the yard like a weird tongue. He couldn't stop staring at Mikey's tan skin, his outie belly button plattered by the hem of his board shorts. They found themselves on opposite sides of the table during a game of flip cup and when they went first, Mikey offered Denny a high-five after they both managed to turn their red Solos over on their first tries. Then, later, Mikey went flying down the slide, fast and aerodynamic, his legs knifed together and raised, strong midsection a crunch of muscle, and he flew off the end of the slide and into some hedges, from which he emerged laughing and grinning.

"It's like you're invincible," Denny said, drunk and bold. He'd brought Mikey a fresh beer without asking.

Mikey took it, swigged deep, and sighed.

"Something like that," he said, examining his chest for cuts and scratches where none were to be found.

—

So many worried emails. His boss asks if Denny will be back after the upcoming spring break. Denny doesn't bother with a reply, not yet. His sick time hasn't expired; he could miss another month of work, he's accrued so many hours.

Jenny calls again, asks about the websites. He gives a perfunctory response, something about useful information. Denny tells her he's been meditating; the lie slips out smooth. She believes him, says, "That's a great tool to use right now."

When his parents call that night, Denny doesn't answer. He puts his phone on silent and leaves it on the kitchen island. Right before bed, he walks through the house again. His phone buzzes against the Formica. Denny turns it off.

—

Saturday, a week after the funeral, Denny's body throbs him awake. Everything feels swollen, as if he's been pumped full of fluid. As he settles into consciousness, the bedroom filled with hard morning light that feels aggressive and ominous, he realizes the tight bloat in his body is centered in his throat, billowing up to his locked jaw and dry sinuses. Mikey kept nasal spray on his nightstand, and Denny reaches over for it without thinking. He lets out an involuntary groan. Where Denny's nightstand is ordered (reading lamp, alarm clock, one book), Mikey's is a chaotic mess of individually wrapped cough drops, used tissues, a tiny jar of menthol rub, spare change. But Denny finds comfort in this terrarium of disorder, relishes waving his hands over these things that were last touched by Mikey's fingers. He's remiss to disturb the tableau, but he can barely breathe.

He tries to drink water in the kitchen, but his mouth is hard and noncompliant, his tongue a dried steak. Denny coughs twice, feeling something hard lodged near his voice box. He manages to down the tiniest gulp of water.

He has new messages from his parents and sister and Calista, all texts. Calista: *Don't make me bring over an axe.* Jenny: *I think you need to see someone.* Mom: *We'd like to have you over for dinner.* None of them mentions Mikey, and he can't decide if this caution is thoughtful or a spearing erasure. How and when does one start to omit the dead? Denny knows that Mikey will fade with time, that his presence will scrub itself out. His clothes will be pulled from their hangers, his toiletries thrown into the garbage, lest they rot to muck in the shower. Eventually his smells will vanish, Denny's nose going blind to their hints in the air and sheets. Someday, even, maybe, Denny will sell their house, move somewhere that has no trace of Mikey whatsoever.

If, that is, he can ever leave.

If he ever wants to.

The locks are plump. They shimmer in the light flowing through the windows. When Denny approaches the back door, he feels his throat undulate. He might vomit, but he clamps his abs and swallows a hard breath that shifts everything from his jaw to his groin. He stares at the lock without touching it, scanning its divots and lines, the cool arc of steel slithered through the hinge's hole. Denny wonders how such a curve is made, so delicate and graceful in something so hard and impenetrable. It involves heat, he knows, and violence.

He can see, through the sliding door's glass, a rabbit trouncing through the grass. Its fur is a glimmering gold, the color of Mikey's skin. The grass is like his eyes, the red of the salvia like the flush that filled his cheeks during the first warm, sunny months of the year. Denny stands there for a long moment, committing the colors of Mikey to his memory, preparing himself to find him in whatever necessary. Denny will stamp him into the world around him, never quite letting Mikey go.

The rabbit tumbles away. Denny wants it to come back, to restore the tableau. A mewl of desire that he tries to choke back ekes out through his lips, and all of a sudden he's moaning, and then sobbing, his nose leaky with mucous, his mouth full of spittle and phlegm. Something is happening in his throat; he can feel the hard bulge that's settled there forming into a shape with bite and pulse. He presses his fingers to his throat, careful at his Adam's apple. Denny can feel the thing with his fingertips, the shape of it undeniable and obvious: a key.

Denny shakes his head. He wants to say no, but if he opens his mouth, the key will surely slide up his throat, fall from his lips, clatter on the floor. Then he will have to open the locks and throw open the doors. He'll have to text Calista and agree to meet and pretend that he can enjoy rum and live music and tacos. He'll have to call his boss and show up on campus, directing lost students to faculty offices they should have found two months ago. He'll have to mow the grass.

So he fights back the crawling sensation in his throat. Denny will open the locks and the doors eventually, but not yet. How can he? He makes a vow of silence, pressing his lips together, gritting his teeth. He swallows, tough and hard, and feels the key slither down, plunking into his stomach like a stone. Denny stands up straight, stares outside, and makes himself into a statue, unmovable against so much forward momentum.

Monarch

My sister tells me she's had sex with the boy I have a crush on. She is two years younger than me.

All I can think to ask her is what it was like, even though I know this information will be useless to me. She knows it, too, but she cocks her head to the side, smiles, and says: "It hurt a lot at first. The second time felt better."

This is how I learn that this has happened more than once.

My sister and I are very different. She is intelligent—we're in the same Algebra II class, not because I'm that stupid but because she's that smart—and blessed with good looks, high cheekbones and smooth skin, no signs of puberty's unpleasantness. When I was fifteen, my face was cratered with so much acne it looked like I had perpetual road rash, and no amount of deodorant could mask the retched, sulfuric smell of my body odor. Jenny, however, is perfect, a modelesque waif who rose to popularity like a rocket ship the moment she stepped into our high school's halls. She is, for people like me, the worst kind of popular: kind and friendly with everyone, her smile the opposite of vapid, her voice soothing and steeped with interest. She is the president of the sophomore class and would be head cheerleader if she wanted to be on the squad, but she does not. Somehow, this choice has made her more popular.

And she is sleeping with Jeremy Cologna.

She tells me this while we both sit on her queen-size bed, cross-legged, something we have done for as long as I can remember every night while our parents cook dinner. It is the one thing that we seem to have in common: we cannot stand to watch the romance of meal preparations. Our parents are young and both gorgeous—our father, in fact, was a swimwear model for a time just before I was born—with full heads of hair, strong cheekbones, and sharp jawlines, and they are desperately in love. They dance around each other in the kitchen while they cook, quite literally waltzing a few steps if they both turn around simultaneously, one from shucking vegetables, the other from stirring a simmering sauce. They laugh and kiss, and both Jenny and I roll our eyes and retreat.

A part of me thinks Jenny is undeserving to feel this disgust toward our parents' public affection, especially now that she has claimed Jeremy Cologna. He reminds me of our father: they both have chocolate-brown hair that rolls back from their foreheads into wavy locks, and Jeremy has a chin so strong it appears cut from marble. His shoulders are mango size, their roundness visible under the thickest sweater. He is, of course, a football star. But he also plays basketball and would be on the baseball team if we had one.

"Well?" she says, picking at the down comforter. We're sitting in front of each other, bodies mirroring each other.

"Well, what?"

"What do you think, Andy?"

"About you having sex with Jeremy Cologna?"

"Yes!"

"I'm not sure what I'm supposed to think."

"You won't tell Mom and Dad?"

"Why would I do that?"

"I don't know."

"Do you like him?"

"Sure, I guess. I had sex with him so I guess I like him."

"Do you love him?"

She wrinkles her brow, and her nose crinkles like she smells something rotten. "Oh no, no. He's really too stupid for me, you know?"

"He's not stupid."

"Well, okay, fair enough, but he's definitely not smart enough."

"Then why'd you have sex with him?"

Jenny cocks her head and looks at me as though I were speaking Russian. "It just seemed like a thing to do at the time." She shrugs and plies the blanket between her fingers like she is spinning silk. "It seemed like it was time."

Aside from being a genius and gorgeous, my sister has been blessed with some kind of extrasensory perception about lost things. She'll be lying on the couch eating potato chips while our mother flurries about looking for her missing car keys, and Jenny will yell out that they're on top of the piano or under a stack of bills, and voilà, there they are. Or my father can't find his key card for work, and she'll declare between slurps of cereal milk that it's probably in the stretchy mesh pocket of his briefcase, and of course she is right. When the neighbor's cat squirted out the front door in pursuit of a loud-tweeting bird in the yard, Jenny was able to pinpoint the storm drain it had curled up in for the night. Mrs. Adams gave my sister a two-hundred-dollar reward, which, to the surprise of no one, she donated to the nearest animal shelter.

There is one exception to Jenny's finding skills: me. When something of mine goes missing, her eyes get wide and she stammers out a suggestion, and she is never, ever right. The first time she realized I was immune to her power she cried, a soft *hyuck-hyuck* noise, not because she thought I had tricked her but because she felt like a failure—this when she was eight years old, already knowing what failure was—and our parents crowded around her with hugs and adorations. They both glanced at me as though I had somehow done something wrong, as if I should have lied to my sister about her incorrect assertion that my Walkman was stuffed under the bathroom sink.

The doorbell rings and Jenny bounds to the front door. I am horrified to hear the sound of Jeremy Cologna's voice in the front hall.

"What's going on?" I ask my mother.

She giggles at my father's hand encroaching across her waist, slapping it away. "Jenny asked if a boy could come to dinner."

"And you said yes?"

"Of course we did."

Jeremy sits across from me, wedged between my sister and mother, and I try not to stare at him while he chews, the muscles in his jaw popping as he bites into his food. He jokes and makes my parents laugh, my father leaning back in his seat, the sharp curve of his Adam's apple bobbing up and down as he chuckles. Jeremy is wearing a white T-shirt embossed with our school's emblem. The fabric hugs his well-toned torso; when he plucks up a forkful of food, I can see the curve of his bicep. While my mother clears plates to make space for dessert, I imagine him and my sister having sex and find myself both aroused and disgusted.

At the end of the night my sister walks Jeremy out, the two of them disappearing from view, and I try to make out their whispers. My parents are settled on the couch, tangled up in each other, watching a sitcom.

"He seems nice," my mother says when Jenny walks back into the room.

"Yes, he is," Jenny says. Her voice is far away, somewhere I would like to be.

———

When the weather is nice, Jenny invites Jeremy over to use our pool. Our father is stretched out on a lounge chair, dripping water between the rubbery slats onto the terracotta brickwork. He's just finished swimming laps, and he is gulping down large breaths, his chest expanding and crumpling like a bellows, the still-taut muscles of his stomach stretching and contracting. Jeremy waves toward us, lifting his chin just so and smiling. He has, of course, a great smile, perfect white teeth and lips that are neither too full nor too thin. Then, before Jenny has a chance to say anything, Jeremy peels off his shirt, kicks off his flip-flops, and makes a perfect dive, slicing into the deep end. I watch from my place next to my father as Jeremy's body slips through the water toward the shallow end, a tan, narrow rocket.

"Nice dive," my father says when Jeremy emerges from the water, eyebrows wriggling as they do when he offers someone a compliment.

"Thanks." Jeremy walks up the concrete steps that fan out on the near edge of the pool, slicking his hair back. I turn my head away just so but look him over. A layer of muscle rolls over his hip bones, upper and lower body separated by a cut in his flesh that until now I'd been convinced could be achieved only by Photoshop, and a small tuft of hair sprouts from the bulb of his belly button (an outie, of course) and trails down to his low-slung swimsuit, blue with white-patterned flower blossoms.

"Either of you getting in?" he asks. Across the pool from us, Jenny is busying herself with laying out a beach towel on her own chair. She's pulled a second one next to it, intended for Jeremy.

"Catching my breath. Just finished some laps," my father says, curling his hands behind his head.

Jeremy turns toward me. "Andy?"

This is the first time Jeremy has spoken to me or said my name, and I feel as though I will melt through the gaps in my chair. I am

immediately aware of the slight sag of my body; I have been running for weeks, thrusting myself through the churning summer
air, clothes clinging to my drooping skin like a second layer until
I nearly pass out. Although my skin has tightened some, and the
push-ups I grunt through each morning have started to give my
upper body more definition, the moment Jeremy speaks to me,
I feel as unattractive as a witch, like every part of me that can
still jiggle—Jeremy, of course, has no such part—is vibrating and
obvious.

So I shake my head and say maybe, then lower my lounge chair
into a fully recumbent position. For the remainder of the afternoon
Jeremy splashes around in the water like a child, Jenny sunbathes,
and I make furtive glances in his direction. Our mother brings
everyone lemonade, like she's some housewife out of the 1950s.
Our father makes a joke to that effect. In return, my mother tosses
him in the pool when he isn't paying attention. There, Jeremy and
my dad compete, swimming laps and thrashing like they're being
assaulted by a gang of piranhas. Jenny shakes her head and looks
in my direction; although we're both wearing sunglasses, I can tell
she is rolling her eyes. I wonder whether she knows I am scowling at her. My skin burns under the sun, and I relish the sharp
tingle.

Jenny brings Jeremy over throughout the summer, especially when
our parents are at work. They have sex, loud, in her bedroom. I've
promised not to say anything.

"I thought you didn't love him," I say one afternoon after he's
left. Jenny's got a towel wrapped around her hair like a turban.
They've just taken a shower together, the bathroom smelling of the
body wash she lathers over him. My body wash.

"I don't. But I've decided sex feels very good once you've done
it a few times. And I'm pretty sure Jeremy's done it a few times."

"Aren't you supposed to be smart?" I turn on the television and lean back, wincing. I'm cherry red from too much sun, but I can't go jogging with a shirt on, it's so hot outside.

"Just because I have sex doesn't mean I'm not smart, Andy."

"Whatever."

"You know," she says, "you're looking pretty fit."

"What do you want?"

"Nothing," she says. "Just wanted you to know that I know."

We stare at one another. Jenny winks, then twirls and marches off to her bedroom. My stomach rumbles.

—

The doorbell rings, and because I'm the only one home, I hoist myself from the couch and open the door.

Jeremy is standing in front of me. He is wearing a homemade tank top, the sleeves of one of our high school spirit shirts shorn off. Jeremy is tan. The veins of his forearms look glued onto his skin.

"Uh, Jenny isn't home," I manage to squeak out. My throat is dry, like I've been running.

"I know," he says, smiling at me.

The look in Jeremy's eyes makes my knees wobble. I recognize the look. I know it because it is how I have glanced at him as he emerges from the pool or chews on a wad of food at our dinner table or smiles at one of my dad's terrible jokes.

As I step back and let him through the door, neither of us speaks, and he reaches out and touches the hinge of my jaw with both hands. They are smooth, warm, and even his fingertips are filled with strength. When he kisses me, his lips are like flower petals.

I am gone then, a ghost of myself, as though I have been knocked unconscious.

—

Jeremy still sees my sister throughout the summer, but I no longer watch their hand-holding and his smiles with envy. When he emerges from our swimming pool, I am no longer worried about being caught glancing at the way the material clings to his backside, revealing the roundedness of gluteal muscle that I have seen and gripped firsthand. If he turns toward me, I resist the urge to smile at him. Jenny has no idea.

I know that I should feel guilty for what I am doing to her; she is happy and yaps on and on about how much she likes Jeremy. She will not admit it while she is twisting the material of her bedspread—where I know they have had sex just the day before—but I think she is falling in love with him despite her insistence otherwise. Her voice is airy and childish as it has never been before, and her cheeks flush when I press her to tell me what she thinks of him, even though I'm not listening. I am picturing him trailing his lips across my neck and reaching under my shirt toward my belt buckle, his hands perpetually warm, and soft, and gritted with capacity, my own hugging at his shoulders that feel like rocks under my touch.

Despite her feelings, I relish in this secret Jeremy and I have because I know in the knit of my bones that it is real and that what he has with Jenny is a deception, his way in. He has told me so through sweated breaths, his voice raspy and tingling. It is the one thing I have that Jenny does not: Jeremy's true affections. I wear this knowledge like a crown, invisible to everyone but myself. But I know it is there, heavy and golden on my forehead.

—

"Why don't you talk to me like before?" Jenny says. I've just emerged from the shower, and she's cornered me in the hallway.

"Huh?"

"Is it Jeremy?"

"What?"

"You don't like him, do you?" Jenny's voice is cracked like she's dehydrated. "You can tell me."

"I don't know what you're talking about."

Her eyes are wide. "You haven't sat and talked with me in weeks, Andy. What did I do?"

"Nothing."

Jenny appears to be shrinking. I look everywhere but in her eyes.

"You look good," she says, poking toward my midsection.

I am saved by my mother yelling for Jenny, wanting to know where the checkbook is.

"You left it in the car," Jenny says, turning away. I use her distraction to slip past, and she lets out a small peep as I surge by.

As the weather begins to cool, Jeremy and I start running together. He teaches me how to do proper push-ups, tucking my elbows and looking forward while I lower my body toward the ground. The first time, I lose my balance and my face smashes into the grass in our front yard. Jeremy darts his hand out and trickles a finger over my jaw and cheek, asking if I am all right. He stiffens and stands up straight, hands on his hips. I squirm up: Jenny is watching us in the window.

"Do you think she knows?" Jeremy says.

"No." I smile. "She has no clue." I turn back to her and wave. She disappears into the house.

When Jeremy and I run, I can tell he is slowing his pace for me. When I tell him this, he acts like he has no idea, but I see through him and I give him a shove, if for no other reason than to feel the slickness of his arm. Jeremy sweats profusely and quickly, and he is drenched, hair lacquered with moisture, only minutes into our route. But he gives off a pleasant scent like he's made of cloves and sugar when he perspires, and I trail after him down the street like a rabid child desperate for a cupcake.

The day is cool enough, and Jeremy cranes his body around to me, abdominal muscles twisting like a wet towel, and suggests we try a longer route.

"I have an idea," he says, winking.

"Okay."

Jeremy leads me into a shaded park with an asphalt trail that snakes through the trees. No more than a minute into the dense foliage he stops and I nearly smash into him.

"What are we doing?"

"Being adventurous," he says.

Jeremy pulls me off the path and into the trees; his hands are wet, and he takes one of mine in his and starts crunching through the brush. After a few minutes of him ignoring my asking where we are going, we emerge in a small thicket, like something out of a movie: the grass is short and mingled with purple flowers, and a felled tree's trunk is covered with a blanket of moss. Somewhere, I can hear the slow gurgle of a creek, like someone is gargling in a hall bathroom.

When I turn to Jeremy he leans in and kisses my throat, and my already-heated body is filled with a different kind of warmth. I return the gesture, the saltiness of his skin like a carnival pretzel. I graze my tongue across his neck and want to taste all of him. But I pull back and look him in the eye.

"I love you," I tell him. He smiles and I can tell he loves me too.

———

"Are you sure I shouldn't stop seeing your sister?" Jeremy brushes a streak of grass from my back. We are still panting as we walk.

"What other excuse would you have for coming over?" I say. He has a smashed flower stuck in his hair, and I pick it out. I hold it up and look at it as if I were staring through a microscope. I take in its ribbing and whispers of veins, and then I let it go and follow its looping drop to the ground. A car wheezes by us, the air billowing at the mesh of my shorts.

Jeremy's hands are cupped around the back of his head as he takes in air, his intercostal muscles stretched to the length of piano keys. "We could just tell everyone we're running partners."

"We are running partners." I try not to grin.

"You know that if I'm seeing her, I'm still, you know—"

"Having sex with her," I say.

"Isn't it weird to you?"

"Is it weird to you?"

Jeremy bites his lip. "A little bit. I mean, I like—well, I don't know."

We turn onto my street and I stop walking. "Jeremy." It occurs to me that I have not really said his name ever, and it tumbles out of my mouth like spilled milk.

"Yeah?"

I swallow, trying to make my voice as silky and unwrinkled as I can. "You still like girls, don't you?"

Jeremy crunches his lip. I can see his tongue rolling against the inner side of his mouth. "I think so, yeah." He presses a smile on like a temporary tattoo. "But that doesn't change anything."

"I know it doesn't," I say, and continue walking. Jeremy follows suit.

———

Jeremy, after a swimming date with my sister, is about to leave our house and is standing at the front door. All he needs to do is keep walking.

But instead he turns around and holds up his naked wrist and says, "Oh hey, I can't find my watch. I didn't leave it around here somewhere, did I?"

I am leaning against the wall, and it takes all of my energy not to slide down it like putty. Everything moves in slow motion and is blurry with fuzz, like I am looking through a white cotton shirt.

Jenny turns around. She is starting to say, "Oh, it's in—"

She slows, like she's stuck in molasses. She stares at me. Jeremy's watch is lost somewhere in my room, probably under my bed.

For which, of course, there is no good reason. Except.

The look in Jenny's eyes tells me she knows. The cavernous O of her mouth tells me she knows. The wash of tears forming tells me she knows.

"Andy?" She squints at me. When I say nothing, she turns back toward Jeremy. He is staring at her with a half-stupid, half-guilty look, and he is paler than I've ever seen, sheeted white. I expect him to puke, but he sucks in a long, piercing breath that whistles through his cheeks.

We stand there together, the three of us statues, Jeremy and Jenny and I in a line, my sister trapped in the middle. I don't feel shame or fear as I expected. Instead, I feel my chest expand, my spine stretch as I stand tall. Jenny wilts like a dying flower, a time-lapse video of its browning and curling in on itself, my smart, gorgeous, loved-by-all sister puttying into a puddle in our foyer. Jeremy hitches his shoulder a few times, wondering whether he should say something, reach out for her, but with our secret revealed to her, there is no reason for him to hold on to her anymore. He and I lock eyes, and I shrug, going for empathy. Months and years from now I will think of his face and recognize the immolation in Jeremy's gaze, the realization that the truth will come out and that he is not ready for that. When I remember this I may even have some sense that in this moment I know we are not destined for each other, that, it turns out, I am strong where he is weak, and that he needs someone like my sister in order to feel right. But not now, not at this moment, when I am the one he wants, and he and Jenny and I all know it. When the only thing I can feel is the power of winning.

Holey Moley

The cheerleaders arrive first.

Bryson is in the kitchen, measuring out baker's yeast for the donut of the day, Over the Raindough, a multicolored glazed topped with rainbow sprinkles, when he hears the door open and multiple—too many—voices: high dithers of laughter mixed with whispers of uncertainty as if to say, *Is this place open?*

It is. Holey Moley is a twenty-four-hour establishment, but things are usually slow from two to five, when he gets most of his baking done before his one employee comes in to help with the breakfast rush and then sticks around while Bryson goes home to his tiny apartment for a quick bout of sleep before returning to wait on the swing-shift doctors and EMTs from the hospital down the street. He only keeps the place open through the quietest part of night on the off chance of bringing in night owls and the kids who stumble out of the downtown bars and want something sweet instead of savory (though he does occasionally manage to come up with a maple-bacon donut or something covered in pink sea salt).

The cheerleaders are all bubbly blondes, the golden wheat of their hair and the spangly blue of their outfits jarring against the brown of the leatherette booths and the off-white counter and tabletops. A dozen of them have made themselves comfortable in the booths, and three of them are sitting down at the counter, spinning on the backless stools that squeal as they turn.

"Hello," Bryson says, wiping his hands on his floor-length black apron, leaving behind yeasty streaks.

"We are famished," one of the cheerleaders says with a Southern accent. She smiles, her lipstick pristine, teeth glaring white. "We would like donuts."

They point at the case, the cheerleaders in the booth coming up one at a time. They take all of the glazed donuts and crullers. A few ask for jelly. Bryson hands them out, presented on paper plates. They ask if he has coffee and clap when he brings out the first pot; they've found the mugs on their own, someone slipping around behind the counter to dole them out.

"This place smells great," the Southern cheerleader says. He thinks of her as the squad captain. "Delicious. You can practically taste the fat."

"Thanks," Bryson says.

"Are you all by yourself?"

"For now."

"Bless your heart," she says, aiming her mug at his chest for a refill.

The bell affixed to the door jangles: lawyers. Bryson can't tell at first that they're lawyers, but their bespoke suits and wool skirts scream "some kind of professional," and they're harried, all of them tired and red eyed, probably from staring at documents. When Bryson emerges from the back with a fresh pot of coffee, having pulled his Raindoughs out of the fryer, he hears one of the cheerleaders asking for advice about divorce. It's like a mixer, the well-dressed, white-collar attorneys schmoozing with the cheerleaders, taking periodic bites out of their long johns and chocolate glazed. Bryson has a hard time keeping up with who owes what, and then, thankfully, one of the attorneys, with salt-and-pepper hair and crinkly eyes, a tight but nice smile, and a tie the color of the deepest ocean, holds out two hundred-dollar bills and says, "Will this cover everyone?"

"More than," Bryson says.

"Keep the change. Good service. More coffee?"

The money rattles into the cash register. Bryson can practically feel the bills pulsing, can smell their leathery odor from living in a damp wallet jammed with Amex Black cards. He finishes up the Raindoughs and sets them out on a large rack to cool. When he returns to the front with a full pot of Colombian, the bell over the door jangles again: a coterie of circus performers. They are led by a lion tamer, who has to lean down as he enters so his gargantuan top hat doesn't clip the door frame. His red blazer is covered in glimmering sequins like thousands of tiny fires. Bryson can't stop staring at the shoulders of the trapeze artists, three men, one in his forties and the others in their late teens or early twenties, all wearing matching green-and-white singlets that make their tanned skin glow. They are accompanied by four clowns in full makeup, a pair of sideshow freaks—a bearded lady and an Elephant Man— and a snake charmer with a yellow boa slung over her shoulders, which is probably a health-code violation.

Bryson is sure there isn't room for everyone, but it is as if the clowns cast a spell on the shop, treating it like one of the cars they manage to spill out of by the dozen. The lawyers make space for the lion tamer; cheerleaders squash into their booth with the bearded lady, complimenting the glow of her facial hair. The trapeze artists treat the empty stools at the counter like pommel horses, mounting them at the wrist and dangling there, looking bored.

Bryson fills mugs and then returns to the kitchen to make more coffee.

The shop's normal aromas of rich, fried dough and snowy powdered sugar are overwhelmed by the sweet-sour smell of human bodies percolating with sweat and excitement. Bryson can hear the din of talk through the kitchen's swinging door; it sounds like a waterfall. He spends so little time among the masses, and the wash of noise makes the tiny hairs on the back of his neck tingle. Running a donut shop is solitary, tiring work. He can't remember the last time he was in a bar, on the lookout for some other lonely heart drinking a wheat beer on his own, eyes equally peeled for someone to share a moment—or, if luck would have it, a night—with.

He is running out of donuts. The jellies have been decimated, the chocolates drilled down to nothing but a sweep of crumbs. Bryson watches a cheerleader bite into the last of the blueberries. The Bostons and sour creams are still holding strong, but he can see how the clowns are eyeing them.

As Bryson finishes topping off coffees—as many as he can before this, his fourth or fifth pot, is emptied—the lion tamer steps up to the counter, muscling his way between the trapeze artists, who have finally sat down to enjoy their apple cider donuts. The tamer has a bristly mustache and tan skin, lined just enough for him to be handsome. He resembles a young Tom Selleck. Bryson gives him a tired half smile. The lion tamer reaches into his blazer and removes a simple black wallet. Like the attorney, he peels several bills from inside and holds them out, wordless, eyes sparkling. Bryson takes them. The lion tamer nods, shoves the wallet back into his inner breast pocket, and vanishes into the crowd. Bryson makes for the kitchen.

When he returns, Raindoughs ready on their tray, the firefighters have arrived. They are bulky and loom large, the smell of ash and smoke clinging to their skin, which is mostly covered by Nomex hoods and reflective pants that flash under the shop's fluorescent lights. The cheerleaders and attorneys make space for them; they jostle past the clowns, who feign courtly deference. Six of them squeeze into the shop, everyone standing shoulder to shoulder, voices a carom of noise that blasts at Bryson's ears. He doesn't bother sliding the Raindoughs into the case and instead starts doling them out without a word; more money appears before him, from whose gloved or manicured or hairy hand he has no clue. The firefighters are desperate for their own cups of coffee, but Bryson is

out of mugs. The fawning cheerleaders, and one of the trapeze artists, offer to share theirs. One of the attorneys asks the firefighters
where they've come from, and they mention a fire in an apartment
building not far from the shop; Bryson recognizes the name.

When he returns to the kitchen for yet another pot of coffee—
he's running out of filters and grounds—he hears footsteps behind
him. He turns: the lion tamer. Bryson is caught off guard; everything in the kitchen is stainless-steel deck ovens and skimmers
and off-white paint, and the tamer's raging red blazer is like a
sun. He stands framed by the swinging door, which threatens to
slam into him as it sways, but it stops just short of his broad back.
His cream-colored pants are tight in the thighs, showing off the
musculature of his legs. His black boots shimmer under the harsh
lights as if freshly polished.

"You could use some help." It isn't a question, but it's not judg-
ment either. The tamer's voice is softer than Bryson expects, pillowy
and kind. When he speaks, the lines around his eyes crinkle.

"That bad out there?"

"It's a happy enough crowd."

"I guess you've seen them turn?"

"Sometimes."

The tamer removes his coat and sets it down in the empty space
on the cooling table the Raindoughs recently occupied. He peels
off his top hat, nestling it gently atop the heap of his blazer, revealing a thick mop of black, wavy hair. His white shirt is tight across
the chest and arms, tapered as if sewn specifically for his body.
Bryson can see the twitch and ripple of every muscle as if it were
mimicked by the fabric. The lion tamer claps his hands together.

"Please," he says. "Tell me what I can do." The tamer makes a
bombastic sweep of the prep station, where the ingredients for the
Raindoughs are still spread out in a messy line: granulated sugar,
eggs, butter, flour, mace, neon gel food coloring. Bryson sets down
his coffeepot at the same time the tamer picks up a sheet of paper:
Bryson's scribbled recipe.

"Oh," Bryson says. "That's just an experiment."

The tamer raises an eyebrow. "You're a scientist? Or an artist?"

"I'm a baker."

"Both then." The tamer rolls up his sleeves, revealing a colorful tattoo along the tender, pale side of his left forearm: a single long red line, plus several shorter yellow ones beneath, interrupted by a few dashes of blue and pink. The tamer sees him staring and points, pressing a finger into his flesh. "People and animals I've lost," he says, offering no further explanation.

The tamer is quick, nodding and grabbing, measuring, adding; he knows how to switch on the sheeter without Bryson having to say anything, and when he catches Bryson staring, he says, "I did this in another life."

"Really?"

"My mother was a baker."

"Was?"

"Was."

"I'm sorry."

"Like I said, another life." He waves Bryson away with a gloved hand; he's swapped out his leathers for blue latex. "Go. I can do this. Make more coffee."

Bryson feels the hot slap of dismissal. His fingers shake as he places the emptied coffeepot back into its cradle, fills a fresh filter with grounds. He wants to watch the lion tamer as he mixes and beats and stretches the dough before sending it through the sheeter, to stare at the twitch of muscles in his forearms, the shift of those colored lines marking tragedy. Instead, he stares at the drip of black as it fills the pot. Bryson shakes himself loose and tries, unsuccessfully, to find more mugs. He returns to the front of the shop and plucks up the used cups discarded by the attorneys. No one has left, but no one new has arrived. The trapeze artists are doing handstands on the backs of the booths, their legs splayed in bendy shapes. The clowns appear to be playing charades, or else performing some kind of theatrical display that is generating laughs from two of the firefighters, the rest of whom are crammed in with cheerleaders, telling stories of bravery and the ravages of housefires. The snake charmer is dancing in a small clearing between the counter and booths. Two of the attorneys sit at the counter, paperwork spread out before them, whispering about liabilities and torts. When he hears the bell above the door jangle, Bryson wants to yell out that he's at max capacity. Shouldn't one of the firefighters see the hazard?

A gaggle of school children enters.

They wear bright school uniforms, the boys in vibrant sunrise yellows and starched navy blue shorts. The girls—three of them, somewhere between eight and twelve years old—wear swishy pleated skirts the same near-midnight color with clean white blouses. Bryson wonders what kids are doing out at this hour, but then he realizes he could wonder the same thing about just about everyone else in the shop, too.

The Raindoughs have already run out, the only remnants on the tray a vibrant array of scattershot crumbs that remind Bryson of space, nebulae and galaxies swirling in the black. He presses a finger into a trough of flakes and sticks it in his mouth. Though the flakes are tiny, they exude fat and sugar and butter. His mouth waters. Bryson stares down at the tray, imagining the clean rows of donuts being plucked up one by one, gnashed against the cheerleaders' white teeth, swallowed down the firefighters' grizzled throats, washed with coffee by the harried attorneys and the flexible circus freaks. Every donut, every ingredient, is a little piece of him traveling through their bodies, providing nourishment and expanding waistlines, sending taste buds into pleasured orbit. And all that he is left with after that is a tray full of crumbs and, at least tonight, a full cash register.

One of the boys manages to muscle his way to the counter and hold out a five-dollar bill. Bryson takes it, and the boy, without a word, shoves his way to the donut case. He waits for Bryson to come over, then points to the last three Boston creams as well as two bear claws hiding on the bottom shelf. A single chocolate-brownie-crumble donut is also hidden in a low corner, and the boy taps the glass with excited vehemence. His five dollars won't cover the cost of all six donuts, but Bryson decides it doesn't matter. He boxes the donuts in a pink Holey Moley box and hands it to the boy, who threads his way back to the other children huddled near the door. Bryson watches them eat, their fingers going gluey with glaze, mouths ringed with cream and chocolate. The boy who bought the donuts is the tallest, clearly the leader of their pack, and he gives the rich crumble to the smallest girl. Her eyes are ringed with dark circles, her hair pulled up into pigtails held fast by pink ribbon. Bryson squints out into the night, expecting, dubiously, a school bus or a car with a harried mother, someone who must pull her weight in carpool at the egregiously early hour of— he checks the clock affixed above the kitchen door—four fifteen. But the dawning day is empty, the streets scattered only with trash and parking meters. Storefronts across the street—a bodega at the corner, a boutique clothing store, a Qdoba—are dark and unmoving. Everywhere except Holey Moley is dead and silent.

Bryson returns to the kitchen, where he can hear and smell the fryers. The lion tamer smiles. His forearms are dusted in flour, and some has made its way into his mustache

"Smells good," Bryson says.

"I adapted your recipe a bit."

"How?"

The tamer shrugs. "Added some of this, subtracted some of that. It is not an exact science."

Bryson's feet and hands hurt. He's not used to moving around this much at this time of night. He can feel burning behind his eyeballs. He rubs them and lets out a breath.

"You are running out of sugar," the lion tamer says.

"I am?"

The tamer shrugs. Bryson wants to rip him open. To stuff his fingers down the man's throat, wriggle them along his tongue and the soft tissue inside. He doesn't want to make more coffee or serve more donuts or take inventory of dry storage. He wants to call his assistant and tell her that he's closing Holey Moley for good, that he can't stand the smell of butter and flour and fryer oil anymore.

The lion tamer is watching him.

"I guess I'll call my supplier."

A small office sits off the side of the kitchen, a windowless room that has barely enough space for a single filing cabinet and a built-in desk with three shelves that are stuffed with paperwork. The little wall space is papered with articles about Holey Moley, good reviews, a feature in the *Post-Dispatch* from a few years ago, a picture of a smiling Bryson leaning in the store's open doorway, arms crossed over his chest. Sometimes Bryson looks at that image of himself, his eyes uncrowded by lines, his back betraying no constant ache. He tries to remember being that version of himself.

Before he can sift through the paperwork on his desk—bills, invoices, a schedule of which hotels and doctors' offices and bookstores have standing orders on file—the lion tamer is suddenly behind him, rapping on the door frame. When Bryson turns, the lion tamer stares down at him, an angle that makes him even more handsome. Bryson feels his stomach tense. He tries not to stare at the tattoo, wonder at the weight of loss in his broad shoulders. Bryson half expects the lion tamer to move into the office, to pull Bryson from his chair, to cup his chin with his dough-wet hands and kiss him on the mouth, shut the door and pry off Bryson's clothes, slam him against the filing cabinet, bruise his back, and leave him spent. Bryson sees then that he's donned his raging red blazer and top hat again, the brim dusted with a faint white outline from his hand.

The lion tamer says, "My people will go soon."

"Go?"

"We can't stay in your donut shop forever."

"I guess not."

"You will be all right without us."

Joe Baumann

"I—yes?"

"Yes." The lion tamer nods and backs away. Suddenly, Bryson is alone in the kitchen, the only sound the gurgle of frying donuts, the only smell their warm, fat aroma. Bryson's mouth waters, but he isn't hungry.

He picks up the full coffeepot and pushes through the swinging door. The sight of the shop is jarring. The children are already gone, the only evidence of their presence the empty donut box sitting atop the trash can by the door, bent open to reveal a mound of used napkins and a smear of chocolate on the interior of the lid. The firefighters are on the way out, their Nomex hoods shining like they, too, are glazed. One of them waves a gloved hand toward the cheerleaders, who wave back, mouths stretched in the kind of grin that can mean only sudden, quick love. He watches one sigh like a princess in a Disney film, the cheerleaders around her tittering like a supporting cast of woodland critters.

Things are happening in reverse. When the firefighters depart, their ashy smell disperses into the dark. The snake charmer and bearded lady slither away. The trapeze artists leave in a flurry of handstands. When the lion tamer reaches the door, he barely looks back.

The attorneys begin packing up. Bryson offers more coffee, but they decline. The one who paid offers up another pair of hundred-dollar bills, and even though Bryson's sure they haven't taken that much from him, he accepts the money. The attorney nods as if they've just settled a case, and then he departs, snapping up his briefcase with a swish as it slides across the counter. His colleagues follow, one woman wiping her mouth with a napkin that she leaves balled on the countertop. Bryson stares at it and the smear of what is either jelly or lipstick.

The cheerleaders rise, their smooth quads flexing as they stand. They thank him for the coffee in hushed tones. He waves, saying nothing. When they're gone, the bell jangling, he stares at the empty store, which seems to pulse like a pair of lungs breathing.

The booths are a mess of crumbs and abandoned coffee mugs. He can't imagine cleaning up. Bryson rubs his face and goes around the counter. He glances at the empty case, a ravaged desolation of crumbs and crinkled wax paper. Bryson pokes his finger into the empty tray on the counter, but the crumbled refuse has gone stale and hard and, when he pops it in his mouth, tasteless. He looks around the emptied store, glances at the sun starting to break through between the high-rising buildings. A few early pedestrians occupy the sidewalk. Bryson swallows the crumbs, hard and grating against the back of his throat. He wonders whether, were he to make more donuts, anyone would really, truly, care for them. In the kitchen, a timer buzzes: the Raindoughs are ready.

Retreat

The closest place to talk to the dead was the artists' colony.

Ronny had been the artist, but Cal was willing to fake it, which seemed easier than flying to Nova Scotia and rowing a boat onto Lake Echo. The other international sites were equally onerous to reach, not to mention expensive. So Cal, at his sister's suggestion, researched erasure poetry and read Ronald Johnson, Jen Bervin, M. NourbeSe Philip. He couldn't sort out any internal logic or structure, so he decided he'd just fiddle around with what he knew, sitting in front of a stack of pages of Perl and Java, swiping over lines of code with a No. 2 pencil, leaving behind gibberish.

He called Laura.

"It's not working," he said. Making erasure poems out of code had been her idea. She lived in Tucson after years of bouncing around Santa Fe and the West Coast: Portland, Seattle, Palo Alto. She'd double majored in nursing and writing, and she took periodic sojourns between jobs on neonatal units to compose poems about premature birth, eclampsia, C-sections, and abortion.

"You could try actual writing," she said.

"Writing what?"

"About Ronny. I know it sounds terrible. But it could be cathartic."

"Painful."

"A useful pain." Laura's voice was soft like a pillow. "Especially if it gets you to the colony."

"I guess."

Cal sat down and wrote. Ronny used to hole himself up in his office, door shut, classical music blasting so loud that when the percussion section got going, the pots and pans in the kitchen rattled. Cal never asked questions about his progress, not even when Ronny came out, smiling, and popped open a bottle of wine.

After he'd written half a dozen pages, he sent them to Laura.

"They're perfect," she said. "You should try to get it published when you're finished."

But Cal had trouble finishing. He didn't know how to tell the end of Ronny's story. His death was eighteen months old, but his absence was still a tender mark, as it always would be.

"So write that," Laura said. "There's your ending."

"But it's not an ending."

"It's the truth, Calvin."

"People don't want to hear the truth. They want a good story."

"Now you sound like a writer."

Two months after Cal submitted his essay, he received word that he'd been awarded a weeklong stay at Talking Woods Artist Colony. The director wrote that his work "plumbed the complicated pain of grief with delicate sophistication," which Cal wasn't sure what to do with. How, he wondered, could grief be delicate or sophisticated? He would never use those words to describe his own pain.

He still lived in the house he and Ronny had bought together, their shared finances—Cal's biweekly salary, Ronny's royalty checks—covering a solid down payment and the mortgage. Cal had more than once thought of selling the three-bedroom house, downsizing to a nice-enough apartment, maybe a loft or a condo, but the idea of shaking apart everything that he and Ronny had built together left him queasy. Ronny's books—those he wrote as well as those he read—took up an entire bedroom, a party of IKEA shelves lining the walls, all the books filled with Post-its covered in Ronny's scribbled notes. His clothes were still in the closet, despite Laura's numerous recriminations that Cal should donate them to Goodwill. But if he did that, he would truly be forced to reckon with how much excess space there was in his house; the master closet would echo like a deep gorge every time a hanger clanged.

He spent too much time before his trip to the colony wondering what he would say to Ronny, or, more accurately, the version of Ronny he would see. People liked to say that the sites—the artists' colony, the Sivalik Hills, the Danube delta, Machu Picchu, one of the dressing rooms in the Sydney Opera House—were places you could actually speak to the dead, but really, they engaged the minds of the living, projecting out versions of those who'd passed away. The Ronny who would appear to Cal—as well as the clothes he'd be wearing, his haircut, the timbre of his voice—would come from Cal, not from some ghost temporarily ripped from the afterlife. Ronny wouldn't be able to answer any deep, epistemological questions about the meaning of life or what happens to us after we die; if he did, they would be Cal's perceptions of the answers. And if Cal were to ask Ronny to tell him about their relationship, the answers that would spill out would be whatever Cal thought Ronny might have said. If Ronny had taken any secrets with him into death, the only answers Cal could pull from him would be the ones he already had or thought were correct.

These realizations had tempered the furor people felt upon the sites' discovery. At first, there'd been pandemonium—in Rio de Janeiro, a small cove on Copacabana Beach had been overrun during the Olympics—but when people realized the limitations of what the dead could offer, the flush of bodies rushing to various points around the world cooled to a simmer. Some called it self-delusion or self-indulgence, shipping yourself around the world just to hear in the voice of your lost loved ones that which was really coming out of your own mouth. Others, especially those who benefited from the increased tourism to far-flung parts of the globe (one hot spot was in the foothills of a small island nation whose name Cal forgot every time he looked it up; flights there were outrageous in their expense and required further travel by ferry), lauded the fact that people wanted to see their dead, remember them in this vivid, tangible way. That, of all things, was perhaps the biggest sustained draw: the dead could be touched. These weren't movie-screen projections or wispy ghosts made of mist that would dissipate at human grope. They had weight. They left footprints. They smelled of familiar shampoos and colognes and body sprays. They had fingers that could rake hair and hair that could be raked. Some questions arose about their ability to copulate, but no one was willing to admit to having tried to boink the dead; necrophilia was still necrophilia, unless maybe in this case it was a kind of masturbation.

Cal drove to the colony on a warm morning, the blue sky marbled with cumulus clouds. Cal rolled his windows down when he turned off the interstate for the winding state highway, the shoulders narrow and alternately edged by woods and farmland. Billboards castigating abortion and celebrating the Second Amendment flashed in black and white and red. He kept glancing into his back seat, where he'd stored his rolling suitcase on its side. He'd been unsure what, exactly, to pack, besides underwear and spare jeans and an old pair of sneakers he could wear to explore the woods and cliffs around the colony. His laptop he'd laid between his socks and T-shirts, and the essay thrummed inside the hard drive; Cal could practically feel its heat.

He almost missed the turnoff for Talking Woods, the sign crumbly, hand-painted, and shoved into the loam of a drainage ditch. When Cal slammed on his brakes to make the turn, his stomach churned, gravel spat, and he thought for a moment the car would roll. It didn't, but he could smell burnt rubber as he caught his breath and clanged onto a dusty trail of a road that slithered through the thickening woods. Even though it was midafternoon, he had to turn on his headlights, the foliage was so dense. As the road swiveled back and forth, he wondered how soon he would be allowed to hear Ronny's voice.

The trees broke suddenly, opening onto a parking lot that was really a field whose grass had been tamped down like a tennis court, with painted lines for parking cars. A squat building in the shape of a yurt had Administration painted on its side. A pond, twenty feet in diameter, was sharp blue, a trio of ducks lazing across the surface.

A handful of cars were parked on the grass, and Cal pulled in between a beat-up Buick and a conversion van smeary with lawn clippings. He left his bag behind and stretched as he got out of the car. The sun was beating down warmth like a heat lamp. Cal could smell the woods, the oaky scent of trees, hints of standing water. His feet whispered beneath him as he crossed the grass and eventually found surer footing on a narrow asphalt walkway leading to the front door of the administrative building-yurt. Inside, he relished the air-conditioning.

"Hello," a voice called out. The interior was plain: a simple countertop like you'd expect at the DMV, with a whirring, idle computer and heaps of paperwork, a filing cabinet, a printer, and a door—ajar—leading to a second, private office. Cal stood with his hands in his pockets.

A woman emerged, midthirties, maybe, wearing a frock dress that, were it not for the air-conditioning blasting from the window unit, would have been unbearable.

"Hello," she said again. "You must be Mr. Barnhart. We've been waiting for you!"

Cal nodded. The woman had him sign some papers, then gave him a key to a cabin and directions.

"We put you in the same cabin that Mr. Barnhart—the other Mr. Barnhart—Ronny, I mean, stayed in when he was with us."

"Ronny came here?"

The woman frowned. "Oh yes. Several years ago. We assumed you knew."

Cal shook his head. "It's fine. That cabin's fine."

She leaned in and lowered her voice. "And I assume you'll want to sign up to see the trees?"

"I—yes, I guess."

"Great," she said. "Of course." She pushed some papers around until she found what she wanted, a printed-out spreadsheet with names handwritten throughout the grid.

"Do you still get a lot of people interested in seeing them?"

The woman sighed. "Some. Not as many as you might think. Like every phenomenon, their time seems to have passed."

Cal nodded.

The woman glanced over the sheet. "How about tomorrow at two? That'll be after lunch, which is served in the building behind us. That's where all the meals are." She transitioned into basic colony protocols, asked if he had any other questions. Cal had plenty, but they all seemed stupid, like, Do I need to report how much writing I do each day? Do I need to turn something in at the end of my stay? Where is the best cell phone service and internet reception?

He shook his head and she smiled, domed her hands in front of her. "We'll see you at dinner then," she said, and before he could say another word, she'd slipped back through the door into the interior office. Cal walked out to his car, gathered his bag, and set off for his cabin.

———

About one hundred yards past the yurt, the trees opened into a clearing where another half dozen small cabins sat in a circle. They were built of pewter wood, each with a sagging front porch adorned with a rocking chair. Cal half expected to hear a banjo's twang, but the only noise was the rustle of tree branches and the scattered sounds of birds trilling and squirrels rustling in the underbrush.

He kept picturing Ronny doing the same things he was, and he wondered why Ronny had never mentioned going to an artists' colony, especially one so close to where they lived. Cal thought he knew everything about Ronny, the sketch of his childhood, the many pinpoints of his international travels when his agent sold his first book in translation, how he preferred to be touched and penetrated during sex. This was such a tiny thing for Cal to have never known, which made him feel more off-kilter for not knowing it.

He found his cabin—number 5—and hauled his bag up onto the porch, the wood groaning beneath his feet. Cal had to work the lock for several seconds before the key would do its job, and then he had to shoulder the door open; it had swelled in the heat. The interior was pleasantly clean, a single large room with a bed in one corner and a door leading into a tiny bathroom in the other. The only other furniture was a small love seat with a round table in front of it and a writing desk beneath one of the two windows, next to a fireplace that he'd been asked to try not to use, at risk of burning the whole place down.

Cal set his bag down on the bed and wandered in a lazy circle, taking in everything from the spiderwebs in the room's corners to the dead leaves scattered like cheap confetti along the baseboards. When he stepped in front of the writing desk, its uncomfortable-looking wooden chair tucked in politely, Cal pictured Ronny. He wondered which parts of his novels or short stories Ronny would have written while sitting there. Cal saw him hunched over a Moleskine, pausing periodically to look out the window that pushed up against the tree line, branches so close that if one opened the window one could stroke the nearest leaves. He turned and looked back at the room, imagining, with a searing intensity, that Ronny had appraised the room just as he was doing, fingers tucked up against his mouth. Cal had long learned to let Ronny roam around the house, make laps through the kitchen, circle the island like a shark, pause in front of the television, bounce on the balls of his feet and stare no matter what was on the screen before returning to his office to scribble more in his notebook.

"Why not a computer?" Cal had asked once.

"It's a different kind of process," Ronny said. "One hand versus two, being able to type fast versus write slow. And," he said, lowering his voice like he was sharing a secret, "I have terrible handwriting. No one can decipher it. No one gets to know how bad things are at first."

After Ronny's death, Cal had found his most recent Moleskine where Ronny kept them stacked in order on a wire shelf in the office closet. For a long time, Cal had stared at the glossy leather cover. When he finally opened it, breathless, he couldn't read any of it. The words were squiggles, as if produced by a seismograph. No matter how long he stared at the lines, endless and repeating until they stopped, Cal couldn't make sense of a single word, not even a *the* or *an*. *Please*, he thought, as he scanned through those impossible words more than once. *Please tell me something, anything*. Cal just wanted the words to mean something, to give some anchoring weight to Ronny's death. His agent had asked Cal more than once via email if Ronny had any posthumous work that might be available—the *New Yorker*, the agent claimed, would almost certainly be willing to run a story—but Cal told her that the only thing was Ronny's handwritten gibberish. The agent groaned but then gathered herself and tried gently asking if Cal might look on Ronny's laptop. Cal, after sieving nothing out of the journals, couldn't bring himself to even try cracking the password to the computer. He hadn't called the agent back.

When, he wondered, had Ronny come here? Sitting down on the end of the bed, Cal tried to do the math. The locations where the dead could be summoned had been discovered in only the previous five, six years—or maybe seven; time melted like this for Cal, the past near decade a pile of sugar dissolved in water—and he'd known Ronny for all of those years, even though there had been a long period at the beginning where they had seen each other only sporadically, still feeling out whether what was blooming between them was something long term or a brief flash, a flick of temporary sexual satisfaction. When they'd first slept together, Ronny admitted he'd just exited a serious relationship (that breakup would become the subject of the book that put his name into the literary stratosphere, landing him on the shortlist for the National Book Award), and he wasn't sure if he wanted that same kind of intensity so soon. Had he come here then? And if he had, whom did he want to see? Ronny's parents were both still alive, and Ronny had never spoken of any hard-hitting deaths in his past. Cal told himself to stop thinking about it before it grew, like a small tumble of snow growing into a giant, impossible avalanche that would wipe everything out.

Cal passed too much time staring down at the dusty floor. His breathing went regular and he felt as if he'd fallen asleep with his eyes open. Dinner time—six thirty—came when the light was still yellow-yolky, the first shifts of evening catching in the windows. He stuttered to life and stood, the backs of his legs giving a quick pinch of discomfort. Cal made sure his keys and wallet were in his pockets, as if he were about to embark on a long trek. He felt queasy as he swung the cabin door open, wondering how fast the actual artists would recognize him as an interloper.

He caught sight of another resident leaving the nearest cabin. Cal waved, and the man trundling out did the same as he hopped down the steps. For whatever reason, the man's youth surprised Cal; he had expected everyone else to be old, wizened and pinched with experience, all gray streaks or receding hairlines, wrinkles and gravitas. But this man, who marched over to Cal and offered his hand, couldn't have been more than twenty-five, his hair dark and wavy, shoulders pinched back and broad, his face clean shaven and wrinkle-free. His smile had the glowing joy of untouched youth.

"I'm Ben," he said. His grip was strong, his palms tough with callouses.

"Cal."

"When did you get here?"

"Just a few hours ago."

"Welcome. First time?"

"It's that obvious?"

"I've been here three times. I can see when someone's taking it in for the first go." He pointed behind them, toward the woods. "There's a wonderment about, you know."

"The dead," Cal said, then thought maybe you weren't supposed to talk about it.

"That's right. Been out there yet?"

"I go tomorrow."

Ben nodded. He was handsome, with dimples that cut into his cheeks. Cal liked his cleft chin, which reminded him of Ronny's. They were similar looking, Cal realized, and then he couldn't help thinking he was already talking to a ghost.

"I went my first time. Saw my mom."

"How was it?"

"Cathartic, definitely."

They grew quiet as they walked the narrow path connecting the residential cabins to the administrative grounds, the only noise the clomp of their feet, the snap of branches beneath them. When they emerged into the clearing, Ben said, "So what do you do?"

"Do?"

"I'm a painter and composer," he said. "Wow. Sorry. That sounded egotistical."

"Just sounded like facts to me."

The colony's other residents were already gathered in the dining hall, a small building whose seating area was hardly bigger than the little office where Cal checked in. The lighting was low, shades pulled down over windows that still leaked frames of sunshine, candles lit and sitting in red sconces on the long, rough-hewn table.

The others introduced themselves: a redheaded sculptor working on a nude self-portrait (Cal wondered how she'd hauled out a large enough rock or whatever with her); a novelist mucking through the second draft of his sophomore effort who spent the entire meal talking about the pressure to follow up the critical success of his debut, a title that Cal recognized but hadn't read; a portraitist who was currently experimenting with crayons; and a mixed-media artist also experimenting, with decoupage and lasers.

"Everyone's experimenting," Cal said.

Wine and water were passed around. The woman from the front office appeared with a basket of fresh sourdough bread. Cal watched Ben tear his slice into hunks. Then came a salad, wild roughage tossed with all number of vegetables; Cal made no gripes about the raw mushrooms, letting them slide to the side of his plate. As they ate, the artists bantered back and forth, goading one another about the progress of their projects. Cal sorted out that they'd each been here a few days, and several, like Ben, were on their second or third stints. Never did they mention the dead, and Cal wondered how many of them had actually gone to visit someone.

Near the end of the meal, the mixed-media artist was talking about her recent show at the Whitney, something called *Blood Sport*. She'd collected menstrual blood, hers and her partner's, for two years, then used it to paint a series of eight-by-eleven sketches of women in throes. That's what she called it: simply, "in throes."

"It was about the sublime experience of womanhood," she said, looking around the table. "Pain and pleasure, joy and anger, how the one exists inside the other."

Cal caught Ben giving the slightest roll of his eyes.

Darkness had fallen by the time they left, the wine gone—the woman had appeared with a third bottle, a sickly-sweet Sauternes—and the plates whisked away. The other artists walked in a clump, laughing and swaying thanks to the alcohol strumming in their blood. Cal felt warmth usher through his cheeks when Ben held back, waiting for him.

"They're a little club," he said when the others were out of ear-shot. "Don't take it personally."

"I don't," Cal said.

Ben cleared his throat. "If you're not busy, would you be inter-ested in a nightcap?"

"There's a bar around here?"

Ben laughed. "I pilfered a bottle of wine last night when no one was looking."

Ben's cabin was identical in layout, but where Cal's felt empty and cold, Ben's had warmth. A laptop hummed on the small writ-ing desk, an easel was perched next to the bed, and a trio of candles sat on the small coffee table, wicks pristine and new.

"Homey," Cal said.

Ben laughed, a deep, syrupy sound that reached out from his throat. He headed to the bathroom, where Cal heard him moving around, and then he returned, the wine bottle in one hand and a pair of plastic cups in the other.

"You bring your own drinking glasses?"

"Also pilfered, but not from here."

"So you're a thief?" Cal said.

Ben laughed. "Aren't we all?" He pulled the cork from the bottle and handed Cal a cup.

Ben gestured for them to sit. When Cal sat on one end of the sofa, Ben threw himself down in the middle. The lighting was shallow, a single bulb in the ceiling that did funny things to the corners of the room. Ben's face caught the light nicely, though; he looked vibrant, happy, but that could have been the wine. Cal took a sip from his cup, a dark, rich red.

"So," Ben said. "You're an essayist."

Cal felt something catch in his throat; he'd been forced to self-identify at dinner under the scrutiny of the redhead, who had, midconversation, turned and stared at him and said, "So, tell me. What do you do?"

To Ben, Cal said, "I guess so."

"What do you essay about?" Ben smiled.

Cal at least got this reference. Laura had told him that *essay* meant "to try." "The truth is, I'm not much of a writer."

Ben laughed. "Well, that makes two of us."

"I'm not much of an artist at all."

"You're here to see someone at the trees, aren't you?"

Cal was suddenly sheened with a clammy perspiration that gathered under his armpits and at his hairline. He picked up his glass and drank, Ben smiling at him. The grin wasn't taunting or nasty. In fact, Ben looked as calm and happy as he had since they'd met, his limbs loose, lips wet with wine.

"It's that obvious?"

"I think most of the people who come here are the same way. Everyone that's here now came for the same reasons at first."

"But they were all so self-assured at dinner."

"A show." Ben drank. "Every artist is deeply insecure about their work. If you don't think of yourself as an artist, maybe that means you are one."

"Doubtful. I write software."

Ben finished his wine. "So who is it?"

"Who's what?"

"Who is it you're here to see? If you don't mind me asking."

"Oh." Cal realized he hadn't thought of Ronny for hours. He'd expected to feel him everywhere, to wonder where he'd sat at the dinner table, where he'd walked through the woods, whether he'd done what Cal was doing—whatever Cal was doing—nestling into another artist's cabin, eyes going slightly woozy from one glass of wine too many, seeing a flirtatious glint in his companion's eye. Had Ronny found himself in the thrall of, say, a potter? A fellow novelist? Had some poet swept in and pulled him into a one-night stand?

But the reality was that Ronny had vanished out of Cal's head until Ben put him back in. For just a little while, for the first time in a long time, Cal had felt pleasantly on his own, freed from the grief-rusted anchor that had pulled at him for so long.

"I'm sorry," Ben said. "You don't have to tell me."

"No, it's okay."

"You made a face."

"I think that's the wine."

Ben's arm was draped along the back of the couch, his fingers close. Cal wanted to reach out and touch them.

"It's Ronny Barnhart," Cal said.

Ben blinked. "That Ronny Barnhart?"

"The one."

"I loved his books."

"So did I."

Ben made a nest of his elbows on the back of the couch atop which he laid his head. The angle made him look even more hand-some. "I'd love to ask him some things, even though I don't write, really. He'd be cool to meet."

At first, Cal thought Ben had misunderstood, thinking maybe that Cal was a fan, someone who wanted to interview a writer slain before his time. Ben was smiling again, his gaze far away. But then Cal figured it out: without having to say so, Ben was trying to skate away from other questions, avoiding dipping into the revelation that Cal's tie to Ronny was something more than that. He, Ben, didn't want Cal to have to say so, to give up the truth.

Cal wondered whether, maybe for a moment, Ben had thought something might happen between them.

"It's getting late," Cal said.

"You've got a day tomorrow."

"I do."

When Cal stood, they were close, like will-they-won't-they leads in a romantic comedy. Could they? Maybe that was the real question, the one no one ever asked. When Ben opened the door, a spry night breeze, thick with the zither of bugs, splashed inside. The coolness was kind on Cal's cheeks, which were hot.

"Thanks for this," Cal said. "It was a nice welcome."

"Good luck tomorrow. Tell me if you learn anything useful."

"Will do," Cal said, standing. But he knew that Ben knew what would happen: that Cal would see the Ronny he wanted to see. That the only things Ronny would tell him were the things Cal wanted to be told.

Outside, he loitered on Ben's stoop and listened. Not just to the sounds of night in the woods, but to the heft of his breathing. To the groan of the planks beneath his feet as he shifted his weight. To Ben, moving around behind the closed cabin door. He sounded like he was humming. Cal left the porch. He wondered, as he made his way toward the door of the cabin where Ronny had stayed, whether he was hearing things. He was sure he could make out the whisper of Ronny's laughter. He wasn't sure if it was relief or excoriation. Tomorrow, Cal would have to ask.

Three Strikes

"What would my superhero name be?" Charlie said. "Or would I be a villain?"

We were lying on the front porch of the house my parents had rented at Myrtle Beach, waiting for the rain to stop. We were splayed in opposite directions, our faces next to each other. The nubby heads of a pair of carpenter's nails bit into the low slope of my skull, and I rocked back and forth so my view of the veranda's defunct ceiling fan blurred. I wanted to feel the sharpness of the nails, pain that would distract me from the heat coming from Charlie, who wasn't wearing a shirt, his nascent muscles—already growing strong and large at fifteen thanks to time spent plucking corn on his father's small farm in Asheville—giving off the smell of suntan lotion and day-old salt water.

"You'd never be a villain," I said. "You're a good guy."

Out of the corner of my eye I saw him lean up on one arm. Soon, his face loomed over mine: his hair was sun bleached and long, curling at the ends. It framed him like a stylish mophead, its light tone a shocking contrast to the deep leather of his face.

"That's awfully kind of you." One of his hands floated in the air as though he didn't know what to do with it. I wished for it to land on my chest, for his fingers to flutter against the fabric of my tank top like the little feelers of a butterfly, desiring, investigating, prying.

Before I could say anything, a shock of lightning ruptured the quiet storm. I felt it in my teeth, in my hamstrings, the heels of my feet, as though the porch itself had been hit. Through the open front window, I heard my father moan out: "Whoa."

"That was close," Charlie said. He looked down at me. His eyes were chocolate, like a pair of tiny bonbons, edible and smooth and dark. "I told you so."

No more lightning came caterwauling down. As soon as the drip from the roof's awning had dried up, Charlie hauled down the front steps and waved for me to follow.

"Where are we going?" I said.

"The beach," he said. Then, without waiting to see if I was actually coming, Charlie took off. I loved and hated that he knew I was there, following him like magnets were pulling me toward his sloping, twitchy back.

The lightning had been close; its crash had surrounded us in a blanket of sound and electricity, its point of origin indiscernible. But Charlie marched with indelible confidence, never once hesitating or looking back at me or reconsidering his route. His feet slapped through the sand in hard, staccato steps. Instead of sinking my feet into Charlie's footprints, I followed off to the side, staring down at the pushed-out sand where his heels prodded away the grains.

When I saw it, my breath flung itself out like I was being crushed by a corset. Charlie stopped, too, but he didn't appear to have been vacuumed out as I had. The thing—fulgurite, I would later learn— looked like a plume of smoke frozen in time, angling up out of the beach like a bowie knife plunged cockeyed into the sand. The side facing the ground was smooth and straight, while the skyward plane reminded me of the ridged back of a stegosaurus.

"Don't," Charlie said when I moved to approach it.

"Is it dangerous?"

"The sand. It'll be too hot."

Another thing I did not ask him about. He simply knew. Charlie always knew. He was charged with something I couldn't touch or understand, like why I yearned to take his hand in mine when he held his arm out to keep me safe.

⎯⎯⎯

Charlie did not want me. That had been clear to me forever. He slept over at my house all the time, escaping his father and uncles when they played poker, smoked cigars, and drank too many heavy American beers, cans gathering in piles just like their betting chips. I had convinced my parents to buy me a set of bunk beds so Charlie and I both had a mattress to sleep on when he came over, and I let him choose whether he wanted the top or bottom. Every time, when we finally turned off the light and tucked under the top sheets, he would wait until he somehow knew I was drifting off before whispering my name. Then he would ask me about girls, inventing insane scenarios that, as an adult, I would realize were absurd in their adolescent boyish understanding of sex: "If you had to get stuck inside one girl in our class, who would it be?" "Which girl do you think would have sex with you the most times in a row?" "If you could make out with only three girls in our class for the rest of your life, who would they be?"

The questions were always about girls. Charlie's eyes always followed girls, strangers in bikinis and long one-pieces who splashed into the surf at the beach, girls in Daisy Dukes walking past us as we left school. Marian Harper, the girl of his dreams, sat in front of him in math class, and her ass was the sole recipient of his attention, even when obscured by the hard curve of her desk chair. When he got going on the subject—of Marian or any other girl, attainable or otherwise, local or televised or projected on the big screen—I found myself zoning out in a glum haze. I imagined Charlie with these girls, his arm slung over their shoulders, fingers dangling with yearning toward their breasts. I saw the lascivious want in his pulsing mouth, the cock of his head and slide of his eyes when he managed to catch a flash of midriff, like a hound catching a whiff of raw beef or a shark sensing a drop of blood. And then my imaginations became more complicated and heated, simmering with his slippery body on top of a girl's, his back straining, buttocks contracting. I could picture his toes, even, curled with effort. And as he talked, I nodded and agreed, adding a periodic *uh-huh* and *mmm* and *yeah, man* while I drifted further and further away.

Charlie invited me—probably at his mother's insistence, a kind of repayment for taking him to the beach—when his family went south for a vacation, all the way down to Louisiana for a plantation house tour.

"It'll suck," he said. "You can say no."

Of course I didn't say no.

The drive was long but expedited by his father's disregard for speed limits except when his probably illegal radar detector started whirling out noise like a broken droid from *Star Wars*. Then he'd hit the brakes and turn things into a game, offering a dollar bill to whoever sighted the cop car first. I was convinced the thing was broken because at least three-quarters of the time there was no Crown Victoria or whatever other bulky vehicle the local precinct had gussied up with lights and a crash bar. We made the drive to Edgard, Louisiana, in just over nine hours, squirting through blazing and glimmering New Orleans along I-10, crossing the gloopy Mississippi River.

Charlie's parents booked a hotel suite in Boutte, a town whose main attraction appeared to be its Popeyes. Boutte had that hardscrabble, falling-down look of small towns on their way to full decline, evocative of tumbling newspapers and empty plastic cups rattling in gutters. The motel, the Southern Style Inn, was surprisingly clean, the lobby smelling of lemon, and not the sort emitted from a spray can. The woman behind the desk, with large boughs of curled hair and fire-red nails approximately half the length of her fingers, smiled and explained the suite's features with a lilt and twang, as though she were singing a sad country song. We each received our own key card, and she gave me and Charlie a wink as we left the office.

The suite was two rooms: the bedroom, which Charlie's parents would occupy, and the kitchenette–living room, where we were banished to the foldout sofa sleeper. I remembered our hushed games of sex talk, the way my body sprung with hot blood when I pictured the things Charlie whispered. Would he do that again, when we were in such close quarters? What would his voice and breath be like so near my ear? Would he be able to sense the tingled arousal emanating from me like some pheromone-laced beacon? But when we turned out the lights, he yawned and rolled away from me, declaring that he was tired. But before he fell asleep, he did say, "It's going to storm tomorrow."

"It's what?"

"Going to strike."

"But your mom said the weather report was great."

"I'm telling you."

"Telling me what?"

"Just wait."

I did wait, sleepless, Charlie and his warm, bready body so close. His breath wheezed in and out, and try as I might, I could not count enough of those exhalations to fall asleep.

The day was blazing, the sun a yolk boiled runny, its heat wavering on the horizon as we drove toward the plantation. Not a single cloud bleached the oceanic sky. Charlie's mom, waving her hand in her face even though the air-conditioning was blasting on high, extolled the gorgeous weather, ignoring the hurricane-level humidity that had left us all with stinky armpits in the short trek from our room down to the car.

The plantation was sprawling, Doric columns holding up second-floor balconies. Attic windows peeked out from beneath the high, pitched roof like little cat eyes. The entire thing had been painted a stark white, including the shutters pinned back from the windows like butterfly wings skewered to a Styrofoam mount. We parked in a dug-out cul-de-sac at the edge of the property and trudged up the long, slithering drive, our eyes shielded from the sharp sun by our oversize sunglasses. But nothing could alleviate the heat.

I glanced at Charlie as we stepped onto the endless veranda, raising an eyebrow and looking back to the sky, still cloudless.

"Just wait," he whispered.

I waited a long while. Charlie's parents paid the suggested ten-dollars-per-person donation, and then we were whirled up and down spiral staircases, led through bedrooms and a library, the kitchen, a formal dining room set for twelve. The air-conditioning here, like in the car, was blasting on high, and I started shivering from the crusty cool that descended on me as my sweat evaporated, leaving me feeling like a vegetable stuffed in a crisper. Our tour comprised Charlie, me, his parents, and a trio of chunky Northerners with Minnesotan accents and blubbering bellies, their noses sharpened to a raw, sunburnt red. Charlie, of the entire assembly, seemed to be the only one who hadn't been affected by the charring heat, his white T-shirt without ringlets of sweat anywhere, his back an untrammeled snowbank. I could see the rise of his shoulder blades through the fabric, the twitch of his rear deltoids. The night before, Charlie slept without a shirt on, and his skin gleamed like a statue where it was hit by the singular beam of moonlight that infiltrated through the curtain. I could see the shift and blip of every muscle in his arms when he twitched in his sleep.

We were dragged outside again to march across the grounds to the former slaves' quarters, a series of squat shacks that, as our tour guide said, would have housed up to twenty people each, a number that seemed astronomical to me: each room was smaller than the main house's little study.

Charlie held back from the rest of the group and cuffed my arm at the elbow. He pressed a finger to his lips and pointed to the sky, which was still an uninterrupted tourmaline.

"What?"

"I told you," he said. He bared his teeth, mouth smiling as it stretched. "Villain. Kaboom."

And then it came, from nowhere: a thunderous crash, much louder than the one at the beach. The noise was jarring, and my vision blanked at the flash of it. Charlie's mother, twenty feet ahead of us, leapt up off the ground, her hands clutching at her chest when she gained her composure.

"Over there," Charlie said, pointing toward one of the slave cabins. "Look."

A thin gray line was rising into the sky, bisecting the cabin's slanted roof. Before I could say anything, Charlie took off, laser beaming his way around the side of the cabin. I chased after him. I could hear the tour group ignoring the preordained route and following, too.

I nearly ran into Charlie, who stood just around the back of the clapboard house. A small copse of trees stood fifty feet away in a small marsh, bald cypresses dripping their curtains of vines toward the stagnant water. But bursting forth from the ground on its own, halfway between the rear of the house and the rest of the trees, was a single zebra-striped birch, its twin trunk rising like a dousing rod from the ground.

It was on fire.

Well, not on fire exactly. It was clearly the source of the smoke, but its wider trunk had been split by the lightning, a long surgical cut down the center of a torso. Inside, the tree's core was filled with magmalike heat, fiery bile charring it from the inside out.

"Whoa," I said.

Charlie stared, wordless. I sidled up next to him and glanced from the tree to him. His eyes, wide and glossy, reflected the warmth pouring out of the tree's hellmouth gash. The heat reminded me of the one time Charlie and I went camping, guests of a friend who later vanished out of our lives when his father took a job in California. I spent most of the evening staring at the impressive fire my friend's father had managed to build. Its smoke kept darting to my eyes, and Charlie told me that the best way to get the smoke to shift elsewhere was to chant "Chasing rabbits, chasing rabbits, chasing rabbits" as your eyes were starting to water. I did it, and the breeze did shift, the smoke pulsing toward Charlie, who sat to my left. I watched his lips, which never moved. He invited the billow and char in, closing his eyes and letting the smoke wash over him. When the two of us shared a tent later, I could smell it on him. I told myself that he had sacrificed his own comfort for me, because this was the kind of thing that showed love.

For a moment, Charlie and I were alone, shoulder to shoulder, the only ones bearing witness to the tree's immolation. I knew that his parents and our galumphing Midwesterners would find us soon enough.

"How long do you think it will burn?" I said.

Charlie didn't reply. He stared, transfixed.

"I knew," he said finally, his lips pursed, Cupid's bow glossy. His mouth flickered with moisture, beads boiling at the close heat.

"Charlie."

"I told you I knew."

"Yes," I said.

And then the others were there. I heard his mother gasp. The Midwesterners took pictures, one of them recording a video that would go viral. I'm in it for just a second at the beginning, my shoulder clipped off from the rest of me. Charlie is nowhere to be found, but I know exactly where he stood.

For two years, Charlie made no more proclamations. On days the weather report called for rain I would ask him during homeroom or chemistry class if lightning was going hit somewhere nearby, and he would give me a ragged smile and shake his head. I never knew if he was saying "No" or "I don't know."

On the cusp of senior year he dragged me to a party at a neighboring farm, where this kid we knew, Jim Cauley—whom everyone called "Gin," for whatever reason—was celebrating that his parents were out of town. We stood on his back porch, the party spilling into the yard that hadn't been mowed in ages so that the Saint Augustine grass licked at people's kneecaps and caught on girls' skirts. Gin didn't want anyone going inside and leaving a mess behind; he stood guard all night, glaring at anyone who came close to the sliding doors leading into the kitchen. Kids peed in the tall grass, girls screeching and worrying about falling over as they squatted.

I lost Charlie after only an hour. I searched the clumped bodies from the porch rail but couldn't see him. I leaned there, nursing a skunky beer. My mouth tasted like pennies. The air swirled with sweetness and the sound of swishing stalks. I thought of rain, but there were no clouds in the sky.

I wanted to ask Charlie if lightning would strike, but he was gone.

He appeared on the porch at eleven o'clock on the dot, like a Cinderella who has forgotten about the end of daylight savings time. His arm was slung over a girl I didn't recognize. It wasn't Marian Harper or any of our classmates he had spent the summer fantasizing about while I twitched and silently moaned on the top bunk in my bedroom. This girl was short, her hair a blazing blonde even in the dark. Her eyes were huge, pupils dilated and inky. She smiled at me and took a sip from her plastic cup, then set it on the porch rail.

"This is Bailey," Charlie said. His words were gummed up like he'd been chewing on saltwater taffy.

"Hi," I said.

"This is my best friend, Ben."

"Nice to meet you," she said, her voice prim like a member of the British royal family. Each word tilted toward the sky as it came out of her mouth. She held out a hand and I took it, not sure how hard to squeeze.

"We're thinking about leaving. You?"

I looked at them. Charlie had given me a ride. The farm was a mile from his house, where my car was tucked in the driveway.

"No," I said. "You go."

"You sure?" Charlie stared at me, unblinking. I had to look away.

"Positive."

He nodded and offered me a fist bump. His skin was electric as always.

I left the party ten minutes later. I tripped twice in large, bent-out potholes, skinning both knees. Halfway to Charlie's house, the breeze picked up and rain started to pour from nowhere. Despite the heat, the drops were cold pricks. I ran the rest of the way. Somewhere far behind me, thunder loosened its earth-moving rumble. I never saw whatever lightning split the clouds apart. Perhaps, I thought, it was too far away for Charlie to feel, to know. Or else, maybe, he didn't want to tell me anymore.

———

Charlie disappeared for six months. What I'd expected to be a one-and-done thing with Bailey turned into a flurried relationship. On the few occasions I saw Charlie alone, he couldn't shut up about being in love with her, how they were applying to the same colleges—she wanted to be an A&M Aggie down in College Station, and so Charlie did, too—how they were going to celebrate Christmas twice, once at his house and again at hers, and how over our last spring break as high schoolers they would abscond alone to Cape Cod or something, all on her dime because her father was some kind of investment banker. I watched from afar as they wandered the halls of our overcrowded high school, hands in each other's back pockets. Instead of waiting for me after school, he waited for her.

And then, the Friday before Valentine's Day, he crashed against the locker next to mine, pressing his forehead into the grille.

"She dumped me, Ben," he said, slamming his fist against the metal, making the combination lock jump.

"I'm sorry," I said.

"It's killing me."

I blinked and fished my calculus book out from the bottom of the stack and shoved it in my bag. Despite the slurry chill in the air, Charlie was in a T-shirt, pilot-light blue. His arms were still stained summer brown where everyone else was pale.

Despite his long absence, I immediately let him back in.

"What can I do?" I said. "Tell me."

A quizzical look passed on Charlie's face, the quickest combination of confusion and fear. His brow furrowed, his eyes narrowed. It lasted only a second, and then it was gone, wiped clean.

"What is it, Charlie?"

"Nothing. Just, you know, bummed. Let's hang out later, okay?" He thumped a hand on my shoulder and squeezed. Then, before I could say anything, he turned and vanished down the hall. The bell rang, startling and loud, warning me that I'd be late for math in just one minute. I let its painful bleat gong in my ears.

After the third lightning strike, I kept circling back to the day of the first one, when Charlie wondered whether he was a villain. At the time, it was nothing. But then it was something.

He didn't find me later. I assumed that Charlie had simply found his own way to mourn the death of his relationship: maybe some illicit beer snagged from his parents' fridge, maybe another girl he could find at a party to which he didn't bother extending me an invitation. I spent the night lying on the upper bunk in my bedroom, staring at the popcorn ceiling and waiting for my phone to ring. Freezing rain tapped at the window, leaving splatters like bird shit on the glass. I decided I was too old for bunk beds and would ask my parents the next day if we could get rid of them.

But then Charlie appeared on Saturday afternoon. The gunmetal had been swept from the sky, the startling sun melting the freeze that had cupped over every surface, leaving runny snowmelt everywhere. Charlie stood on my front porch in combat boots and a hoodie.

"Aren't you cold?" I said.

"You busy?"

"No."

"Great. Let's go."

I put on my shoes. I didn't ask where we were going. Charlie swept around the side of my house, his boots sinking into slucky pools of mud. I skirted around them, clambering along the paving stones my father had installed the summer prior. They were slicked with black ice, and more than once my toe hit a slippery patch and I nearly fell into the desiccated banks of melting snow.

"What are we doing, Charlie?" I said when we rounded into my backyard. My parents didn't own a farm in the same sense that his parents did, but our wedge of grass—maybe twenty yards by twenty yards—backed onto a wild field of untamed wheaty stalks blended with scutch and ryegrass. We had a small slab of patio on which sat a glass-topped table and a quartet of chairs, all of which were covered in uneven lumps of snow. One tree, a weeping willow, fawned over a third of our yard, on the left side. Charlie stood in the mucky grass on the right side, facing the field, where the snow had dribbled into mangy heaps.

I did not approach him at first, standing a good ten feet away. The air was dead, the silence total except for the periodic *slip-slide* of icy slush from one of the draped branches of the willow tree.

When Charlie spoke, he said, "I don't know what's wrong with me, Ben."

I took a few careful steps toward him, trying to avoid the thickest of the wet sludge.

"What do you mean?" It came out a whisper.

Charlie turned to me. He'd been crying. "There's so much wrong with me. You don't know."

"I don't?"

"Come here, will you? Please."

He didn't need to tell me twice. I stood close to him, our faces only inches apart. My blood pounded. In the sharp, cool air I could smell his musk, a cedar that made me think of a closed room. I shut my eyes.

Charlie wrapped his hands around my biceps, his thumbs pressing into my muscles so hard I let out a little weep of noise.

"Please, Ben."

I opened my eyes. His were shimmering and scared. My heart thumped. I felt like an orchestra was blasting in my chest.

And then he kissed me. Quick, hard. His breath was hot, sour with saliva. Then it was over, so brief that I couldn't so much as open my mouth to invite him in.

Then he pushed me, so hard I reeled and nearly fell into the muddy snow.

"Move away, Ben."

When Charlie turned from me, I scrambled away. I knew what would happen. The air took on a tingling charge, like it had been spritzed out of an atomizer. From nowhere the wind blustered, sending snow swirling up around our legs. I looked up to the sky, expecting an interloping cloud, but there was nothing. Still, I tore backward, tripped, and fell, hands splayed in the cold chill. I shut my eyes.

And then Charlie was struck by lightning.

I felt the heat on my cheeks, as if I'd stuck my head in an oven door. The crackle of noise was immense, like I was sitting inside a timpani. My ears rang and I felt a dizzy nausea. The last thing I wanted to do was look, but I did.

Charlie was on his back, head cupped by the wet earth. I stood, body slucking out of the muck with a noise I felt more than heard. Charlie's hoodie was frayed and blackened, and his hands were covered in Lichtenberg lines. His face was scarred and burned.

His eyes were vacant.

When my hearing returned, I could make out the bustled yelling of my parents. One of them must have called 911 because eventually, as my ears cleared, I could hear a siren.

Charlie wasn't breathing. His body was still, his face trapped in a look that mixed confusion and grace. Despite the heat radiating off of him, I pressed a hand to his chest and felt my palms burn. But I didn't pull away. I looked at his face, which was bloated with burnt flesh. To anyone else, he'd have looked horrid, craggy and swollen and charred. But when I looked at him, I could see only the softness of his lips, the pure whiteness of his teeth. I wondered what he wanted, and why he felt so wrong. I touched my own lips, wondering whether the saliva there came from me or him. And then I wondered whether he'd known about the lightning, if he'd brought it down on himself. My stomach pitched and wobbled.

I blinked and told Charlie he was no villain, but by then, there was no one left to hear me.

There Is Love Under This Mountain

"Turn on the television," Clyde said when he burst into my apartment. I'd given him a key two weeks ago over dinner.

I was working on a jigsaw puzzle, sitting in the crook between my couch and the coffee table, legs tucked up beneath me. Clyde liked to laugh at the fact that I still sat like a child, but at thirty, I thought it was a fashionable display of flexibility and youthful bones.

"The remote's over there," I said, pointing to the recliner. "What's up?"

"Something's happening."

I was about to tell him that this was not a movie, that whatever he wanted me to see wouldn't magically be on the screen because he needed it to be, but lo and behold: when he clicked the television on, the very story Clyde was concerned about was being discussed on CNN. A shaky camera was panning over blurry footage of Leh–Manali Highway in the Indian Himalayas. Rain was pelting down, and the lens was fuzzy.

"What the heck am I looking at?" I said. Clyde didn't answer. He stared at the television, tapping his left foot on the carpet, hugging himself, the remote up near his face like a telephone.

On the screen, the side of a cliff had been blown away, demolition that was meant to be the opening phase of a construction project. I could tell immediately what the subject of the ruckus was: from the depth-charged mountain was oozing some cartoonishly purple substance. It made me think of chewed bubble gum.

"What is that?" I said.

Clyde turned to me. He was grinning. "That, Dennis, is love."

On the screen, the side of a cliff had been blown away, demo-lition that was meant to be the opening phase of a construction project. I could tell immediately what the subject of the ruckus was: from the depth-charged mountain was oozing some cartoon-ishly purple substance. It made me think of chewed bubble gum.

Clyde and I went out to dinner that night, and he couldn't shut up about the discovery in India. He asked our server whether she'd heard about it before ordering the chicken Kiev. She nodded with manufactured enthusiasm.

"Please stop that," I said, before diving into my Cobb salad, which they'd forgotten to leave the blue cheese off of. I shoveled it into a corner and ate around it.

"Stop what?"

"Asking people about India. You're freaking them out."

"I am not."

"Well, you're freaking me out."

He frowned, bit into his chicken, and said, with his mouth still half-full, "Sounds like someone needs a dose of love."

"That sounds like a bad song lyric. The kind of thing a hair band would scream into a microphone." But I thought, for a second, about what a dose of love might be. What that might feel like. And I found I couldn't.

Clyde swallowed. I liked watching him eat because he had a strong, long neck, and his Adam's apple moved like it danced with each bite. He always shook out his hair, black and floppy and a mess over his eyes, before cutting into his food. When he didn't say anything after one, two, three bites, I sighed and leaned back, resisting the urge to press my thumbs into my eye sockets.

"Okay," I said. "So what do you think it means?"

"What does what mean?"

I waved my hand at a television near our booth even though it was airing a baseball game. "The love business."

"I'm not sure."

"But what does it mean that it's love? How can love be a substance?"

Clyde shrugged and blinked. His eyes were a sapphire blue that reminded me of something from a cologne commercial. All he needed was a sandy beach and a Speedo.

"What's it supposed to do?" I said.

He set down his utensils, crossing them over his half-eaten chicken breast. I looked down at my own plate, where my salad was a minefield of ham cubes and hard-boiled egg.

"The kinds of things love does," he said, as if that were an answer that would make any sense to me.

I woke in the middle of the night, emerging from a dream I immediately forgot, except for the flashing feeling that I was drowning. Clyde was curled away from me, his body in a tight C. This always happened, and I tried not to blame him that his unconscious found comfort in moving away. Most nights, I found myself staring up at the ceiling, one shoulder pressed into his back like a lance. His body was always warm and slick with sweat no matter how far down I plunged the thermostat or whether I peeled off the comforters and top sheets. He slept in boxer briefs, solid colors that hooked high on his thighs and low on his hips, the fabric bunching at his crotch. Getting through the night without interruption was hard for me, so when I jolted awake, I always spent some time looking over Clyde's body in the dark. His legs were lean but strong, muscle drooping around his knees like a tennis player's. He had a hard stomach covered in the smallest film of fat, peskily clinging on no matter how many carbs he cut or miles he ran. I liked this little imperfection of his; it made him feel more accessible and human, and I enjoyed the way my hand slid across his stomach: I could feel rocky muscle beneath a just-mobile layer of flesh, like Clyde was my own mountain that maybe, somehow, I could mine. What, I wondered, would I find inside?

More than once I'd found my hand heading toward the band of his underwear while he slept, a hard, sexual urge floating between my ears in the middle of the night, but instead of molesting him, I would slide closer. He would often mumble in his sleep but never wake, his body shrinking into an even tighter ball, as if protecting himself from an assailant he couldn't see.

How did they know it was love under that mountain? Well: two of the workers on site when the detonation was cleared had seen the viscous liquid oozing from the broken earth and, in the spirit of idiotic, nameless victims in a slasher film, had marched straight up to it, letting it soak into their hard-soled boots. One of them reached out a gloved hand, clearly mesmerized by its color, convinced apparently that nothing the hue of clematis or wisteria could possibly be harmful. Neither man touched the stuff directly, but it glommed into their clothing and then diffused across their skin. Hours later, they were madly in love with each other.

All of this Clyde told me over breakfast.

"So it's like a potion?" I said. "Something from an old witchy story?"

He shook his head and bit into a piece of sourdough toast. "No, you don't get it. It's, like, pure."

"How can something that makes people feel things they didn't previously feel be pure? Isn't it manipulative?"

The men in question, Clyde went on, had apparently both felt attraction for each other before but had been unwilling to verbalize their feelings.

"The love just allowed them to verbalize what was inside," Clyde said.

"So how do you know it's not just a truth serum then?"

Clyde yowled in frustration and grabbed the back of my neck. He pulled me up, kissing me.

"You're so annoying," he said, smiling.

"What if someone tries to weaponize it?"

"What do you mean?" he said.

"Like, what if the United States makes Putin fall in love with us or something?"

Clyde shook his head and rolled his eyes. "Only you, Dennis. Only you could imagine weaponizing love."

Clyde smelled of borax and tanners. He was apprenticing to be a taxidermist, and even though he insisted that he wore gloves and washed his hands up to his elbows at least half a dozen times at work, he still carried a sharp chemical odor with him. It seeped into my bedsheets. He tried to cover it up with heavy colognes and smears of deodorant not only under his arms but across his chest and stomach, but the tart bitterness of formaldehyde and degreaser and the earthy, queasy aroma of intestines and blood always loomed beneath arctic blasts and spritzes of Curve.

"You're like a slaughterhouse," I said when he appeared at my door with takeout Korean barbecue.

A week had passed since the discovery in India, and although Clyde had stopped talking about it every other minute, he still insisted we watch the news while we ate, just in case there was anything breaking.

"I read online that a company wants to bottle and sell it," he said as he slid onto the floor next to me.

"Sell it?" I said, licking a smudge of sauce from my thumb. "They think it's safe to do that?"

"No one has cancer yet. No one who's been near it has died or anything."

"I think cancer takes more than seven days."

He chewed a strip of bulgogi, his eyes closed. I wondered what Clyde was seeing in that darkness. Sometimes, I wondered what it felt like to work with dead animals, freezing them in time, digging into their bodies, rooting around beneath the surface to make them look pristine and lively.

"Stuff anything interesting today?" I said.

"A woman brought in a peacock," he said, eyes blinking open.

"A peacock?"

"We didn't ask questions."

I gnawed at a piece of spicy pork. I looked at Clyde's hands. Despite where they'd been, rubbing through animal carcasses and marinating in embalming chemicals and hair cleansers, his cuticles were carefully trimmed and clean aside from the driblets of ssamjang on his knuckles. He took good care of himself.

"Here," I said, pulling a napkin from the bag. "You've got a smudge on your lip."

Clyde leaned toward me. "Why don't you take care of it." But when I reached out with the napkin, he grabbed at my wrist, darting his hand in the air to cut me off. "No, no." He grinned, the saucy splotch widening. "Not with that."

I squirmed from my seated position and ran my tongue across his skin.

"Better?" he said.

"You know," I said. "It's not like leukemia or radiation poisoning show up in a week or less. That stuff could really be anything."

He bit down on his last bite of meat. "Oh, Dennis," he said, shaking his head.

Clyde did not like his apartment, a grizzled little efficiency in an old building. Everything creaked: the stairs leading to his second-story unit, the floor covered in carpet that reminded me of a golf green that had been worn down by thousands of cleated shoes, the refrigerator and the two cabinets that held his tiny cadre of plastic plates and bowls. If you weren't careful in the coffin of a shower, a stray elbow could knock one of the handles or the show-erhead right off the wall, sending hard sprays against your back or chest.

"You need to move out," I said. We were at his place because Clyde had fallen ill, perhaps from the Korean barbecue but more likely the flu, even though it was summer and I had never thought of the hot months as a time when anyone would really get sick.

Clyde was curled in his bed, sweating. His mattress was on a low platform he'd built himself from scraps he scrounged from a lumberyard owned by a friend of a friend. He'd messed up one of the sides, facing it the wrong way so pink and orange graffiti announced half a cuss word when he lifted up his comforter.

"Tell me how I can help. What can I get you?" I said. "Soup? Medicine?"

"Just be here," he said.

"I don't think that will help you feel better."

"Dennis."

"And I could get sick."

"Please."

I sighed but did what he asked, but not before insisting I lie down outside the blankets. I also told him to keep his mouth and nose safely within the confines of his duvet.

"Okay," he said, voice snotty. "It's not supposed to be a hardship."

"Sorry."

He held me tight, slipping one lizard-clammy hand out from the blankets and shoving it over my shoulder like a heavy pashmina.

"TV?" he said.

"You want to see what's going on in India, don't you?"

"I've been too messed up to track."

"You won't even be able to see the screen," I said, but I picked up the remote from the floor anyway.

"Just turn up the volume."

For once, the daytime news channels weren't focused on the Leh–Manali. Clyde groaned. I could feel his breath on my neck. Eventually it leveled out, and his arm went dead heavy. I wanted to slither away but stayed still. His body was weighty and warm, and the apartment was cooled only by a tiny window unit. Soon I felt sweat building behind my knees and wallowing under my arms, which were slick and seal-like. Clyde's breath was ragged, doggy. I turned up the volume on the television a few clicks, wondering if it would wake him, but he slept on, breath hitching and catching. He started snoring.

The news did circle back, as it always did, to the love under the mountain, as it was being called by then. This always made me roll my eyes; it sounded like the name of cheap, off-brand perfume or some terrible sex toy. Plus, the love was inside the mountain, a hidden inner layer, not something stuck underneath. I didn't say this out loud, as I knew Clyde would roll his eyes and let out a leaky sigh of frustration at me being so particular.

The most recent development was that everyday citizens were scrambling toward the mysterious goop, young men and women—mostly men, and mostly stupid, I thought—who were convinced that a slopped-up handful of the stuff would make their greatest romantic wishes come true. The authorities were trying to keep people at bay with armed guards and complicated construction equipment that formed a makeshift perimeter, but desperate people were, well, desperate. Tricky. They kept slipping in, and the love goo kept slipping out.

It took Clyde three days to get well. He dipped in and out of fugs of sweat and nausea, his body thrumming with chills. More than once I suggested he needed to go to the hospital, but he swatted that idea away, moaned about his shitty insurance and crazy deductible. His apartment stank worse than usual, and I imagined all the chemicals that had seeped into his skin, all the dead, eviscerated insides of the animals he'd gutted and pelted, spreading their miasma across his blankets and boxer briefs and his tiny writing desk where he paid bills the old-fashioned way. I had to hold my nose at one point, so I trundled out to a nearby pharmacy for heavy-duty air fresheners that I sprayed until I felt dizzy. I didn't say so, but I imagined that maybe he'd fallen ill because he had too much love built up, that whatever he felt for me was making him sick somehow.

When he was better, Clyde thanked me for my caretaking. We were once again in my apartment; he had once again let himself in.

"What have I missed?" he said.

I turned on the TV.

"You could just tell me," he said.

"I don't want to misinform you."

He leaned in close; I felt his breath against my ear. "I trust you."

"I know you do," I said. "But maybe you shouldn't."

He pulled back. "What does that mean?"

"Nothing," I said. "Just that I don't care about all this love stuff."

Clyde slung his arm over my shoulder. I could still smell his chemical odor, which he'd tried to mask with a heavy dose of some new cologne that reminded me of fermentation and rainwater.

"I just find it all very suspicious," I said.

He kissed the side of my head. "It makes me think."

"About what?"

"What love even means."

I turned to look at him. Clyde's eyes were like the wavery bottom of a public pool. "I wish I could tell you," I said.

———

When we first got together, I asked Clyde why he would want to be a taxidermist. All that blood, the guts, the chemicals. The dead animals.

"People come to me heartbroken," he said. We were eating sushi at a noisy place in the Central West End. He snagged a piece of spicy tuna roll with his chopsticks, which were delicate and tiny in his large, strong hands. "They've lost their beloved pets."

"And you fix them? The people, I mean. Or, I guess, maybe also the pets."

Clyde laughed. "I wouldn't go that far. But I do think I give them something back." He twirled his chopsticks in the air, then aimed them at me, pointed together like a beak. "It's more like, I help them keep something that's slipping through their fingers." He thought for a second. "But then there are the hunters. They're just excited about their kills. What's the saying? Two kinds of people in the world."

I almost said, And which kind are you? Instead, I drank from my water until we had something else to talk about.

———

"This is for you," Clyde said. He held out a small bird, frozen in time, one tiny clawed foot attached to a six-inch length of cypress. "A songbird."

I didn't know he'd been doing mounts on his own. I said so.

"First one."

"How did you get the bird?"

He shoved it forward. The bird was fat, its chest puffed out like a swollen weight lifter. The breast was a hot yellow, the head and wings the gray of an overcast sky.

"It looks alive," I said, holding it up close. The eyes were marbled and tiny, the size of peas.

"That's the idea," Clyde said. He cupped his hands beneath mine, his thumbs working at the cords of my wrist, pushing against the veins worming toward my hands.

"What do I do with it?"

He shrugged. "It's yours. You do whatever you want with it."

I didn't like the bird. I could appreciate the craftsmanship—I couldn't see any sutures or any signs that Clyde had done a single thing; the bird looked like it could fly up into my ceiling fan at any moment—but the idea of keeping a dead thing somewhere in my apartment made my stomach flip-flop.

"There's something else," Clyde said. He released my hands and rummaged in his jeans pocket, wrestling with whatever was in there. His belt buckle jiggled. He produced a small, glinting key.

"What's this?"

"To my apartment. A key."

"Oh." I took it in my free hand, letting the jagged side bite into my tender palm.

"You're the one who gets to decide what to do with it."

"I assume I'll use it to get in and out of your place."

Clyde shrugged. "That depends, I guess."

"On what?"

"On how you feel about barging in on strangers."

I frowned. "Now I'm confused."

Clyde smiled. The look on his face was the one he used when he explained things to me that I didn't understand, like the causes of World War II or trigonometric functions or the difference between stewing and braising.

"I'm going to move out, Dennis," he said. He took a step closer to me. I could smell aftershave, cologne, chemicals: the boiling cauldron of Clyde's various smells. Intoxicants, repellents, and pleasures all rolled into one.

"Okay."

Clyde's fingers gobbled at my fist closed around the key. I opened it, and he poked at the key, which was pressed against my palm, its harsh edges still chewing at my tender skin.

"The question," he said, "is whether I should go somewhere else."

"Or?"

He squinted, then sighed. I closed my fingers around his. "Or whether you should come here," I said before he could.

"Yes, that's the question."

"You're inviting yourself to live with me?"

"Dennis."

"That's what it sounds like, is all."

"I'm asking if you want to live with me. Whether that's here or not."

"Will you try to poison me with that love juice if I say no?"

He wilted and I felt a salty sting in the back of my throat. I never said the right things, I realized. Not once had I ever done that.

"Of course you should live here, with me," I said. I looked around the room: my walls were bare. Between two end tables there was only one picture frame, a snapshot of my mother. "But I'm not sure what to do with your bed."

Clyde smiled, but I saw a shadow behind his eyes. "That's an easy question."

"You can get rid of a bed just like that?"

"Please stop," he said. Then he pulled me to him, the bird, still in my hand, squashed between our thighs. I could feel its little feathers bending against my jeans. "Please, no more talking."

———

I kept waiting for something to go wrong. Clyde, as he started boxing up his meager possessions and plopping them in the various rooms of my apartment, would realize he'd made a terrible mistake; he would accidentally lop off his thumb or forefinger at the taxidermy shop, or burn his palms or face with some skin-melting acid while trying to clean a pelt, leaving him horrifically mutilated and convinced that he should never see me again; the love substance would prove to be some ancient evil that would eat away at people's insides or turn them into zombies or sociopaths and he would have a mental breakdown when what he'd believed about love was turned on its head.

But nothing happened.

We marched through summer. Clyde spent time on my tiny patio with his shirt off. We had lots of sex. He brought home another stuffed animal, this time a small, white rabbit that he set on the entertainment center next to the television. It looked ready to hop down at a moment's notice. When Clyde was at work I stuffed it in one of the closed cabinets below the TV so I didn't have to look at it, but I was always careful to pull it back out before he came home. Its eyes were black with a little hue of ruby, just enough for me to think the thing was demonically possessed and waiting for an opportunity to come to life and chew at my jugular vein while I slept.

On the news, the story in India lost momentum. Clyde took to the internet, gobbling up whatever manic conspiracies and fake stories he could find. One website claimed that its bloggers had gone to the mountain and there wasn't anything, that the whole story about the love was faked, some kind of publicity stunt for some movie. Another stated that those who had come into close contact with the substance had started disappearing. Yet another claimed that the gooey liquid was, in fact, caused by nuclear radiation thanks to the dropping of the atom bombs during World War II.

"Wasn't that Japan?" I asked when Clyde read that one aloud. We were lounging in my bed on a Sunday morning. Clyde's skin was sticky; we'd opened a window and left off the air-conditioning. The room smelled salty.

"Could have been from fallout."

"That has to be thousands of miles."

"I don't know what to tell you."

I swatted at the phone. "Maybe stop reading those things. They rile you up."

"They do not," he said, holding his phone away. But then he darkened the screen and set the phone down. Clyde swung toward me and kissed my neck. My body tingled. His fingers tickled toward the elastic band of my underwear, my hips pushing upward at his touch. I couldn't help this; he knew it.

"Seems like someone else is getting riled up," he said. His fingers pressed into my pubic hair. I let out a hot, shuddered breath.

"Not fair, Clyde," I said.

He kissed my throat.

"I love you, Dennis," he said, but then he wasn't listening to me, so I said nothing, Clyde's mouth suctioned to my collarbone.

———

I woke one morning way before Clyde; we'd had gin rickeys the night before while we sat on the patio and swatted away mosquitos. Clyde drank too many too fast in celebration of the end of his apprenticeship. He could now take his own orders and work his own mounts. His eyes went glossy fast, gummy and stupid with joy. He kept leaning over and pressing his weight against my right knee, threatening to cant over onto the concrete. I had to sling him into bed on his stomach, a trash can nearby. Even though he didn't puke, the bedroom smelled like a locker room the next morning. Clyde was snoring, head pressed sideways into the pillow.

I turned on the television in the living room, the volume low, while I drank a glass of water. That was when I saw it: in Illinois, near Decatur, a highway construction team demolishing part of I-72 for rebuilding had taken out a small mound of rock, too tiny to have a name. When the small boom settled, there it was, seething beneath the surface: the same purple substance.

"Love," the news anchor said. "Closer than ever."

His coanchor nodded and let out a satisfied noise. She leaned back and closed her eyes for a second, hand pressed to her solar plexus. Her eyeshadow was an overpowering green, like seaweed.

She blew a noiseless raspberry with her painted lips before sitting up straight and moving on to the next story.

I walked, dazed, to the bedroom door and looked in. Clyde was still twisted in the sheets, his back billowing up and down as he took snoozy breaths. I looked toward the bedroom window, where the light was bright and powerful. Somewhere out there, so close—just a few hours' drive—was the substance that had captivated him. "Love," his voice had said. "The physical manifestation of love." I imagined his joy. He would want to go and see for himself, and I would have to go with him. It would be the ultimate test, my willingness to get up close to it if we could. To slingshot down the highway, our hearts beating to the rhythm of the rolling road. He would look at me, clamp a hand on my leg in excitement, and wonder aloud what it would mean for us to be near it. He would expect me to have an answer.

My stomach roiled as though I were the hungover one. Then Clyde groaned. He turned onto his back and blinked at me, his face bleary.

"Good morning," I said.

He smiled and rubbed his eyes, then said, "I feel terrible." He patted my empty half of the bed. "Will you come here?"

I took a deep breath and glanced out the window one more time. "Of course," I said, and to Clyde I went.

The Sad State

As soon as our car crossed the border, I could feel a new glumness pushing into me. Jess, driving, let out a low sigh. We'd had sex last night for the first time in weeks, but it had been strained, arrhythmic, our bodies incapable of finding the kind of fitted-puzzle-pieces pace we used to. Right as we finished he looked past me, toward the ceiling, squeezing his eyes shut. I wondered who he was picturing.

For most of the drive the weather had been bright, crisp; Jess had even rolled down the windows so the early-fall air, always making me think of fresh apples, could filter into the car. But as soon as we entered the Sad State, the sky cluttered with cumulus clouds, gray and pregnant with the threat of rain. The temperature ticked up with unpleasant humidity. Jess closed the windows.

We'd planned the trip before things went south. I know Jess thought I was cheating on him, even though I wasn't; I was just tired from work all the time. I was teaching extra classes at the community college, and I was serving as interim chair of my department (communications) while the current chair was on sabbatical. I liked teaching, but I hated handling everyone else's unhappy students, the requests for prerequisite waivers, sorting out the next semester's schedule, being dragged into meetings with the dean when students complained about an adjunct. Jess, too, was bedraggled. He worked in human resources at a small IT company, and his boss and one of his coworkers had recently quit. In order to save money, they weren't going to be replaced. Jess was promoted and received a small salary boost, but he was doing the work of three people. He was, by training, a benefits specialist, able to navigate health insurance and retirement plans with aplomb, but he'd had duties way outside his range—sexual harassment training, sick leave, Family and Medical Leave Act filings, conflict resolution—dropped on his desk.

The border town we entered was all ramshackle split-levels and dilapidated ranch houses. The interstate had funneled down to a two-lane road buttressed by sad strip malls whose curbs were littered with garbage. Jess, without consulting me, pulled into the parking lot of a tepid-looking diner whose windows were in need of a hearty washing. Inside, the air smelled of fryer grease and smoke. The waitress on duty wore a gray smock like some peasant from revolutionary France. She stood behind an empty counter next to a coffeepot whose contents, based on the odor, were deeply scalded. Her hair was burnt blonde. She gestured for us to choose whatever booth we liked; they lined the walls, their red pleather cracked and unbecoming, and every single one was empty. Jess chose for us, a table at the front window directly across the from the space where he'd parked.

The waitress dropped a pair of sticky laminated menus in front of us and then stared, waiting for us to order something. I asked for a Coke, and Jess nodded, staring down at his menu. They were printed on piss-yellow paper with tiny black lettering that was all italics; it made my eyes hurt, as if I'd been smacked in the temple. There were no pictures. When the waitress came back, she practically dropped our plastic cups full of soda and barely any ice onto the table, liquid sloshing onto the menus. She tapped her foot and extracted a pencil from the beehive of her hair and glanced from Jess to me and back.

Jess chose the burger, medium, and I opted for the patty melt with a cup of chili instead of french fries. The waitress nodded, the closest she'd come to any form of human communication, and then disappeared through a swinging door behind the counter.

"Cheers," I said, picking up my drink. Jess rolled his eyes but offered his cup in toast. The soda was flat, warm, the ice cubes already melted to slivers. Jess slurped a third of his down without pausing for breath. I watched his throat undulate as he swallowed. When he was finished, he looked out the window. The sky hadn't changed its rain-threatening color, and no cars passed on the main thoroughfare. For all I could tell, he, myself, and our bored waitress were the only people left in the world.

Traveling through the Sad State had been his idea. A way—he had said as a joke then but that seemed pointed now—of seeing just how good things were for us. We lived together in a compact apartment in a complex of duplicates, the carpets a fuzzy beige gray that felt like no color at all, the kitchen galley style with a tiny window peeking into the living room. We'd decorated our walls with prints of my favorite Vermeer paintings—*The Music Lesson*, *The Milkmaid*, *The Little Street*—and shelves containing my books, which towered on either side of the window looking out onto our metal-railed balcony. We had two bedrooms, and the extra was crowded with my desk and his exercise bike, which he'd stopped using, citing exhaustion from his long working hours. Our apartment smelled like red pepper, Jess's favorite spice, which he put into everything he cooked. It was a pleasant-enough life we had together, even if it was a dusty suburban existence.

The waitress brought our plates. They were chipped and tinted gray. When Jess asked for ketchup, she pointed a lazy finger toward the end of the booth, where a sticky sugar caddy held Sweet'n Low and glass bottles of condiments. She left without another word but then reappeared with fresh sodas, as flat and warm as their predecessors. My chili was layered with a skin of orange grease, beans poking through like ice floes. The french fries on Jess's plate looked limp and cold, and he confirmed as much when he picked one up and it sagged like an old carrot. His bun released an audible crunch when he bit into it, and I could see the beef was overcooked when he set the burger down on the plate. My patty melt was actually pretty good, but it was slathered in so much Thousand Island I couldn't taste the onions or meat.

"Well," he said after drowning his pathetic potatoes in ketchup. "Here we are."

"The Sad State," I said.

"Living up to the name, that's for sure."

"Yes."

"Think this place makes milkshakes?"

"The milk would probably be sour."

"And the ice cream's probably low fat or something." He smiled and used his fork to pry a fry from the lake on his plate. Jess nodded as he chewed. I wanted to reach out and put one of my hands on his, but my fingers were greasy. We had no napkins. I looked around for our waitress, but she'd vanished. We could have walked out without paying, probably.

We drank our terrible sodas and ate our terrible food in silence. My chili was watery, the beef stringy and the beans undercooked so they popped between my teeth. The waitress returned through the kitchen's swinging door—I glimpsed a grimy sink and a flat-top grill studded with grease—and took our plates away, leaving behind a handwritten bill that didn't include any tax. When I pointed this out to Jess, he said, "You didn't research anything about this place, did you?"

The Sad State hadn't really interested me, despite its proximity, only an hour from our suburban enclave of repetitious home architecture, desperately manicured lawns, and fresh-painted gables. I knew enough, I thought: the Sad State was a sad place, with sad weather and people and landmarks. I said so.

"Well, there's more to it," Jess said, pulling out his wallet.

"Let me," I said. I felt the heavy glumness pressing down on me from all sides. It came in weird waves, periodically spiking like I'd just run a sprint or was remembering a recently deceased pet.

"You can cover the tip."

"Do they do tips here?"

"It's still America, Donovan. We didn't go to Europe."

I plucked a handful of bills from my wallet and settled them atop the twenty that Jess had placed on the receipt. I was always a generous tipper, having spent my teenage and college years working in various bars and restaurants, first as a busboy when I was sixteen, stacking plates and pint glasses in my arms, dredging my skin and uniform shirts with streaks of ranch dressing and salty grease. Jess, when things were good, mentioned multiple times that my generosity was what had first attracted him to me. We met at a bar, a sleepy hole-in-the-wall in a strip mall squashed between a manicurist and an insurance firm. I was there with a trio of friends, celebrating one's impending divorce. We'd ordered two buckets of beer, and when those were gone, I ordered a platter of shots from the bartender. The place was weirdly packed, drinkers jostling for the attention of the brunette in a white tank top who was bustling back and forth, filling tankards with frothy Anheuser-Busch products and mixing well drinks. The bar was dimly lit, half of the fluorescents replaced with colored lights, greens and reds and blues that gave everyone an alien glow. The walls were covered in Cardinals regalia and foam fingers supporting Mizzou and Southwest Missouri State and the Fighting Illini. Seating was limited, and my friends and I had managed to snag one of the leatherette booths along one wall. When I slipped up to the bar, I found the tiniest sliver of space but still managed to accidentally elbow my neighbor. That neighbor was Jess. He glanced over at me, the bones of his face catching the psychedelic light, making his angles sharp and striking. When I smiled through the colored gloom in apology he smiled back, mouth flashing a fruit-punch red. Then he turned away, back to his friends. But he saw me order a quartet of shots of Jack Daniels and lay down too much money, and as he would tell me later, he took note of where I went.

Jess led the way out of the restaurant. We were met with a burst of humidity, the air smelling of impending thunderstorms.

When we were back on the road, Jess said, "I guess we should check into our hotel."

"Isn't it a motel?"

"Semantics."

"I think there is, in fact, a difference."

"Fine. Our motel."

The building was a saggy two-story, its front facade's red paint peeling. One of the columns holding up the office's awning had a chunk taken out, as if a car had recently clobbered it. The interior smelled like wet dog, and the man slumped behind the desk took his time attending to us, staring down at his phone for a good five seconds while Jess stood on the other side of his desk, fingers rapping on the oak surface. I looked around: the room was hardly larger than a jail cell, feeling even more cramped thanks to the scratchy chairs lining two of the walls, the square kind that occupy doctors' offices and are never comfortable. A coffee maker sat on a low table, along with dusty packets of creamer and individually wrapped stirrers. A television was mounted in the corner opposite the check-in desk, a film of dust gathered along its lower lip.

"Okay," the guy said. His hair was long, pulled into a tight pony-tail, his head shimmering with grease. "One room, yeah? Two nights?"

"That's right," Jess said. I frowned. We'd talked about spending three nights in the Sad State. I said nothing.

The clerk handed Jess two old-fashioned keys with plastic tags, blue diamonds that had the motel's name—the Super

Stay—written on them in shaky black Sharpie. Jess handed me one and pocketed his own.

"You're on the far end, back side," the clerk said. "Near the pool, though it's closed."

Jess drove around in silence. There were no other cars in the lot. Our room was, in fact, as far from the office as possible, right next to the ice machine, which I would later discover made a lot of whirring noise but was incapable of actually dispensing ice.

The room smelled of cheese and must. It contained two beds, full size even though Jess mumbled something about requesting a single king, which I took as a good sign: he wanted us to sleep in the same space. For the previous several weeks, I'd woken multiple times to find myself alone in our bed, discovering Jess sprawled on our living room sofa, knees bent, elbows tucked up beneath the throw pillow upon which his head was cocked at what looked like a deeply uncomfortable angle. I never woke him, and in the morning, I always found him back where he belonged.

The carpets were an ugly sewage brown. Everything was mid-century modern, from the wood-paneled walls to the table lamps with their bloated shades. The bedcovers were slippery and thin, and the television tube backed. When I tried the remote, nothing happened.

"Lovely," I said.

"Sad," Jess corrected, tossing his suitcase on the bed closest to the window, whose shades were drawn tight. The air-conditioning was letting out a low, rattling growl, something loose in its bowels. I thought about setting my luggage on the other bed to see what he'd say, but instead I propped it next to the doorless closet, where half a dozen wooden hangers waited for something to do.

I peered into the bathroom, which was surprisingly clean. A faux-marble vanity with a clamshell sink had been scrubbed, the stainless-steel faucet winking in the harsh fluorescent overhead. A box of tissues, unopened, and a trio of tiny lotions and shampoos stood in decorative array. The tub was generously sized; I could picture Jess and me hunched together in steamy water, feet tickling each other beneath the surface, but then I also couldn't possibly imagine us that way, either. The showerhead looked a bit low—when I stepped into the tub and stood before it, it came up to my chin. I got out and turned the knob experimentally. Water came gushing out like I'd opened a fire hydrant.

"The pressure's good," I said. Jess was lying on the bed, dead center, staring up at the ceiling. I followed his gaze to a sizable water stain.

Jess had taken off his shoes and socks. He had nice feet, nails he kept manicured. He buffed his soles twice a week. He'd played some tennis in high school and college, purely recreationally, but it had beat up his toes, and he'd quit shortly after graduating, nursing his callouses and blisters away. He enjoyed the periodic pampering of a pedicure, a fact he'd admitted to me sheepishly on our third date. I'd watched him wince as he spoke, clearly expecting me to laugh at him. I nodded and said, "That does sound relaxing—rejuvenating," and sipped from my beer. He stared at me for a long moment, his face betraying nothing. He had an ability to go stone still, unreadable. Then he smiled and drank from his beer, too, and said thank you.

"For what?"

"Not laughing."

I shrugged. "Enjoy what you enjoy."

We went home together that night.

I stared at his feet, toes pointed toward the ceiling. Jess looked like a dead body, set to be reposed. For the briefest moment I yearned to grab his big toe and give it a quick tug; I used to do that all the time, when he was sprawled in an afternoon nap or watching a movie or reading a book. He would blink at me and smile.

"What should we do now?" I said.

"There's probably a museum or something around somewhere."

"A museum for what?"

Jess shrugged. "The history of the state, maybe? I don't know."

"This was your idea."

He threw a forearm over his face. "I know that."

"Well. We've got lots of time."

"Maybe a nap is in order," he said.

"I'm not really tired."

"You didn't drive."

"Maybe I'll take a walk."

"Sure."

Jess had recently become very good at feigning sleep, or pretending not to hear me, or doing anything that would cut short a conversation like a switch had been flipped. I let out a huff of air and left the room, letting the door close behind me before I realized I hadn't taken my key, which I'd set down somewhere. I tried the knob, carefully. It turned generously in my hand. Of course the motel didn't have automatic locks.

The day had gone fuggy. The oppressive gloom felt heavier, like I was draped in a lead-lined blanket. I started walking around the motel the way we'd driven in. The parking lot was full of cracks through which grew weeds, most of them choked brown. A vending machine next to the office was streaky with soot, its brand name and image of a wet, inviting can faded to a washed-out shadow.

I hadn't read up on the town we were in; I had no idea its population or what there might be to do or see. In either direction ran a sad line of businesses, most of whose lots were as empty as the motel's. Past their pitched roofs I could see the tops of houses, so I crossed the street and wandered, peering at the back end of the commercial lots until I saw a break in the fence line. The neighborhood was separated from the business district by a thick line of trees about ten yards deep that offered no easy, discernible walking path. I pushed through, brambles and branches and sharp leaves scratching at my arms and face, and emerged into a backyard that was fortunately not fenced in. The grass was thick, not lush but unkempt, dotted with dandelions and children's toys:

a trio of kickballs sat abandoned, a bicycle with purple streamers spewing from the handles lay on its side. A back patio that was nothing more than a concrete slab was home to a glass-topped table in need of a deep cleaning, a puddle of rust-orange water covering the surface. I slipped through the yard fast. Neither the house in question nor either of its neighbors showed any signs of life. The siding was uneven and not affixed all the way to the raised foundations, against which brushed white-painted boards that were suffering from wood rot. Dead hydrangeas lined both houses, brown bulbs slumped.

I stopped as I emerged in the house's front yard. At the end of the driveway, a single slab of weather-stained concrete, a little girl had set up a lemonade stand.

She didn't see me. She wore a strawberry-red sundress, the most vibrant thing I'd seen so far, spaghetti straps hooked over her bony shoulders. I couldn't tell the girl's age from where I stood; her back was to me. She was standing behind a low credenza that had been dragged to the curb, her arm shaking as she stirred a pitcher. I could hear her humming but couldn't make out the words; they were like radio crackle a room away.

I took a few steps through the grass, hunched down as if I were tracking an animal. Then, deciding I would look more terrifying in that craven, predatorial pose, I stood up straight but kept walking at a diagonal away from her, into the yard of the neighboring house, whose front porch featured a hanging wooden bench swing that was lilting in the slight breeze that had picked up. The sky was a seasick green. I glanced at the girl, who I could now see in profile. Maybe seven or eight years old, upturned nose, thin lips, hair the color and texture of straw. She was staring in concentration down at her pitcher, whose contents she stirred with a wooden spoon gripped in her right fist. As far as I could tell, the only thing inside was water.

The driveways up and down the narrow street—there was no curb or sidewalk, just a smash-up of grass and uneven concrete—were all empty. Two mailboxes across the street— driven into the ground at an angle so they resembled stumbling drunks—had their flags raised, the only indicator of normal, lived life I had seen so far. I was about to slink away from the girl, but then she looked up and saw me. Because I was looking right at her, I could do nothing but wave. Her face was impassive. I could see in her eyes the almost physical manifestation of something sad. It had been in the clerk and waitress, too: not quite sorrow, but an absence, a void of hope or optimism.

"Mister, would you like some lemonade?" Her voice was raspy, as if she were a smoker, but it had a songbird quality that offset the dirt in it. Without looking, she reached down to a stack of Styrofoam cups and pulled the top one. She stopped stirring, tapped her spoon on the pitcher's lip, and set it down on the credenza.

I walked over. The credenza was battered and scraped, as if a roving gang had kicked and punched it. The wood was gray, like an anemic pork chop, the squat legs scuffed, one of them angled crookedly and threatening to snap.

I wasn't sure what to say to the girl. Kids were not my flavor, which had been a point of contention between Jess and me recently. Although we'd both been against child-rearing when we started dating, a point we had quickly agreed upon and toasted more than once while listening to our friends' horror stories about their newborns and prepubescents, his feelings had begun to shift. He would drop hints, some of them carefully testing the waters and others gargantuan cannon balls that raised tsunamis. Eventually, I'd had to tell him that I simply wasn't interested, and I went so far as to say that if he wanted a child, he'd have to raise it on his own.

"Shouldn't you be at school?" I said.

The girl stared as if the concept were foreign. She thrust the cup forward. "It's only twenty-five cents."

"What flavor is it?"

"Lemonade flavor."

"Isn't lemonade usually yellow? Or pink?"

The girl frowned at this critique. She set the cup down. "Do you want it or not?"

"Well, considering the dearth of options, sure."

I watched her struggle to lift up the pitcher, her little arms straining. I was sure it would tip over, splash all over her dress and the credenza, send my cup flying, but she managed, with only the tiniest slosh out of place, to fill it.

"Here," I said, pulling a dollar from my wallet. "Keep the change."

She took the bill with solemnity, as though I were passing her a piece of the Shroud of Turin, and set it beneath her stack of cups, which was teetering precariously in a sudden wind. Then she handed me my lemonade and stared at me, challenging me to drink it. I did. Surprisingly, it was full of tart flavor. My tongue practically curled in on itself.

"Delicious," I said.

The girl blinked at me, pressed a hand down on the cups, and picked up her spoon, started stirring again. I glanced around me, wondering whether I was in a horror movie.

"Is it usually this quiet?" I said.

The girl shook her head and kept on stirring.

"Your parents home?"

"I'm not supposed to talk to strangers."

"Aren't I a customer, not a stranger?"

"You can be both."

"Fair enough." I sipped again. Something about the lemonade's astringent flavor was welcoming as it jolted down my throat.

"You like it?" she said.

"It's certainly memorable."

The girl scowled but kept stirring, turning her attention toward the tiny whirlpool of liquid in her pitcher. I was dismissed.

I walked along the edge of the street. The houses reminded me of the neighborhoods that had surrounded my tiny liberal arts college in northern Missouri: peeling paint, slanting porches, roofs on the edge of collapse. Most of the sad, sallow homes in that town had been rentals; the wallpaper in the kitchens was perpetually peeling, the carpet thin as putting green, paint chipped along doorframes and archways. The interiors always looked cobbled together like a kid improvising a Lego building.

The girl was the only person I encountered. No cars drove by. The breeze picked up, the cloying wetness notching up with each blast of wind. Despite the fact that I'd walked for maybe only ten minutes, I decided to turn back so I didn't get caught out in a storm.

I didn't make it.

I was soaked through by the time I reached the motel, my shirt pasted to my chest, hair flattened, underwear drenched as if I'd wet myself. I was sure my cell phone had drowned in my pocket and that the money in my wallet was limp, the ink runny. Jess had to let me in because he'd locked the door. His hair was tousled with sleep and he wasn't wearing a shirt. Despite his lamentations over not being able to exercise, he was still in excellent shape, though I could see the tiniest softening around his hips and shoulders.

"Jesus," he said and stepped aside. The room was frigid. Jess liked to sleep in the cold, whereas I preferred warmth, a disagreement that hadn't really arisen until we moved in together. Eventually we compromised; I got a quilt that he tended to kick off, and he got a fan propped on the dresser, aimed only at him.

I went to turn down the blast of the air, but Jess said that it was broken, refused to do anything but churn out arctic spray. I pretended not to hear him and fiddled with it anyway. No matter which knob I turned or button I pressed, it kept chuffing out its cold air.

"Did you call anyone about this?"

He shrugged.

I went into the bathroom and peeled off my clothes, strewing them over the shower rod. I stared at myself in the mirror; I looked like a drowned rat. Back in the room, Jess had lain down again, head propped on the heap of pillows he'd stripped from the second bed.

"So what now?" I said. "What are we doing?"

"You should probably put on clothes," he said.

There'd been a time where me standing naked in a hotel room would have elicited a very different reaction. When we went on our first vacation together, a trip to a tiny island off the northeastern Atlantic, we stayed in a quaint bed-and-breakfast. Everything was handmade quilts and framed photographs, and I stepped out of the bathroom after a shower in only a towel, slung low on my waist, and Jess practically threw himself at me. We'd had to change the sheets to the spare set in the room's tiny closet afterward.

I sat on the edge of the bed. My skin was unpleasantly slick.

"What are we doing?" I said again.

"It's raining. What are we supposed to be doing?"

"That's what I've asked myself this entire time."

"Come on, Donovan."

I pounded my thighs with closed fists.

"We can always go home, if that's what you want. Tell me what you want to do."

"I don't know what I want," I whispered.

"I'm well aware."

I sat down on the edge of the bed. Jess had his hands behind his head, elbows splayed out like wings. "And you do? Know what you want?"

"Of course not. Who does these days?"

So long ago, we had both been sure. When we went back to his apartment at the end of that third date, we made out in the front seat of his car, headlights boring on the front windows of his downstairs neighbor before we clattered up the steps, the wrought-iron banister groaning as we bumped our way up, kissing and tumbling. Our clothes flew with abandon, scattered about his living room and dining nook. In the morning, he brought me coffee without asking if I drank it (I did) and then asked if I wanted to go for donuts (I did) before kissing me hard, again. I felt like I was full of warm stones.

Jess cleared his throat. I laid back, head bumping his knees, his feet at my hips. My body ached.

"You should shower," Jess said. "You smell like a sewer."

"Must be the rainwater," I said. "It's sad."

"Everything here is sad. That's the point."

"Is it a point or a state of being?"

"I don't know."

I turned to look at him. His eyes were still on the ceiling. I shook my head and stood, then went to my suitcase and pulled out a pair of underwear. In the bathroom, I yanked at the faucets. The water was lukewarm. I threw myself into the shower, the spray hard on my back. The tension in my body didn't release no matter how many times I sighed and rolled my neck and wrung my arms. I thought of the look on the waitress's face, on the clerk's, in the eyes of that little girl with her stinging lemonade, the horrible lack of joy. I blinked through the water, pulled the shower curtain open, and tried to see myself in the mirror, but it was steamed over.

The night I met Jess, our second encounter took place at the door of the men's room. I was on my way in, my bladder screeching. As I approached, the door swung open and there stood Jess, tall and messy haired, all cheekbones and broad shoulders. The bathroom was tucked back in a dark, quiet hallway, like a bomb shelter, the noise of the bar tamped down.

"Oh," he said. "Hey."

"Hi," I said. "Sorry about earlier."

He frowned. "Oh. That? Nothing." Jess was wearing a red-and-cream jacket that reminded me of a jock's high school letterman minus the bad fit and pompousness. Jess reached up and scratched at the back of his neck with his left hand.

"I'd love to talk to you," I said, trying to sound sober. "Really. But I really, really need to pee."

He let out a small laugh and stepped aside. I hustled into the bathroom and practically leapt to the nearest urinal. I heard the bathroom door close, and I assumed Jess was gone. Something cold swirled through my stomach, a black hole of missed opportunity. After I washed my hands and pulled the door open, though, there he was, leaning against the wall decorated with vintage Busch Stadium memorabilia. The lighting was dim, but I could see the look on his face: unadulterated excitement. When he looked at me, he was smiling, coy flirtation in his eyes. He reached up toward his neck again and his smile grew larger. I felt a flare in my sternum and took a step toward him, knowing that something wonderful was about to happen to me.

A Tough Man to Love

The investment banker tells Timothy to take off his clothes, so he starts with his shoes and socks. The hardwood floor is cool against his heels. Real wood, the investment banker was quick to point out the first time Timothy walked in the door, like he were trying to sell him the place. The only lighting comes from the almost-crepuscular glow of a trio of pendant lights above the kitchen island and the magmatic aura of the gas insert in the fireplace, where the flames are real but the embers are not. Timothy twists his torso for the investment banker, who is leaning back on his Nella Vetrina sofa, to highlight his abs. The apartment smells of fresh flowers, carnations the investment banker says he pays a woman to arrange in a Baccarat vase twice a week. The unit is on one of the upper floors of a downtown St. Louis high-rise, one wall entirely windows, and Timothy can see the outline of the Arch through the darkness, its red light blipping to alert low-flying planes to its location.

When they met in person after messaging back and forth, Timothy knew they would not fall in love. He's never had an easy time falling in love, and he's always known he is a tough man to love. He has never felt the weightlessness in his heels that indicates something deep and moving in his heart. Also, Timothy isn't stupid. When the banker suggested an expensive steakhouse, and then paid for their expensive Wagyu strips, and then suggested a nightcap, Timothy knew exactly what the deal was. He had no problem with it. The investment banker was handsome and in excellent shape. Sandy hair, broad shoulders, icicle eyes, crater-huge dimples. All things Timothy was, and still is, happy to work with. But then, that first night, as soon as Timothy's lips were on the banker's, he was jolted to find that the banker started to lift, just so, as they stood in the kitchen, a pair of rocks glasses filled with expensive whisky left abandoned on the granite countertop. The banker didn't actually rise off the ground, but Timothy had to hide his surprise.

Timothy steps out of his boxer briefs. He looks at the investment banker, who wears a loose white oxford, sleeves rolled to the elbows, buttons undone at the throat to expose a wide triangle of smooth, bronze skin. The investment banker is clean shaven, sharp, even though tonight they went to a sports bar and watched a Cardinals game. They ate onion rings that oiled their fingers. They drank Budweisers, and now the investment banker sips Macallan. The only sound is the investment banker's slurping, his loud swallow. He smiles over the glass.

Timothy knows it's servile, perhaps degrading, to fall to his knees in front of the banker and work at the button of his pants, a pair of beltless black dress slacks. The sound of the banker's zipper descending should feel shameful or silly, like they're in a ridiculous porno. But as the investment banker rolls his hips so Timothy can peel away his underwear, revealing his erection, Timothy doesn't care. Isn't the point to do what you want? And, as he grips the banker, he knows this is what he wants.

The investment banker's body is warm, radiating more heat than the fireplace. When Timothy places his left hand on the banker's thigh—just as smooth as his jaw and chest—the skin is practically smoldering. Timothy feels the air of floatation in the banker's body as his thighs and ass start to buoy just so. When Timothy glances up, the investment banker is staring toward the skyline, refusing to look his way; he says nothing about what is happening to his body. Instead, the banker brings his free hand to Timothy's cheek. His fingers are like matchsticks. When Timothy kisses his knee, it feels like he's brushing up against a radiator. When the investment banker lets out a shuddering breath as Timothy takes him in his mouth, Timothy feels his own shudder, but he remains firmly planted on the ground, his kneecaps like lead weights. He shuts his eyes and listens to the banker moan, a song that gives him momentum and confidence. In a few minutes, the banker's breathing is shallow, and one of his hands is in Timothy's hair, and he's telling him to wait, wait, to be careful. His body isn't quite floating, but he's close. Timothy isn't careful, not at all. He can feel the recoil in the investment banker's body, the tension in his legs and the contraction of his abs and then the hot spume of the banker coming in his mouth. Timothy keeps going, and he hears the sound of the banker's heel thumping against the hardwood that makes every noise reverberate. It sounds like heavy applause.

———

"So does he, like, pay you?" Timothy's brother is stirring eggs in a pan. They've shared an apartment for two years now, mostly because Timothy can't afford to live alone on his high school teacher's salary and neither can his brother, who is still in graduate school for music and receives a stipend that barely covers groceries and crappy beer. In return for Timothy paying most of the rent, his brother cooks and, apparently, slut shames.

"I'm not a prostitute."

"Next you're going to tell me he gives you gifts. Like teenagers give cash on their friends' birthdays because they're too lazy to find an actual present."

"It's not like that."

"It sure sounds like that."

Timothy's brother is the taller of the two, broader but lanky. He's a better cook; the eggs are always fluffy, scrambled and drizzled with shredded cheese. They eat in relative silence until, in a lull, his brother says, "I just don't want anything bad to happen to you."

"That's nice of you."

"Jesus, Tim."

"How's Amber?"

His brother frowns. They both know that things have been rocky; the walls of the apartment are thin, and their bedrooms are smashed next to each other. Instead of sex noises, Timothy mostly hears the whispered edges of arguments, the stomping of Amber's feet as she marches out of the apartment late at night. Unlike the investment banker's, their apartment is claptrap, small, covered in worn carpet. The kitchen feels like a prison, and the living room can fit a sofa and recliner and TV stand and nothing else. Timothy remembers finding his brother so light and airy once that he had to haul him down from the ceiling by the ankle. Apparently, he and Amber had said "I love you" to each other for the first time the night before, which sent them up, practically slamming their heads into the ceiling. His brother was all smiles then. Now he's like someone chained to the earth by heavy cinder blocks. This makes him both easier and more difficult for Timothy to understand.

"She's fine."

"She's not here," Timothy says.

"She had to work."

"On a Saturday morning?" Amber is a receptionist at a swanky spa in the Central West End, where most of her job involves booking appointments for seaweed baths and deep tissue massages. Sometimes, Timothy believes, she folds towels. She never works on weekends.

"She's got a second gig."

Timothy raises an eyebrow and eats a bite of eggs. "I guess that makes two of us."

"Not that kind of gig, asshole." His brother takes the plates away even though Timothy still has food left on his. A bit of cheese falls from the tines of his fork to the table. "She's bartending."

"A career change in the offing?"

"Expanding her horizons."

"Maybe that's what I'm doing, too."

"She's not getting some stranger off for dough."

"He's not a stranger."

"What's his last name?"

Timothy feels blood rising to his face, which makes his body sink deeper into his chair. When he says nothing, his brother smirks. Timothy holds his fork, hand leaden. His stomach growls, but if his brother cares or hears, he makes no indication.

As a kid, Timothy heard stories.

Couples in parks lifting off of benches, so caught up in their burgeoning love that they didn't notice how high up they were. Legs kicking in the air as they slipped further into the sky, then calling out in fear and worry, desperately grabbing for treetops. Others rocketing up toward ceilings in churches after exchanging vows, the flood of love so great that they shot straight up to the peak of the nave, heads cracking on woodwork. New mothers feeling such love for their newborns that their IVs snapped out of their wrists and elbows as they flew out of the their hospital beds, children cradled in their arms like tiny weights not heavy enough to keep them grounded. He watched his mom and dad periodically lift off the ground as they stood next to each other in the kitchen or hover above the couch as they cuddled and watched a movie.

Timothy tried to understand. He tried to make himself feel the love that would send him buoying upward. For anyone, anything:

his teachers, the family pets, athletes on television and movie stars on the big screen. He experienced the same adolescent lusts as his peers, for the beautiful men and women around him and out of arm's reach, but always these produced a heavy heat, an earthiness in his heels rather than something lifting. If nothing else, he understood the radical difference between lusty desire and love. And he knew others knew he knew.

The first time his brother floated, he was on the phone with a girlfriend, splayed on the bottom bunk in their shared bedroom. His head thunked against the slats of the upper bunk. Timothy was fifteen, his brother a year and a half older. He spent the rest of the night splayed out on his bed, trying to will himself to float. He thought of his parents and their kindness and protection. He thought of Sabrina Heller, the girl who had asked him to homecoming and kissed him tentatively in the dark gymnasium during a slow song, who cocked her head at him when their lips parted, her hips in his hands feeling light. He thought of Bradley Weller, his teammate on the soccer team who wandered the locker room shirtless more often than not, how Timothy had to stop himself from staring at his midsection. None of these did a thing. He felt heavy, weighty, something to be swallowed into the ground.

The investment banker sends him a text, inviting him to a wedding.

A wedding? Timothy texts back.

Wear a tie. And a jacket.

Timothy stares at his phone and feels a jiggle of something tight and uncomfortable in his stomach. He's sitting at his desk during his planning period, a stack of student responses to the first chapter of *The Catcher in the Rye* looming at his side.

Is it a Catholic wedding?

Nondenominational. Ten-minute ceremony. Open bar.

He tries to picture himself and the investment banker sitting at a reception hall, surrounded by tulle and centerpieces. Friends of the newlyweds asking about their connection to the bride or groom. Couples dancing, lit up by the neon strobe of a DJ's lights. Chewing wedding cake and mass-produced chicken products and rubbery pastas. Clapping after the various unfunny toasts and heartfelt speeches. Rocking back and forth to a silly love song with violins and a twangy guitar and swelling lyrics. The slip-slide of his body against the banker's, who stays anchored to the floor thanks to heavy, expensive loafers.

Sounds good, Timothy writes.

The banker wears a glossy tie, gold with flecks of blue. Not dots or lines; they're like stars, almost, the tiniest fuzzes of color buried in all that precious sheen. Timothy slides into the passenger seat of his Maserati, and the investment banker hands him a cream-white envelope to hold.

"The gift. Sorry I didn't think to include your name on the card."

"I don't even know these people."

It turns out, though, that he does, at least vaguely; he went to high school with the groom, who played basketball, not very well (no one on the basketball team played very well). He is tall, red haired, and blasted with freckles. Good at math, if Timothy remembers correctly. There had always been rumors about him, that maybe he snuck around with his teammates in a romantic-sexual kind of way, but here he is, marrying a cheery, short woman who, according to the maid-of-honor speech, loves CrossFit. Of course, Timothy thinks during the first toast, sipping his Schlafly Pale Ale, anyone can marry anyone, and it can mean something or nothing.

When the couple comes around to their table, faces shiny with sweat from all the walking and talking and first dances and mother-son dance and father-daughter dance and dollar dance and the entrance and the vows and photographs and the barely eating, the groom hardly notices Timothy. The investment banker makes no introductions; the music is loud, the people at the table

Joe Baumann

are munching on cake, and the bride and groom are quick to
move off.

The investment banker drives them back to his apartment,
insisting he's sober, having consumed only two cocktails and a single glass of champagne. Timothy is bloated on beer. They arrive
safely, and in the elevator, the banker takes his hand. The investment banker's fingers are light and airy like an inflated latex glove.
Timothy looks straight ahead at his reflection in the stainless steel
and feels like a kid desperately holding on to a runaway balloon.
Weddings do this, he knows: all the heartfelt talk, the romantic,
swooning ballads, the first kiss, the second kiss, the tears. Couples asked to come to the floor, whisked away one by one until the
elders whose marriages and lives have endured for half a century
are tottering alone to Celine Dion or Rascal Flatts.

Inside his apartment, the investment banker pulls a bottle of
brut from the refrigerator. Despite feeling turvy and wasted, Timothy accepts a glass. The investment banker offers a cheers and then
threads his arm through Timothy's. They drink at the kitchen island
the size of a ping-pong table. A bowl of fruit sits in the center. A new
arrangement of flowers exude their fresh smell. Timothy feels dizzy.

And then the investment banker leans close, breath tingling
with champagne, and says, "I think I'd like you to fuck me."

The hair on the back of Timothy's neck rises. The investment
banker sets down his glass and rubs Timothy's arm. His touch
is light; he's practically dancing into the air. Without a word
they shuffle down a long hall. The investment banker's bedroom
features heavy drapery and an expensive throw rug framing a
queen-size bed that's all lush satin sheets and a hand-hewn oak
headboard. The only noise as they undress is the banker's excited
breathing. When he pulls off his shoes, his heels bob into the air.
Timothy feels a coil in his stomach.

From his bedside nightstand the banker pulls a bottle of lube.
Timothy, standing in his underwear, says they should shower. The
banker nods, a sheepish smile on his face. "I've never, you know."

"I'd be the first?"

The banker blanches.

"Tell me," Timothy whispers. "Tell me I'd be the first."

He does. Timothy kisses him, hard, then takes his hand—he's so light, bobbing—and leads the way into the bathroom.

Under the hot spume of water, Timothy watches the banker float, a buoy pushed down by the pressure. Timothy lathers a loofah and scrubs the banker's back, then helps him clean himself. Without a word, Timothy presses two fingers into the banker, who lets out a small noise that Timothy barely hears over the water. He sets his chin on the banker's shoulder to keep him grounded. Although he knows they're crossing into something that should make him lighten, transformed like a balloon filled with helium, Timothy feels heavy, as if every hair on his body were absorbing as much water as it could, keeping him logged and low.

The sex is good, the banker's nerves palpable as Timothy enters him. Even as his stomach fills with silver warmth, and numb pleasure funnels into his groin, and the investment banker's breathing goes shallow as he uses his hands on himself, and even as Timothy crumples over atop the banker and their inhalations mingle, their chests touching, chins clicking like the champagne flutes at the reception, his torso is steel. He feels the investment banker's body rising against his, pressing like a bird trying to fly away. Timothy closes his eyes and demands that he do the same, that they curl toward the ceiling in blissful romance. But all Timothy can do is dig his heels into the bedspread, his toes curling and feeling every thread, every warp and weft.

—

Oftentimes, he finds himself thinking about weight, heaviness, the plumb nature of his body. Seeing others bobbing along in pairs, bodies ready to rocket into the sky, Timothy wonders what it's like to feel that joyous lightness. He steps onto the scale in his bathroom every morning, seeing the numbers hover and tilt around the same 170 pounds, give or take a few depending on his diet and devotion to exercise. Never does he experience a sudden plunge out of the thickness of his bones.

He watches birds, reads about the hollow nature of their bones, how that is what allows them to take flight. So different, he thinks: they don't have to rely on a feeling he can barely understand in order to leave the earth behind.

As he enters his apartment, he hears a squeal. Walking through the door, Timothy sees his brother down on one knee, squashed between the coffee table and the sofa, Amber standing with both hands over her mouth, nodding with ridiculous vigor. Timothy watches, silent, as his brother stands and the two embrace, bodies floating off the ground in a tangle of tight arms and pointed toes.

When they finally land, Timothy's brother turns to him and says, "Good timing."

"Congrats, I guess?"

Amber is busy admiring the tiny diamond on her finger. Timothy wonders where his brother got the money.

"You were gone all night," his brother says.

Timothy has already decided he won't see the investment banker again. Last night, he had trouble sleeping. The banker's body kept levitating off the sheets, his shoulder bumping into Timothy's nose. In the morning, though, it was as if the night before had never happened. The investment banker offered Timothy breakfast, but then when they were finished with their egg whites and turkey sausage he said, "Why don't you take off your underwear?" Timothy stripped, morning sunlight and the steely glare of the Arch in the background. They didn't kiss goodbye. Timothy's mouth was salty as he took the elevator down, and he felt as if he were plummeting like an anchor dropped into a lake.

How he wished, as the elevator kissed the ground floor and the doors rolled open to the gaudy lobby with its parquet flooring and lilac walls, that he could hover.

His brother and Amber stand shoulder to shoulder in the kitchen, mixing batter for waffles. They fill the maker, then heap them with syrup and canned whipped cream before they've properly cooled. She smears a white glob on his nose, and he retaliates with his sticky fingers, which wriggle toward her cheeks. Amber shrieks and laughs. Timothy wants to shout at them that they were just fighting days ago, slamming doors and threatening severance. And now they float through the room, feet barely touching the floor, as if they were figure skaters gliding around a rink. When they sit down on the couch, they have to tuck their feet under the table to stay grounded.

"Want some?" Amber says. There are sprinkles atop the whipped cream.

"We have extra," his brother says. "We made too much."

"No," Timothy says, already halfway down the hall. "I'm full." He shuts his eyes, letting his head thunk against the back of the door as it closes. Timothy lets out a deep breath. He thinks of the banker's body, its yearn to rise against him. He pictures its curves and dips, its muscles and lines. For a second, Timothy thinks he's going light, but when he opens his eyes, he's still standing strong, planted to the scuzzy carpet whose feel against his feet is all too familiar.

Gethsemane

Every fourth Wednesday, Trent and I bury our sister Gretchen in the garden in one of our mother's cracked red clay pots. This week we drag out one of the largest, in which she used to grow peppers, blending the yield into a briny soup that we always ate too fast, burning our tongues. We fill the pot with the tumbled black soil we keep tilled in the garden so that our sister can slip in, dipping her foot like she's entering a bath. She wears a pair of white panties pulled that morning from one of the bulk packs we buy at the discount store, our cheeks red as the emaciated-looking clerk with sunken eyes and tangly blonde hair runs the plastic package over the scanner. Trent says he wants to have sex with the clerk, and I laugh and agree even though I find her bony elbows frightening as brandished knives.

Our sister stands up straight, hands covering her naked breasts even though we've seen them many times and only the three of us are in the garden. Nothing else grows here except clover and dandelions, weeds that our sister tells us over and over we should remove but neither Trent nor I ever do. She reviews the plan, that she will need to be watered every morning and night, and we remind her that Trent and I have already sorted this out. We remind her that we've done this before, every month since our mother and father died, even the evening following their joint funeral after our aunt Ethel finally left when we convinced her we would be fine without her. Gretchen cried at the funeral, briefly, a single gulped sob that she swallowed like an inappropriately timed belch. Neither Trent nor I shed any tears, sitting shoulder to shoulder and glancing at each other throughout the eulogy. I didn't know what to do with my hands.

Once Gretchen is settled, nodding that she is secure, toes wriggled down deep, Trent and I trudge back to the house. Evening has settled in, the sky turning a sleek orange that will soon drift into gray then black, the temperature knit into the low sixties and falling. I imagine our sister's bare arms dangling near her stomach, hands bristling together for warmth. For a moment I worry, but then I picture her paste-white skin undergoing its monthly transformation, hardening and browning as if she were being baked, dapples rising like shingles as her flesh turns to bark, a thick, leathery exterior that will not shiver in the dewy night.

When we were young, Gretchen seven, and Trent and I five, our father took us out to look at our mother. We knew she disappeared for days at a time, an absence ingrained in us since we were toddling masses of dumpy flesh that fell over every few steps we took in our droopy diapers, and so her monthly vanishings were simply a part of our lives. But we did not know until we traipsed after our father—Gretchen right behind his bright-red flannel shirt, me following, and Trent bringing up the rear—that she had been so close all along. "Your mother," Father said, patting the trunk of the cherry tree sprung up in the garden. We thought, for a moment, that she would spring out from a hiding crouch, surprise us with candies and hugs and smiles, but our father kept smacking the tree until we understood. He waved for us to come closer, to touch our mother. Her bark was gritty like concrete.

Our father spent his evenings during our mother's transformations staring out the bay window in the dining room that offered an unobstructed view of her place in the garden. Gretchen stands there now. Unlike him, Trent and I do not look; we pull shut the heavy drapes so we do not have to see Gretchen change, her body stretching and morphing. She becomes a maple tree, the hand-size leaves perpetually green and full, even in the winter months. She will sit dormant for four days, her roots bursting the clay pot like a thick balloon, and Trent and I will clean up the pieces, sling them into a trash bag and toss them out before she is our sister again.

I defrost hunks of the first of three casseroles Gretchen has prepared for us, a mix of cheese and stale tortillas and ground beef, while Trent uses the restroom. He whistles while he shits, a pitchy, squeaky noise I can hear through the crack under the door. No song in particular, at least not one I recognize, but the music has a marching beat to it, and I find myself tapping my foot to my brother's song while I spoon our dinner onto paper plates that sag under the greasy weight. When Trent emerges, still whistling, hands wet from washing, we sit at opposite ends of the gargantuan table that fits eight. The room feels sticky and glommed with perspiration even though the air outside is cool and dry, Gretchen's absence moistening the space around us. Trent does not seem to notice, scarfing down his food with hardly a breath between each gnashing forkful, and before I've taken more than two bites, he is finished, crumpling up his plate. He tosses his fork into the sink, the metal clattering like a rambunctious wind chime.

While Trent is locked upstairs in his bedroom, probably masturbating while looking at porn on our slow-moving computer, I fill a pitcher of water. This month Trent will rise at daybreak and do the same, pouring the water into the already-fracturing clay pot so that Gretchen can soak up the cool liquid. The air outside is sharp in the darkness, the autumn sun's absence leaving the sky quaky and depleted; I can smell the far-off odor of a bonfire from the neighbor three acres behind us, separated by a thick batter of trees that, even in winter, obscure any view of their yard except for flashes of movement on their grandiose deck.

When she underwent her first transformation, Gretchen would let only our mother be with her. They had spent the months before it happened sharing hushed whispers, sitting side by side on the lumpy sofa in the living room, voices cutting to silence if me or Trent or our father walked in. I felt pangs of deep jealousy: I was ten, Gretchen twelve, and Trent and I had started to drift apart. Although we still looked the same, both bore identical five-pointed clusters of freckles on our left cheeks, he had thrown himself into youth football; I drove him from our shared bedroom with my squeaky clarinet practice, trying to pour dexterity into my fingers to play my first chromatic scale. Our father spent afternoons with Trent, tossing him passes in the narrow strip of grass between the house and the garden that, under my mother's capable green thumb, sprouted tomatoes, ancho peppers, bushels of basil and rosemary. I would watch them from the dining room, the ball spiraling through the air like some bloated bird, my father's throws sharp and perfect, Trent's wobbly at first but smoothing out like ironed sheets as weeks went by. Sometimes I would sit in the foyer, my back against the wall, while my mother and Gretchen whispered in the living room. I drank up the hissing sounds of their voices even though I couldn't understand what they were saying, closing my eyes and pretending to feel their breathy whispers cresting my cheek or neck. I wished someone would tell me whatever my mother was telling Gretchen. I felt jealous, tremulous waves shudder through my shoulders at their intimacy, silky like fresh-spun ice cream.

The air feels like whipped frosting when I carry the pitcher out to Gretchen, whose face is already lost in the bark that surrounds her, hair swallowed by leaves and budding branches that will fill and reach toward the morning sky, eight, ten, twelve feet over the next two days before beginning to retract, slimming down and slowly fading back to pink on the fourth day, when Trent and I will stand before Gretchen and catch her, each of us gripping one arm so that she doesn't tumble to her knees when she is herself again.

The transformation back, she says, is like riding in a rocket ship, and she comes out woozy and wobbly, sometimes even vomiting up a translucent slop that wets the soil.

I spend about an hour with Gretchen, walking slow circles around her, my fingertips brushing her bark skin where I imagine her stomach would be, although I know Gretchen's body is nowhere to be found. I talk to her as if she were able to hear me, even though she has never indicated that she has ever absorbed a word I've said. But I speak anyway, because I would not want to spend four lonely days by myself, and I know Trent spends no more time watering her than he has to, sometimes chucking the pitcher of water from yards away, letting it splash somewhere in Gretchen's vicinity.

We fought over that once. I watched Trent from my bedroom window as the water arced through the air and splattered on the ground, none of it coming close to Gretchen's outstretched roots where, having burst through the clay pot, they tunneled into the ground like crooked forearms. Before Trent could come through the kitchen door I was outside screaming at him that he wasn't being careful and what was wrong with him and before I knew it he had socked me, his knuckles clipping the left side of my face right by my eye socket and a curtain of black sewed up half of my vision and my head felt suddenly scooped out, my hearing muffled like my left ear was packed with cotton. Instead of crying out or falling over as I think Trent expected me to, I lunged at him and pushed him to the ground, falling on him, pinning his hands with my knees. Then I punched him hard in the nose so he bled and so did my knuckles, and that was when I howled in pain and he took advantage and threw me across him, rolling us both so he was atop me, and he slapped me with his fingers wide, swiping across my cheeks, twice on each side, then we were huffing, silent, chests expanding, blood everywhere. Then for no good reason Trent smiled and helped me up and went inside and filled a new pitcher and was careful to pour it so Gretchen could soak it up. When she changed back, I had a black eye, the left side of my face the color of radicchio. Trent's nose was the size of a toucan's beak. She cried but we laughed and told her everything was okay, and she made us promise not to fight like that ever again.

On the first morning I wake to the sound of Trent letting the heavy kitchen door slam as he takes water to Gretchen. I watch him. He stops a few feet from the crumbling pot and tosses the water in a thick, low arc, but I do not feel a squirt of rage reaming in the back of my throat. This is Trent's way, I know. That night, I tell Gretchen this, patting the bark, little bumps digging into my skin.

On Friday Trent skips school. He doesn't do this too often because he wants to keep playing football, and if he's truant he could get kicked off the team, but sometimes he fakes being sick when Gretchen is transformed because he can call the school secretary and pretend to be her. He mimics her voice well, raising his pitch just so, winking at me while I sit at the kitchen table and eat soggy cereal, shaking my head while he explains that Trent has a fever and won't be in. I ride the creaky bus by myself, ignoring the cacophony of chatter and gossip, setting my bag down next to me so that no one will slip in. No one talks to me, but this is unsurprising, as I don't speak to them.

Trent is gone when I get home that afternoon, the yard dusty and the grass crinkly and overgrown. He doesn't return until dark, and he is not alone: the girl from the dollar store stands behind him like a ghost, hair matted and sweaty, hooded eyes sunken and surrounded by dark, smeary skin like she hasn't slept in days. Her spine is curved over so her neck juts out at a sharp angle, her face thrust before her body like a slumping jack-in-the-box. I can't quite look her in the eye.

Somewhere, somehow, Trent has acquired a six-pack of beer. Neither of them says a word to me when they plant themselves in front of the television, turning the volume up loud, letting the beer-bottle caps fall to the hardwood floor with a tinkle. I stand in the kitchen doorway, leaning against the jamb while the pitcher fills in the sink. As I turn to walk out, Trent rolls his arm over the girl's shoulder, pulling her toward him.

When I come back inside—I do not spend more than a few minutes in the garden, patting Gretchen, saying hello, then rushing away—they are gone. I hear the creak of Trent's bed a few minutes later. As I move through the first floor, flicking off the overhead lights, snapping off the television, plucking the bottle caps from the floor (the two beer bottles are empty, set on the floor by the couch, but the rest of the pack is nowhere to be seen), the rocking of the bed picks up speed and the matted sound of groaning presses through the ceiling. At the base of the stairs the sound is stronger, and it increases as I take each step with a slow exactness, careful to skip the plank third from the top, the one that squeaks under the lightest of weight.

I stop by Trent's door, which is not quite shut. Like most of the doorways in our house, the frame has swollen over time so the door won't close without a careful jiggle, and through a tiny sliver of space I can see the blurry outlines of their bodies. The girl is perched atop Trent, and he is making deep grunting sounds, his hips bucking, while she hovers above him. At first I think Trent is the only one making noise, but then I hear a small, constant murmur like the whine of a refrigerator, which must come from her.

I tiptoe past and shut my door. I can still hear them, Trent's rising groans and the girl's plaintive, constant whir. I add a singular long sigh to their song, then turn off my lights and slip into my bed, the mattress squealing beneath my weight. Outside, Gretchen is silent and tall.

⎯⎯

Sharp and bright like a glimmering snowbank the sun shines through my window, pulling me from a feverish half dream in which I am incapable of rising from my bed, my limbs frozen like felled lumber, chest heavy with a weight as if a thick, snaking chain had been draped atop me. When I do finally wake, the clock on my night stand stares at me: past ten in the morning. I shoot up, rocketing myself off my mattress, the sheets trailing after me like billowing shrouds. I turn to the window, and the weight of my dream comes to life, pooling at my ankles.

I scream for Trent, yanking my door open. Before he can respond, I barge through his still-cracked door. The girl is gone, all trace of her vanished except for the cloying, moist smell of sex. Trent is face down, empty beer bottles and two condom wrappers—and their gummy, used wares—arrayed on the floor like a gruesome Christmas display.

I scream at him again. And then again, until he finally groans and rolls over, palms rubbing against his eye sockets. Trent's body is starting to bloat with muscle from football practice, his trunk thicker than mine, his chest two hard plates, the heft of his biceps easy with strength.

But I leap toward him anyway, the memory of his slaps fresh, and my cheeks sting as if he just hit me. That he is naked beneath the blue satin sheet is of no matter to me, and I begin to batter him, whacking him with clenched fists across his temples, knuckles smashing against his shoulders, jabs connecting with his obliques and ribs. He hardly fights back, caving in on himself instead, his groans louder, voice pleading for me to stop. Then he finally roars, hands shooting out and pushing me off. I teeter and fall from the bed, wiping out two of the beer bottles, which leak small guzzles of thick, lazy liquid onto the floor like dribbles of urine.

Trent expects me to lay there, panting and limp and docile, but I think of what I saw outside my window and it stirs a twangy strength in my muscles and I push myself off the floor. I pounce in one springing motion back onto him, but rather than punching Trent, I wrap my arms around him, locking my elbow around the back of his neck, dragging my body weight down by gripping my one wrist with my other hand. I pull on Trent, hauling him toward the window. He doesn't resist, and the sheet falls away. His legs are thick with muscle, rounded where mine have remained thin and wiry, but he offers no resistance as I press him to the glass.

I tell him to look. He squints, groaning when the light hits his face, and I tug on his neck, pushing his nose to the window. "Look," I tell him. "Damn it." My mouth feels like copper when I curse at him.

He blinks and his breathing grows shallow, so I let him go. Normally, Trent would shove me away, puff out his chest like a peacock making a show of his glossary of feathers, but he blinks again and again, laying his hammy hands against the glass.

"I hope it was worth it," I say and march from the room.

In the hallway, my stomach clenches, a nervy quease that has been bubbling beneath the surface of my rage, and I let out a cry.

Filling the pitcher is pointless, but I do it anyway, especially because this task—such a simple thing, a minute or two's commitment—is all Trent had to do. I want him to enter the kitchen and see the ease, the smallness of it, its breezy effort. But he doesn't appear, not even when the pitcher is full, threatening to overflow into the grimy sink. I tell myself I will not scrub the metal basin no matter how crusted with slaked off crumbs and smeary sauces it becomes, because Trent creates plenty of those messes and never cleans them and it is time for him to learn what life is like: hard, and gritty, and nagging.

I push open the kitchen door and am hit by a blast of warm air: an unseasonably frying day, the sun a blistering pearl in a sky the color of a chlorinated pool. The grass waves, in need of mowing, another chore I banish from my list of tasks, along with vacuuming and scrubbing the bathroom sink and hauling bloated bags of garbage to the curb. All things Gretchen and I have done ever since our parents died five years ago.

We received the news of their death from a phone call; I'd always assumed such information was delivered in person, on rainy nights like the one on which our father, having drank too

Joe Baumann

much at an office party, barreled through a metal rail and dumped their car in a ditch, where it crumpled into a stand of trees, the imploded engine and wiring and other guts pinning them both. Instead of a droopy police officer gripping the brim of his cap in his hands greeting us with a heavy, unexpected knock on the door, the phone rang, and Gretchen, the only one allowed to answer when our parents were out, was the first to hear.

I stand before Gretchen's place in the garden and dump out the water, but I can already tell it will do little good. The water is only four hours late, but the bark on Gretchen's trunk has already gone a stale brown like a hard crust of bread, leaves drooping with a pinkish-beige tinge, several of them fallen in a splattered ring around the tree's base. I do not reach out to touch Gretchen's pebbly, brittle skin for fear that it will begin to slake off, that I will be raking away my sister's gasping, thirsty body.

Trent makes loud, thrashing footsteps as he kicks through the grass and stands beside me. He offers no apology. He says nothing. His breathing is ragged.

"Will she be okay?" he asks, reaching out his hand. I slap it down and glare at him. My grip on the pitcher tightens, and I picture myself clubbing him with it, blood pouring from his ear. He deserves it for this betrayal, this sloppy mistake.

Once, I sat outside and listened while my father gave Trent a throwing lesson. He was kneeling before my brother, arms around Trent's ankles, shifting his feet just so through the grass.

"Everything is about balance," my father said. "The slightest shift can change everything, send it toppling over or setting it true. Success is in minutiae." He stood, patting Trent's shoulder, and ran to the other end of the yard. A few minutes later, as they continued throwing the ball, I went inside, where Gretchen and my mother were baking cookies.

I shake my head and drop the pitcher, which rolls and bumps against Gretchen's tangle of parched roots like a boat nosing a dock. Trent does not follow me, and I look through the kitchen

186

door's porthole of a window as I lock it behind me, as I will soon lock the front door and all of the first-floor windows. I leave the kitchen, not looking back, the last image of my brother his head bowed in meditation and regret.

Shrinking

My parents' house is shriveling, like a burning strip of paper or a cashmere sweater that has been tumbled in a dryer.

I first noticed when my mother asked me to come over and help with their taxes. She was taking an apple pie out of the oven, and when she set it on the counter, I leaned over to smell the tartness that made my jaw tingle, and I smacked my head against the frying pan hanging overhead.

"Fucking shit," I sputtered, rubbing at my forehead. My mother clucked at my language. "Since when have these things hung so low?" She shrugged and handed me an ice pack the size of a dollar bill.

—

"No, no," my father said, waving a hand at me as though he was casting a spell. "Everything's fine, I'm fine."

This, two days after he'd rear-ended someone while approaching a stop sign.

"Just a bit of misjudging distance and speed and all that," he said, adjusting his glasses. He looked presidential in an ancient way, like someone you'd see on paper currency or in a gilt-framed oil painting. We were sitting in his study, he behind the oak desk he'd had since before I was born, I crammed into a high-backed chair that had once felt like an expansive, squishy ocean but now had the give and space of a baby's high chair.

"What's wrong with all the furniture, Dad?" I said, tossing a leg over the side of the chair.

"I don't know what you mean."

"Everything's smaller."

He squinted. "Are you feeling okay?"

I cleared my throat. "Is the car damaged? Will your insurance go up?"

He waved me away and shuffled some papers. "They didn't even call the police." The forms in his hands, too, had shrunk, the pulpy life sucked out of them.

———

My parents were shrinking along with the house. They called me over for dinner, a thank-you for dealing with the taxes as well as the calls from the insurance company that flustered my father and left him twisted and turned about what forms he needed to fill out (none) and who he needed to call (the body shop). When I tried to sit down at the kitchen table, I couldn't fit my legs between the chair and the table.

Neither of them noticed, slipping into their seats like perfectly aligned puzzle pieces.

Mom had baked a chicken, and my portion—a leg, plus nearly half the breast—looked like the plastic food that would come with a child's kitchen play set. I looked from one parent to the other; they were awash in their mashed potatoes and green beans—mine resembled matchsticks—and didn't seem to notice that they, and everything around them, were smaller.

"You okay?" Mom asked as she took a sip of water from a cup that looked right in her hand but whose equivalent was shot glass size in my own.

"Uh, yeah."

"You're hardly eating."

I wanted to say that was because I had hardly any food, but I glued my mouth shut and ran my tongue over the backs of my teeth.

"Everything's great, Mom," I said, picking up the drumstick. She watched me, her eyes slitted like a snake's. I took two bites of chicken and all the meat was gone.

"We need to talk about Dad's driving."

Mom sighed through the phone, a mist I could almost taste in my mouth.

"Really, Mom. Two fender benders in two weeks."

"It was raining, and you know how hard it is for him in the rain."

"I think he can't see."

"I know, but—"

"And has he been to the audiologist yet?"

"He missed the appointment. He said he didn't need it."

"But you have to practically scream at him in the morning to get up. He doesn't even hear his alarm."

My mother was silent long enough that I had to ask if she had hung up.

"Yes, yes," she said. "But look, I have to go. I have that doctor's appointment."

"Okay, but talk to him. And let me know what the doctor says."

"I will." She hung up, the click echoing like a ringing bell.

Part of me hoped that perhaps I was just getting bigger, even though my last growth spurt was when I was a junior in high school and suddenly none of my jeans fit. My mother was the first to notice, and she tsked at me when I didn't say anything about the fabric of my pants hovering just above my ankles, like I was wearing fishing waders.

"You look ridiculous," she'd said. "We're going shopping after school." I'd been weighted down by so many bags that my arms and back were sore the next day.

But it was clear that it was, in fact, my parents and their house, because the rest of the world was normal size. My car fit in my driveway, but I had to park on the curb in front of their house because my tires dug trenches in the yard if I tried to squeeze onto the concrete; even the grass had been reduced to stalks the size of cat hairs, and I could barely fit my hand in their mailbox to grab the bills.

The day I had to stoop to enter the garage, I called my sister.

"I think you need to make a trip out to see Mom and Dad."

"Why? Is everything okay? Tell me what's wrong."

"They're shrinking."

She scoffed. "Old people do that, Sam."

"No, I mean everything is shrinking."

"Is this one of your jokes I don't understand?"

"No, it isn't."

"What about Mom's blood tests?"

"White-blood-cell count was slightly elevated, and her blood pressure was still high, but nothing the doctor said to worry about."

"Okay, see?"

"I don't think you understand."

"Sam."

"Really, something's going on." I sighed. "Please. Come out? I'll pay for the ticket."

"I do not need you to do that for me, thanks."

"So you'll come?" I said.

"Let me check my schedule."

"Hurry," I said. "Who knows if you'll even be able to see them without a microscope by the time you get here."

She hung up without saying goodbye.

⎯

My sister moved to the West Coast after she finished college, my last image of her a pink hand waving like a stiff streamer out her car window. In high school, we'd made jokes about whether it would be me or her checking in on our parents like nurses watching them grow old. For the longest time I'd been sure it would be her, and for a while, it looked that way: I moved all the way to Louisiana for a graduate degree, while my sister opted for Mizzou, just ninety miles down Interstate 70, close enough that Mom and Dad went out to see her every other weekend for lunch and to play with Wilfried, her dog. But then, when I received a job offer not twenty minutes from my parents' house, and Karen landed a big gig in Portland at a start-up company right in her wheelhouse, the script was flipped.

"See you at Christmas," she'd said, slapping me on the back and giving me a wink as she got into her car to make the trek out. She was taking very little with her, just a carload of clothes, Wilfried, who was worrying a stuffed chicken's head that squeaked at every bite, and Tutu, a beloved stuffed monkey she'd had since birth. My parents stood in the grass, waving until she disappeared down the road.

⎯

"Seriously, Mom," I said. "I don't think Dad realizes how bad of a driver he's become."

"He's always been a bad driver," she said. She was visiting my cat, an impromptu stop after a trek to the mall. I'd thought about giving the bathroom a quick once-over but decided it didn't matter.

"But it's not the same anymore," I said. "He used to deny that he was a bad driver, but he always knew. Now he just has no idea. Besides, we're not talking about being an aggressive driver. He just doesn't, like, see things. Or hear them, for that matter."

My mother sighed and leaned back on the sofa. Here, outside of her house, she looked like my mom again, tall, lean, with only a few wrinkles lining her swannish mouth and neck. I wondered whether it was a trick of the lighting: the early evening sunlight from the patio door, paired with the peach glow of only two table-side lamps, didn't highlight or draw attention to signs of age: droops, wrinkles, spots, and splotches. She had accordioned out back to normal size, as seemed to happen whenever she wasn't in her house.

"What do you expect me to do?" she asked as she was leaving. "Steal his keys?"

"I don't know, Mom. I don't know."

———

While I lived in Louisiana, my grandmother came to live at my parents' house, taking up my old bedroom.

"She doesn't like me very much," my mother told me.

"What?"

"She thinks she could still live in North Carolina. Doesn't have a clue."

"Oh."

"You don't want to hear this," she said.

"Of course I do. You have to tell someone. So tell me."

My grandmother died less than two years after moving into my parents' house, a ghost of herself: her hair shocked white, arms nothing but bones under skin the color of bleached leather. I hadn't been home much while my grandmother lived there— graduate school was a time for being poor, and Louisiana was a long, twelve-hour drive filled with radio stations that were nothing but twangy country music or religious preaching—but my grandmother had become a different person, a mumbling, incoherent whisper of herself. She called me by the wrong name more than once, and she didn't understand what was happening on the television, even when she watched *The Price Is Right*, which had been her favorite for ages. She would mumble, her cracked lips wiggling like hooked worms, her voice a murmur. Everyone ignored her, like she was an expensive vase bought for the price rather than function.

When my mother told me my grandmother had died, she said it like a fact, no different from that the weather had been good or that she'd gone to see a movie with one of her friends. She told me not to worry about coming home; there wouldn't be a service. Her voice was pregnant with relief, and when I saw her next she seemed energized, like she'd slept for days. Her lips were full and red.

———

"Sam, it's your mom."

At first I thought my father was telling a bad joke, which was the only kind he knew.

"You're funny, Dad."

"No," he said, and then there was a long pause. He breathed heavy into the phone, air crackling in my ear. "Your mother's had a stroke."

She was tucked into her hospital bed, resting. The doctor was looking over a chart, making notes, checking his watch. He was young, dark haired, tan as a leather couch, his voice like pulled toffee. He said the stroke was minor, that she should recover with little to no problem, but she might feel some numbness in her fingers and possibly struggle with some aphasia now and then.

"What's that?" I asked.

"She might misuse a word here and there. Say *pencil* when she means *car*, that sort of thing."

"Oh." I pictured my father driving a massive pencil, sharp, down the highway, popping tires like they were balloons.

The doctor nodded to dismiss himself and brushed past me, white coat swishing.

The shape of my mother's body under the blanket was only three feet long, a child's, and I mentioned this to my father, who was sitting in one of those square wood-and-pink-fabric chairs that is never comfortable.

"People always look smaller when they're vulnerable, Sam."

I sat down in the chair next to him. He was curled in on himself like he was collapsing into a single point of light, his bald head heavy on his neck. His size matched my mother's. He held her hand, rolling her skin under his thumb.

He and I must have been thinking the same thing: we were surprised that he was comforting her rather than the opposite. My mother was active and flighty, a hummingbird of activity: knitting, book club, even a small garden with peppers, toma-toes, and a chocolate mint plant that was suffocating everything else. She knelt and stood with smooth ease, brushing off jeans or Capri pants with a smile that betrayed no aging pains; my father creaked, his knees groaning, when he so much as tottered to the bathroom.

My mother came home two days later, and while I helped ease her onto the couch and found the TV remote, she told me to relax.

"I'm not dying, you know."

"Yeah, well." Her body was almost weightless, like a pillow I might thwack against a friend during a sleepover's requisite fight.

─────

"You're really not going to come? Our mother was in the hospital, for goodness' sake."

Karen sighed. "Jeez, Sam, who even says *goodness* before they're fifty? Besides, I called Mom. She told me not to come."

I looked around the cramped kitchen; I could hardly reach the fridge anymore without squashing myself against the center island, and squeezing into a chair at the table was out of the question. I could take the stairs to the second floor four at a time, and my heels hung off them.

"So you're not concerned about our parents' health?"

"No, I am not. Not any more than I have been for years. They're getting old, Sam, that's all."

"A stroke is not that's all."

"Come on, she's not even showing the signs of—what did the doctor call it?"

"Aphasia."

"That. She's doing just fine, isn't she? Can you honestly say you would know she'd had a stroke by looking at her?"

I glanced into the living room. My mother had a bowl of salty popcorn in her lap; her legs dangled off the couch, not quite reaching the floor. She swiped her palm against the nearest armrest and laughed at a joke, lips pulled wide. Dad was in his office; I could have picked up his desk in one hand and juggled it. I was permanently stooped because of the height of the ceiling, and I could see into the second-floor windows if I hopped like I was taking a jump shot.

"Sam?"

"Fine," I said. "Whatever."

—

The walls of my parents' bedroom and the hallway upstairs were polka dotted with photographs, and during my visits after my parents started shrinking, I would slink upstairs and stare at them, my face inches away. I took in my father's sharp hairline, the deep chestnut color of his locks, which had turned gray and lost their tight curve. My mother's cheekbones were sharp, her face smooth. They were both tall in another life, towering over me and Karen in photos from when we were prepubescent, the person taking the photograph having to stand far away. In one such picture, we're all wearing dorky Christmas sweaters, Dad's arm hooked over Karen's, my mother's hand trailing toward the center of my back. We are smiling and ridiculous, my glasses too large and Karen's nose upturned like a pig's; she hadn't sorted out her good angles yet.

I sighed. I wondered whether, given another day or two, it would become impossible for me to enter the house at all.

—

"See?" I said.

Karen had finally come, recognizing a real, deep concern in my voice when I called and pleaded. Our father had dislocated his hip while he was mowing the lawn. Because our mother was still recovering, they'd had to hire someone to help around the house, a woman named Leanne who was just as bite size as they were and who agreed even—without compensation—to take my father to physical therapy. She swished around the house in sea-foam green scrubs, hair pulled tight in a ropy ponytail.

Karen and I were standing on the lawn. She had her hands on her hips.

"I don't get what you're saying, Sam."

"You've got to be joking." The oak tree in the front hardly reached my waist. The entire place had become microscopic, a toy I might have sat in front of when I was six.

Karen looked at me, shutting one eye as though the sun were blinding her even though it was overcast.

"I know that this is hard for you."

"Well, duh. Our parents are—"

"Getting old, Sam. That's what parents do."

"That's not what I'm talking about, Karen."

"Then I don't know what to tell you, Sam."

"How can you not see it?"

"I do see it, Sam." She stepped onto the grass and started to shrink. "You're the one who can't."

I stared at her, unable to follow, as she continued to wilt into a tiny figurine, hips and arms and legs slimming and curling up with each step. "Are you coming or not?" she squeaked when she reached the door. I could have put her in my hand, along with my mother and father, like they were marbles. All I could manage was to shake my head and stare at the ground, at my sizable feet.

"Fine," she bleeped out, and the huff of air she let out was like squeezing everything out like an inflated balloon, a high, wheeling hiss. "This is how things are, Sam."

She opened the door, went inside, and shut it behind her, the sound a tiny clapping noise, like a child excited about the prospect of ice cream.

Glass Hammers

When my mother called to tell me my uncle Rex had died, I first remembered something he used to say when we would watch *Wheel of Fortune*: "Why are Black people always so bad at this?" He said it any time an African American guessed a letter incorrectly or bought the wrong vowel. It didn't matter if the other players had made the same kinds of mistakes, or if the Black person was winning. He also questioned their names—"Never heard the name LaShonda before"—and had things to say about their hairstyles. Whenever he spoke, my mother would glance my way from her spot on the couch—my uncle sat in my dead father's recliner, clutching the remote in one hand and a beer in the other—and sip from a can of Diet Coke that was probably half whiskey. I sat on the love seat, legs tucked up under my feet, and allowed my jaw to unclench only when I solved a puzzle, always figuring out the solution before my mom or Rex, who would shake his head and say, "We gotta get you on this show," as if I would share my winnings with him.

"What happened?" I asked my mother. My boyfriend Berk stared at me from the couch. "Same as Dad?"

"His heart gave out, yes," my mom said, but I could hear it in her voice: *No, not like your father.*

"Do you want me to come for the funeral? Will there be a funeral?"

Berk raised an eyebrow and shook his head to push his hair out of his face, which he'd let grow long. I couldn't decide if I liked it or not, and I had then decided it didn't matter what I felt about it. When I'd said so, Berk thumped my sternum with the heel of his hand as if he were trying to restart my heart.

My mother sighed. "Of course, Danny."

"Of course what?"

"What do you mean?"

"Of course there will be a funeral, or of course you want me to come? Tell me."

Berk, with dramatic flair, threw his head back, tongue sticking out the side of his mouth.

"Do you really need me to tell you that?" my mother said.

"I wouldn't ask if I didn't."

"The funeral is this Saturday. You and Berkeley can stay here."

"Generous."

"Please, Danny," she said, her voice finally cracking. "Please do not make this difficult."

I told her we'd be there. When I hung up, Berk shook his head. He didn't need to say anything else.

———

My uncle was a big man, six-three and over 250 pounds, a diabetic like my father. Like my dad, he didn't take his medication or his diet seriously. Nor did my mother, who served him heaping plates of biscuits and gravy for breakfast and gave him a double portion of whatever entrée she made for dinner: twice the heap of beef stroganoff, a second cheeseburger on a flaky white bun, an extra slab of meatloaf or breaded chicken cutlet. His mashed potatoes towered higher, his ranch-drenched salad—really just iceberg lettuce and shredded cheese—took up extra space on his plate. The only things he didn't expect more of were baby carrots or bowls of raspberries. After *Wheel of Fortune*, he liked to turn on Fox News, which was always my cue to leave the room. When I brought my first boyfriend around, Rex looked bewildered by Tommy, as if he were some kind of extraterrestrial and not the striker for our varsity soccer team, already committed to playing at Texas Christian. Rex asked him, pointing at me, "Has he ever tried to turn you into glass?"

"I'm sure I've told you all of this," I said as Berk drove us across Missouri. The drive from our Overland Park apartment to my mother's home in St. Peters was a straight shot down I-70, interrupted only by Columbia, the roadside dotted with gun-show adverts and billboards for Mizzou and Birthright. We left after lunch on Friday, Berk taking a half day at his engineering job. I burned a sick day at the high school where I taught English, leaving a handful of writing exercises for the substitute.

"No, you haven't," Berk said, shaking his head. "But I'm not surprised."

"I really thought I'd brought it up before."

"You? Bring up your uncle?"

The weather was nice, and Berk had the windows cracked so air whistled through the car. He didn't like listening to the radio while he drove; he preferred to talk. I preferred not to. Yet somehow he managed to make me talk while he listened. Berk had those kinds of skills.

He flexed his hands on the steering wheel, knuckles popping. His lips were pursed, teeth clenched.

"Just say it."

"Say what?"

"Whatever it is you want to say."

Berk shook his head and laughed. "You English majors. Too observant." He looked at me. The road was clear ahead of him, aside from a semi on the horizon. We were rolling past gold fields of grain. "Except, maybe, about yourselves."

"Please don't," I said.

"Gonna turn me into glass if I do?"

"Only if you want."

"We'd probably crash."

In high school, people knew what I could do, thanks to the time I accidentally turned my biology textbook into a block of glass, dropping it as I was pulling it from my locker so that it shattered, spreading across the hall. I'd been angry, as I had to be for it to happen, pissed that I'd forgotten about a math quiz. Plenty of people saw. Some said I was a freak, others that I was a real-life *X-Men* character. But most people ignored me, still, which just proved that once the world decides where you belong in it, there's nothing you can do to change things.

———

Mom met us at the door. She hugged Berk, tapping him on the back and telling him how jealous she was of his tan, then kissed me on the cheek.

I expected the house to feel different in Rex's absence, but mostly the air felt unchanged. Rex had always loomed so large, stuffing himself into my father's armchair, rattling the walls with his heavy gait when he came stomping down the hallway after a bathroom break, his breath and groans loud, wet, sickening. He carried a certain smell, a funk, not exactly bad but somewhere between sweet and sour, like he waited one day too many between showers but still changed his clothes and put on deodorant.

Mom had laid out some afternoon snacks on a cutting board: soda crackers, a soft yellow cheese, hard sausage still in its vacuum-sealed pack. As we walked through the living room toward the kitchen, I glanced at the recliner, which was still in surprisingly good shape for having carried two overweight men through to the end of their lives. I could still see, in the green fabric, the slightest outline of my uncle's rotund ass, as well as the depression where his head lolled when he was drinking and watching TV.

We sat down, but not before my mom offered us beers, wine, water. Berk asked for the last of these, and I nodded agreement. She had already opened a can of soda for herself, which she would have spiked prior to our arrival.

"So what happened?" I said when she sat.

"What do you mean?"

"To Rex."

"I told you."

"But what happened, exactly?"

"Danny," Berk said.

"What?" I looked from him to my mom. "He was my uncle. I want to know."

My mother sipped from her drink, and the tart, wooden smell of expensive bourbon floated across the room. "You don't need to pretend to care more than you do."

"I'm not pretending."

"Are you sure?"

"Pretty sure. But maybe I'm more curious than anything else."

"English major," Berk said in a stage whisper, but my mom didn't laugh.

"He was sitting in his chair," my mom said. She pointed into the living room.

"Dad's chair."

"It's been his chair for a while, Danny."

"It's Dad's chair."

"Fine. Whatever." She drank again, this time long, hard. The can was practically empty when she set it down. "He said his arm felt weird, and then he started breathing, I don't know how to describe it. Hard and shallow at the same time? I called 911." She paused. "But it was too late."

"Sounds like you did what you could," Berk said, but he was looking at me. I reached out and held my mother's wrist. She, along with Berk, was one of the only people who, knowing what I could do and had done before, let me touch her without flinch or hesitation. Her skin was hot, as if she'd just been lying in the sun.

"Sorry you had to see it," I said.

"You should be sorry your uncle is dead."

I had nothing to say to that.

———

After my dad died, Tommy had preferred talking on the phone. He didn't say so, but I knew it was because that way I couldn't turn him to glass. Before the incident with my father, he liked me to tap his fingertips and give them the slightest blue sheen; he would make little jokes about me being gangly and thin in order to juice me up just enough that I could pour that little bit of cool freeze into his body. Once, when we were making out on his bed, he said: "I hate that I have to make you mad. If only there were other ways to make you change things." His fingers were tickling at my waist.

"You'd be glass by now," I'd said. He'd laughed. Later on, we stopped joking about it.

Berk was less concerned and less interested than Tommy.

"That's cool," he said, like he didn't believe me. I told him to say something mean about me. He told me that my haircut wasn't good for my face.

"Meaner," I said.

"Your shoulders could use some work. They're not proportional to the size of your biceps."

I felt a flush, but it was embarrassment, not anger.

"You're not good at this," I said.

He rolled his eyes. "Pardon me for not wanting to make my boyfriend angry."

"I won't stay mad," I said. "I promise."

"But Danny," he said. "You're always mad."

"No I'm not."

We were sitting on my couch. We didn't live together yet.

"It's hilarious you think that."

I felt a small pulse, the tiniest shiver, starting in my hip.

"What do you mean?" I said.

Berk shook his head; he'd just cut his hair, and being able to see his wide open face and forehead all at once was discombobulating.

"You don't see it?"

"See what?"

I could feel it spreading, cresting across my belly button and heading toward my crotch. It was just enough. I grabbed Berk's wrist and could feel it pour through, calcifying the ends of his ulna and radius, the skin there going a hard, almost-clear blue.

"Whoa," he said, staring down. We looked for a minute, and then I pulled it back, his skin returning to its rich tan, the little hairs at his wrist wiry and gold again.

"Did you really mean that?" I said. "About me being angry?"

"Did me saying it make you angry?"

"You saw."

"Well, then." Berk shrugged. I expected him to say more, but he just stared at me.

—

The funeral home was situated on the northern frontage road off I-70, the building long and low and looking more like a country club than a place of mourning, all cream paint and golden sconces, green shutters pinned against exterior walls. The portico gave relief against the heat of the day, which was swampy and harsh for mid-April. My uncle had already been cremated, in accord with his will—"Rex had a will?" I asked over breakfast; Berk slapped my shoulder and my mom ignored me—and the service would be brief: a visitation and a short eulogy from my mother. I had no idea how many people to expect. To my knowledge, my uncle's only friends, if one could call them that, were a group of guys with whom he'd played poker every third Wednesday of the month.

The room where the service was held—all white, just like the building's exterior, almost blinding in its snowy consistency (even the chairs had white upholstery on the backs and seats)—was jammed when we arrived, even though my mom had insisted that the three of us leave the house forty minutes early.

"What the hell?" I said.

Berk grabbed my wrist.

"I'm just surprised."

"You could express your surprise in a whisper," Berk said. People nearby had glanced our way.

The confusing thing for me wasn't necessarily the size of the mourning crowd—of course, somehow, Rex would have a far-reaching net—so much as its composition: not just single, overweight men with unkempt beards and bad haircuts like I'd expected but families, trim couples with two or three kids in matching funerary garb. A surprising number of aloof, single women my age or even younger. I whispered this to Berk as we slid into seats in the front row.

"Maybe," he said, adjusting the knot of his tie, "they're here for your mom."

"Oh. Right. Maybe. I bet you're right."

"Not that it really matters. Maybe people liked your uncle."

"I can't imagine," I said. "I can't imagine why."

"We don't all see everyone the same way, Danny," Berk said. Before I could respond, he laid his hand on my thigh and pressed a finger to his lips.

The memorial was, as expected, brief. My mother said a few words, none of which I really absorbed. She wasn't shaky or slurry, nor did she shed any tears. Her voice reminded me of the hardness I felt whenever I was angry, whenever I could turn something—or someone—into glass.

My dad died three months after I accidentally transformed him. The service, like Rex's, was brief, nonreligious. That day, the sky was annoyingly bright and cheerful, thick braids of light shafting through all of the windows in our house. My mother hadn't wanted a reception, but Rex insisted. People came armed with casseroles and beer. When they left, they told her not to worry about getting the Bakelite dishes back to them any time soon. Months later, when my mom finally did return them, she hadn't bothered washing a single one.

I thought my uncle had left with some of my father's buddies to go drown their grief in Miller Lite and pool at a smoky bar, but when I headed toward the hall bath to pee, the door opened and suddenly he was standing in front of me. I backed up against the wall, banging my head against a family photo. He and I had not spoken at the service, and I'd spent every moment we were in close proximity since my dad's death avoiding him.

He glowered at me. "What's the matter?"

I swallowed but couldn't speak. I looked away from him, adjusting the photo I'd bumped into even though it was already level.

"Look at me," he said. When I didn't, his hand shot out and grabbed my jaw, his thumb and forefinger gripping me tight, sending shocks of pain up through my gums and teeth. "I said, look at me."

I stared at my uncle. He and my father had the same bone structure: prominent cheeks, a hard, wide nose with nostrils that were perpetually flared, giving them both a dragonlike look. My uncle had thicker eyebrows that gave him a caveman vibe, though where my dad's eyes were green, his were the color of ice. Or glass.

"You may have everyone else fooled, but not me."

"What?" I said, but it came out garbled, my jaw trapped by my uncle's hand. He let go.

"You say it was an accident. I know better."

"It was an accident," I said. "And I didn't kill him."

My uncle huffed. "Whatever you have to tell yourself."

I felt it then. The iciness slithered up my body like a snake was chuffing through my bones. Rex must have seen something shift in my eyes because he softened and leaned back. I didn't dart out a hand to grab his wrist or to push my palms against his chest or shoulders, but I did cantilever forward just so. Just enough for him to wince and step back. He let out a growl of noise but then shoved past me, careful not to touch me as he went.

I told Tommy about it, and he offered to come over, having skipped the funeral because he needed to take the ACT. I tried to turn him down, but he showed up anyway. My mom, caved up in her bedroom, didn't notice the caul of the doorbell or our footsteps as we shuffled into my room. Tommy said nothing, and instead, as soon as the door was closed, he started kissing me. I was still wearing my shirt and tie, the latter of which he started to unknot.

"What are we doing?" I mumbled, his lips still mashed against mine.

"Quiet," he said, tugging the tie away from my collar. "You need this."

"Need what?"

He pushed me onto the bed and straddled me. This was new. He was wearing athletic shorts and a plain white T-shirt, as if he'd been on a basketball court instead of hunched over Scantron sheets for the last four hours. I could see the outline of his erection through the mesh of his shorts.

"Now?"

"Stop talking," he said and unbuttoned my shirt. His hands, when they found the plane of my stomach, were hot. Or maybe, I thought, I was just very, very cold.

Berk and I waited while my mother accepted condolences. We stood in the funeral home's lobby, which looked like some kind of LA mansion, a pair of staircases swooping down from a second floor on either side crowning another viewing room straight back from the building's entrance. Bouquets of chrysanthemums and gladioli stood on half columns.

"I guess you can tell who's who now," I said.

"What do you mean?"

"Rex's friends all left without saying a word."

"Maybe they already said what they had to say."

I raised an eyebrow. Berk shrugged.

"Maybe they wrote. Or called."

I scoffed. "Not Rex's type."

Finally, my mother freed herself from her friends. She was still clear-eyed, and she huffed up to us, letting out a tired breath. "I could use a drink, yeah?"

We drove to a nondescript pub: oak bar top, heavy chairs that offered no lumbar support, too many beers on tap to choose from. My mother ordered a whiskey and diet soda, Berk a sour ale, me a hefeweizen.

"To Rex," my mom said, holding up her glass. She blinked at me. Berk's foot poked my ankle.

"To Rex," I said.

The bar was mostly empty, a few men slumped over shots of gin or whiskey at the other end. The bartender, a thick-necked guy with tattooed knuckles in a black T-shirt a size too small, leaned against a cooler, rubbing at a spot on the bar.

"Funeral?" he said.

"My uncle."

He nodded. "Sorry for your loss."

"Thanks," Berk said. His shoe was still digging against my foot. I felt a small flare in my chest, but I made sure to touch only my glass, because what else could I do to it but let it be what it already was?

———

We drank too much, our bodies matching the slump of the men at the far end of the bar as the hours dragged on and the seats around us filled. When my mother asked the bartender whether they served food, he offered us a platter of onion rings and toasted ravioli on the house, which we ate with reckless abandon, fried dough and spiced meat mingling with the beer and booze slough-ing in our stomachs. My mom shouldn't have driven us home, probably, but it was still light out when we strode out of the bar, the early-evening sunlight playing tricks on our drunken vision. The trek was only a few miles, and my mother held her hands tight around the wheel at ten and two, her head pitched forward, eyes squinting.

"I need a nap," she said as we walked in through the garage. She tossed her purse on the recliner and then stood staring at it for a long moment, Berk and I flanking her like sentinels.

"It's so empty," my mom said. Berk put his arm around her before I could. He looked at me. I looked down at my fingers, then threaded them through my mom's. She gripped mine tight, goug-ing her fingernails into the backs of my hands. Her skin was warm, her cheeks flushed. I wanted to cool her down, but I had nothing inside me that could do anything but make her feel way too cold.

⸺

"This is where I did it," I said.

Berk was sitting on the edge of the bed, the old twin I'd slept on throughout high school replaced by a queen. The bureau and writ-ing desk were still in their respective corners, the latter still home to the trinkets and toys I'd collected as a child—crappy things, like an inflatable baseball bat I won during a trip to Six Flags—and the walls were still their same cerulean blue. Berk was pulling his socks off, one leg beveled over the other.

"Where you did what?"

"Ruined my dad."

Berk patted the bed beside him. When I sat, he rubbed my shoulders.

"Tell me."

"I've told you before."

"So what? Tell me again."

We'd fought, in the living room. I'd asked my dad if I could get a job at a restaurant or a department store or something. He'd been sitting in the recliner at the time, and he shook his head and said he wanted me to focus on school. I'd begged and pleaded. I had some money but not much, just whatever I'd managed to save up keeping score at basketball games at the middle school where he taught sixth grade. My parents were hardly rich, but they didn't worry about paying their next bill. My dad took pride in this.

"If you need something, we can buy it for you."

"But what if I want something?" I said, which yielded only a shake of his head and a demand that I get my history grade up—his favorite subject. I had an eighty-nine average.

He turned his attention to the television, where some terrible action movie we'd seen a million times was reaching its climax. He rocked back and forth, unaware of the hardening happening under my skin, the familiar built-up calcification of my innards blooming far and wide, stunting my ears and filling my fingers and toes. I felt like I was made of stones too heavy to move, but I did move, stomping past him and huffing out teenage anger in a miasma of meaningless sound. I slammed my bedroom door, which I knew would make him angry.

"You have a way about that," Berk said, fingers digging into my shoulder blades. "You know how to make people mad."

"Is it that I make people mad or that I'm mad?"

"Little bit of A." He tapped my side. "Go on."

"Do I have to?"

"This will be cathartic."

"For who?"

Berk cleared his throat.

My father had let me stew for a while, probably thinking that it would ease my temper. Instead, I spent twenty minutes staring at the popcorn ceiling and then at the posters lining my bedroom walls—Albert Pujols; the cover of *The Great Gatsby*; Ryan Adams's *Heartbreaker*—and then the ceiling again, blank and white and giving me nowhere for the chilling, heavy anger to go. When he knocked and called my name, his voice gruff and flat, I threw myself off the bed. He opened the door without me saying anything, which made me only more upset, and he was halfway in the room when I grabbed him by the shoulder and let it all pour out. The release was swift and painful, like I'd been punched in the stomach. When I let go, he teetered and nearly fell, but I managed to grab him again, my breathing hard and labored. I concentrated, the anger slucking back up my arm and out of his body, which returned to its cool peach color, my dad's arm hair and mustache freed to waver. He blinked at me and gasped, eyes wide. That night, I dreamt that I hadn't caught him in time, that instead he had shattered into millions of pieces, his clothing a limp dressing covering a wound that would never heal.

—

I could never sleep after drinking craft beers, their fruit flavors, bourbon infusions, and various floral notes burbling in my stomach. I woke at three in the morning, mouth dry. My fists were pressed against Berk's back, which was slick with sweat in the rivet of his spine. He was snoring, his breathing wet and liquid. I slipped out from beneath the sheets, which stuck against my waist and tried to knot up against my ankles. Berk snarfled and rolled over onto his back but didn't wake.

On my way to the kitchen I stopped at the door of my uncle's room. When I pushed it open I expected my mother to be inside, but it was empty. You'd think I'd have felt his presence among the mess—clothes dripped from the bureau's drawers, old sports magazines and *Playboy*s slid from its top; the nightstand was cluttered with a bottle of men's Vaseline lotion, an old alarm clock blinking the time in hard red light, a darkened metal lamp with adjustable, snaky bulb—but I just smelled the must of unwashed skin and heard the tinkling settle of things that haven't been touched. My mom hadn't mentioned what she would do about his stuff, and I hadn't asked.

The living room was sliced with moonlight that cut through the window blinds. At some point, my mom had moved her purse from the recliner, which seemed gargantuan in the dark, a throne.

I sat.

The material was warm, like bread just baked. I put my forearms on the plush side cushions, dug my elbows into the fabric. When my dad died, I had refused to sit there, though sometimes I would stand behind the empty chair and rock it forward and back, wishing that it were my dad and not me moving it. I tried, several times, to turn it to glass, but whenever I looked at it all I felt was sorrow.

But that night, sitting there, starlight flickering off the black of the television, the walls kaleidoscoped with moonglow, I felt a well break inside me. My father was long gone, and my uncle was too, and that meant it was my turn in the chair. I dug my fingers into the polyester, feeling the threads against my nails.

I was full of poison. My lips were chapped. My head throbbed. It took nothing to spool it out, let it snake out of me like water from a hose. In no time the chair changed; I felt it underneath me, the glassiness spreading like a fast-moving frost over the surface of a pond. Beneath my thighs the material went cold and slick, slippery and smooth. I stopped rocking for fear of breaking it.

Because I didn't want to break it. It would have been easy—so easy—to lean back and crush the chair with my hips, my shoulder blades, the strength of my triceps. I could have used gravity to tip it, send the chair falling over, let it shatter beneath me, pierce my skin, cut me to ribbons, embed into my spine and bones and muscle, dig into all of the tight, sprung parts of me. But instead I stood and turned around, stared down at it like I was looking at the glossy surface of a lake. I saw my dad, I saw my uncle, I saw me. I saw the sorrow of my mother. I saw Berk. I saw all the things I'd fractured. How easy it would have been to leave it that way, to turn away and walk into the kitchen for the glass of water I was desperate for and then to slip back into bed, to leave with Berk in the morning, to leave my mother.

I leaned forward, one hand on each arm of the chair, and drew it all back up. I felt bloated, like a cow in need of milking. Like Santa's sack as he headed out on Christmas Eve. Like I might finally be able to hold onto something without letting all of it crack out of me, edges bursting, bristling. I might sink, but I would at least take no one else down with me.

We Are Rendered Silent

When I was eighteen, the man my mother loved died. She and I were standing in the kitchen, a bright, airy space thanks to the open floor plan and bay window in the breakfast nook. My mother was stirring a pot of risotto, steam rising toward her face, as she told me about the pottery class she was taking on the weekends, when her voice simply stopped. She turned to me, eyes wide, and cupped her throat with her free hand. I was sitting at the kitchen island and felt my stomach flop.

But then my father came home from work as usual, his arrival signaled by the growl of the garage door. I stared at my mother, who stared at me. We both stared toward the kitchen door.

———

As early as third grade we were prepared. Most of the instruction went to the girls, because, our teachers said, they were the ones who would lose their voices. What, we asked, about the boys whose fathers died or their best friends or grandparents? Our teachers shook their heads and said, "That's a different kind of love."

It would happen immediately, whether you knew about the death or not. Love, its absence, was like that: striking, hot, sudden. The loss, our teachers said, could not be stopped.

We were taught American Sign Language. The girls needed it so they could express themselves, the boys so they could listen. We were separated by gender, the girls given advice for going through life mute, the boys taught how to handle the silence of their wives. I was too young to know, exactly, that I might love another boy one day, but something gnawed at me as I watched the girls march to a different classroom. When they came back, I yearned to ask them what they'd been taught. But even when I figured out I was different from my classmates, I kept my mouth shut.

———

My mother's eyes were teary when my father started yelling, his voice crackling and scratchy.

"Tell me the truth," he said. "Tell me who he is."

But my mother just shook her head.

I should have left the room, but I was pasted to my chair like the risotto soldering itself to the saucepan. A burning smell filled the kitchen, and eventually my father's exhortations were interrupted by the bleat of the smoke detector. He turned away, leaving my mother to solve the problem of the alarm, and disappeared into his office upstairs. I listened to the noise of his stomping footfalls and watched my mother's silent, heaving sobs; I could see her shoulder blades pike in and out as she took in hiccupping breaths while she fanned her hand near the smoke detector. I pulled myself down from my stool and went to the sliding door leading to our back deck and drew it back and forth. Finally the noise stopped, and the house was dazzled in an eerie silence. My mother looked at me with relief, her eyes bloodshot. I could see the desire to say something on her face. Her hands remained on the lip of the countertop. Her silence, like that of the whole house, was deafening.

———

By eighth grade, I was terrified of losing my voice. One girl in our class, Miranda, had already gone silent, though none of us knew who had died; her parents and teachers were concerned because she was so young. My classmates hounded her, demanding she write down a name, but she sat on her hands and refused to pick up any pencil or pen shoved toward her chest. Seeing how my peers swarmed at her like angry insects jostled worry inside me, particularly because I'd been harboring a crush on Timothy McNaulty, who sat in front of me. He had a gentle laugh and kind eyes, and he always turned around to work with me in math class when our teacher gave us worksheets. Most of the time I said little, not because I didn't know how to solve the problems but because I was worried I would say something stupid. Already I'd managed to take away my own voice.

———

My father left for two weeks. He came barreling downstairs while my mother and I were eating a pizza. We'd each barely been able to swallow down a single slice, and when my father appeared at the foot of the stairs with a rolling suitcase, the cheese had already gone waxy, lakes of orange grease congealed in the bowls of sliced pepperoni. My mother, of course, could say nothing to stop my father. My own throat was scorched dry, and so we both watched from the breakfast nook as he dragged his luggage across the hardwood, the wheels letting out a sustained screech. When he slammed the door, the sound echoed through the room. My mother looked at me with sorrow on her face, her cheeks still damp. She had offered no explanation, no identification. I didn't press; I had my own secrets, too.

———

The first boy I kissed was not Timothy McNaulty; he moved to Kansas City after eighth grade. In high school I tried out for the boys' volleyball team because the coach were desperate for players and I was tall. I discovered I was good at blocking and a decent server, so I was put on the varsity team even though the coach had to spend tons of time teaching me how to approach the net and read the opposing setter. Despite the ragtag way the roster was filled, we managed to gel and perform well, better than our basket-ball and football teams, and we started drawing crowds, especially when we reached the district playoffs. Rumblings of a state title started to wend their way through the halls. I became popular, people I barely knew trying to edge their way into my orbit. Rather than feeling like I was at the top of the high school pile, I was terri-fied that someone would discover the secret of my wants.

Kenneth Woodrow was our setter. He was lanky, had good hands, and was committed to Cal State Long Beach. When we won the state championship our junior year, he threw a party for the team, rife with cheap beer and spliffs of weed. Kenneth had fed me the ball on championship point, a perfect thirty-two set, his jump pulling away their outside blocker so I had a one-on-one net, an easy put-away. He'd been the first to grab me in excited victory, his sweat-slicked arms tangled in mine. His face had been close, hair greased with perspiration, but he smelled sweet. I'd held on tight.

At the party, he found me in a corner slowly drinking my nasty beer. Kenneth's eyes were glossy and his limbs were loose. When he practically yelled my name, he poked a finger at my cheek and then rested his hand on my shoulder.

"You, sir," he said, "are a stud."

My face was hot. I smiled.

"Seriously, dude," he said. "Pro material."

He nearly tumbled over. I reached out my free hand to help him balance, pressing it against his left hip. Kenneth glanced down at my hand and smirked, then tilted and swiveled so he stood next to me, hip to hip as if squaring to set up a block. But then he leaned up and kissed me on the cheek. Before I knew what was what, he had managed to turn my face toward his, and suddenly our lips met. Kenneth's mouth tasted of beer, tangy and metallic. His lips were sticky and slick. The kiss didn't last long, and no one else seemed to notice, or they were all too drunk to care. When Kenneth pulled back, he was grinning. Saying nothing, eyes hooded with half sleep, he wandered away. In the following weeks he said nothing about it, though I remembered the taste of his saliva and the warmth of his breath. I wanted to ask him why he'd done it, what it meant, but just as he kept quiet, so did I, and soon enough it was as if it never happened.

Every afternoon while my father was gone I came home to find my mother staring out the window above the sink, eyes squinted as if she were trying to read something in the clouds. She would turn to me, gesture toward the pantry and fridge. I would shake my head; my appetite seemed to have vanished like my mother's voice.

I scoured local obituaries from the day she lost her voice, staring at the names of dead men, reading their life stories captured in bite-size chunks, wondering whether any of them were the man my mother had loved. Of course, proximity meant nothing; he could have moved across the country, or to Europe or South Africa, and searching global deaths brought up too many names. I finally gave up and tried to instead imagine the kind of man my mother would want, but all I kept seeing was the kind I wanted: someone soft spoken and tall, richly voiced, with strong arms but gentle features.

Eventually my father came back, and we existed in a stony silence, as if the loss of my mother's voice had spread like an infection. We ate dinner together, but the only sound was the scrape of our knives and forks. My father was always first to leave the table, holing himself up in his office. Sometimes, after helping my mother wash the dishes, her passing me bowls and spoons one at a time, the only noise the slosh of water and the tinkle of soap bubbles bursting, I would slip upstairs and stand near the door of his office, listening. I could never hear a thing.

By the time my mother lost her voice, I'd kissed two more boys, both of them in hidden dark corners, secret moments that no one else saw. The first was a server at the restaurant where I found a job bussing tables during the summer; he invited me to his apartment one Saturday night. We sat on his couch eating Doritos and playing video games, and in between rounds of Halo, he set his controller down and looked at me, a ring of cheesy dust around his lips. He kissed me, unprompted; I kissed him back. He had gelled hair and strong fingers that rested on my forearm like the claws of tiny birds. But then, a few weeks later, he was fired for knowingly serving alcohol to underage kids, and I never saw him again. I found out just as I clocked in, and I was sure I wouldn't be able to speak, but my voice appeared as I cleared away a table's detritus and someone nearby asked for a refill of their water. The second kiss happened at my senior homecoming dance, in a dark hallway near a bathroom of the labyrinthine reception hall. Music was pumping, and lots of kids had snuck pulls of vodka before arriving. A soccer player stumbled into me as he lost his way to the bathroom and he kissed me hard before wandering away. I stood in stunned silence, wondering what it was about me that signaled to these boys that I wanted them to kiss me, and what it was that sent them away immediately after, and what it was that kept them silent after the taste of their lips had long faded.

Right before I left for college, my parents sat me down and told me they were divorcing. My father, of course, did all the talking.

My mother nodded and looked down at her hands, folded as if in prayer. She could have written something down, scribbled notes of defense, but instead she stared at her fingers. To my father's credit, he did not place blame. His voice cracked, and his eyes watered, and his hands, at one point, gripped the edge of the table so hard I wondered whether his fingernails wouldn't crack. But he kept his cool as he explained that sometimes these things happened. That relationships weren't what you thought.

I wanted, then, to say something about myself. To tell them about my crushed longing for Timothy McNaulty and my kiss with Kenneth Woodrow, whom I'd watched on television win the national championship for Long Beach just a few weeks ago, crowded by his teammates in a dogpile at the ten-foot line. Or about my dreams and fears and wondering what it really meant to lose something, or to simply feel lost.

But when my father asked if I had any questions or anything to say, I shook my head. He nodded and left the table. So did my mother, who pressed a hand down on my shoulder as she walked away. I sat there for a long time, no words coming to my throat, no thoughts passing through my lips.

———

At a grungy frat party my freshman year of college, I found a drunk boy in a white T-shirt and ridiculous cargo shorts who kept staring at me from across the room, his plastic cup obscuring the lower half of his face. With enough liquid courage swirling in my belly I introduced myself, words slurred, body loose. He apparently lived in the house, and with no more than a handful of words shared between us, he took my hand, guided me up to the house's second floor and, in his dark bedroom, pulled off my pants. The room smelled of stale cheese and marijuana, the funk of dirty clothes hovering above our bodies. My senses were dulled by the beer, and for a brief moment I paused, felt the tiniest tinge of regret: did I want this first moment, this first dive into real physicality, to be with a stranger, to be tamped by the fact that I was sloshy with alcohol? I'd learned all about consent, and I wondered, briefly, whether I was doing something I didn't want to do.

He smelled of sweat, and even in the grim darkness of his room I luxuriated in the lean musculature of the frat boy's body, of his curly brown hair, of the earthy loam of his groin and all of the heat and hardness there. Once we were atop his mattress he had nothing to say and neither did I. He took me in his mouth and the most I could do was let out a groan and, later, return the favor, pretending I had any idea what I was doing.

He fell asleep shortly after we were finished. I lay on his bed, dazed, unable to sleep, unsure if I was supposed to sleep: did he expect me to be there when he woke up in the middle of the night to pee or vomit? Would we go to breakfast, or at least awkwardly trade phone numbers? Would we pretend nothing had happened? What had happened? What had it meant to him?

The room was dark. It teetered and spun just so when I sat up, careful not to disturb him. I felt stupid and silly climbing around him, stumbling across a pair of old running shoes when I managed to get to the floor. The party was still going on—I could hear the muffled, underwater-sounding noise of music and laughter—but I managed to slip down the stairs and out a back door, unnoticed.

I never learned his name. I never went back to that house, and I never saw him again. It was a story I wouldn't ever tell anyone, burying that first encounter deep in my memory, sealed away like a prisoner sentenced to life in a grim hole. In a way, that momentous thing was its own silence.

Several years later, I told my parents, one at a time. I sat with my mother in the breakfast nook, as if we had no other place to arrange ourselves in a house that felt echoing and empty without my father present. It took me several tries to speak, but I did, finally. And once I started, everything spilled out: my crush on Timothy McNaulty, the secretive high school kisses, Kenneth Woodrow. I left out the nameless frat boy. Though unable to say a word, my mother stared at me with a level, open gaze, her eyes wide. She nodded several times. When I was finished, I half expected her to share her own secrets, to let the story of her slain love out into the open, fingers and palms and gestures telling the tale that words no longer could. But instead she stood and quietly grabbed me in a hug, her hand tapping my back in a code I couldn't break.

My father, in his condominium, smiled and said, "I was wondering if you would ever tell me." His nonsurprise was a surprise to me, but I asked him no questions. He went about his business after that, cleaning up from the breakfast he'd cooked for us: sausage and gravy and biscuits that broke open soft and steamy. Once again, I couldn't think of a thing to say, struck as I was by his seeming prescience and awareness.

By then I'd met men who had lost their voices. I'd read about them online. Schools had started teaching boys how to live with their own silence, a wave of curricular reform that seemed to sweep through primary and secondary schools in the immediate wake of my departure therefrom. I was glad for this, but I felt the slightest, tartest regret and recrimination: if only someone had thought sooner about us boys, the ones who might quietly fear for their own lost voices, maybe I would have taken less time to articulate my wants to my parents. By then I'd had boyfriends, some serious, some not, all of them hidden away from my mother and father all because I had no idea how to share with them who I was. The words had spent so much time stuffed down my throat, choked like a terrible clog in an old drain.

Joe Baumann

I never did learn who took my mother's voice. When she died in my late thirties, of a brain aneurysm that had been lurking but never detected, she took that secret with her. I asked my father, after her funeral, if he had any idea. It was the first time I'd asked him any questions about it. He had gone gray, and his posture was a little stooped, but he was otherwise a spry man in his early sixties. He had not remarried.

He took a long, deep breath. We were sitting at the breakfast nook, him in the same spot he'd been when they told me about the divorce. He hadn't been in the house in years—he moved out, into a smaller condominium that I visited a few times a month until I left for college, and then my appearances were sporadic—but he fit right in.

"Your mother was complicated," he said.

"So you didn't know who he was?"

"Would it make you feel better if I did?"

"I have no idea."

He patted my arm and stood. He was staying in the guest room, finally cleaning out his office, which had remained a tomb of his books and old tax documents after the divorce. My mother, too, had never remarried, but I was never sure if that was because of the loss of her husband or the loss of the man who took her voice.

My father lumbered off to his office to mull through his abandoned papers. I stood and went into the kitchen and grabbed a glass from a cabinet; I still knew where everything was because my mother had not been the sort to rearrange. She may have upended our life in one way, but she had been a woman of routine and sameness otherwise. I drank, staring out into the dark of the night, unsure what to think or say to myself. My eyes hurt from crying at her funeral, and my stomach was empty. My throat was scratchy, my body achy with grief. I couldn't believe I could still speak, even

226

though I knew that mothers, wives, and girlfriends did not take voices with them when they died.

I heard a floorboard upstairs squeak and thought I should go find my father, offer him my help. But instead I stood where my mother had when her loss had left her empty and silent. I shut my eyes, thinking of my own silences, how one day, if I was both lucky and not, someone would demand so much of my heart that they would eventually take more than that. That the loss would be so great, so stripping, that I would be hollowed out so deeply. Or maybe I would die and leave someone else without words. Which would be better, I couldn't decide. I drank down the rest of the water, letting its cold shock expand through my throat and chest, letting it grab everything hard and raw and flush it away. I opened my mouth to scream, but nothing came out. I filled another glass and drank it, too, listening to my body as it passed down my throat, imagining all the sound inside, all that rumbling and endless noise. So much noise.

Keep Your Last Breath Close

I

Chantal's last breath was the most secure of the three, kept in a tightly screwed, emptied-out Burt's Bees tin the size of a half dollar that her father had soldered to a gold chain she kept around her neck. Every year on her birthday she sat before him, his beery breath cascading against her throat as he wheedled extra links on with a splicer and joining tool. Max kept his in a pepper-spray canister looped on his keychain. When he asked his parents why, they laughed and said they'd been young idiots—"Probably high, too," Max liked to add—and had thought it would be quirky, weird, memorable. They had emptied the canister in the backyard of their little bungalow, thinking that being outdoors would prevent their eyes from watering, but they failed to take into consideration the frenetic Midwestern wind and found themselves crying and coughing and laughing until the spray was gone.

No one talked much about Holden's, especially not around his parents, who didn't like it. They believed that one go at life was enough, so they had not extracted his last breath when he was born. He'd had to fork over several months' worth of allowances to have it removed, and he could think of nothing ideal to put it in but a black fanny pack that he won as a door prize at the eighth grade's field day. Chantal and Max always rolled their eyes when he emerged from his house, the fanny pack slung low on his hips, a horrible accessory whether they were going miniature golfing, to a movie, slumming around the mall, or sneaking into a party. Holden would offer a sheepish smile and shrug as they piled into Chantal's car, Max always skipping ahead so he could claim the front seat. Holden, patiently and without complaint, climbed into the back, his long legs folded up so he felt like a crumpled paper crane, the fanny pack pressing against his stomach.

———

The trouble was, Max was in love with Chantal, who was way too tall for him. Chantal was in love with Holden, who was her height and played outside hitter for their high school's state champion boys volleyball team, his lean arms and narrow chest struggling to fill out his billowy sleeveless uniform but excellent at crowding the net and finding seams in the opposing block. When Chantal met up with Holden and Max, it was always the former she threw her arms around in greeting first, the Burt's Bees tin kissing his chest.

But Holden was in love with Max.

No one knew that the reason he sat behind Max in Chantal's car was so that he could stare at the back of Max's neck, where narrow corded muscle strained when he talked and turned his head. No one knew about his furtive glances toward Max when they all went to the park and Max, a kicker on the football team, tore off his T-shirt, revealing nascent abdominal muscle and strong pectorals. More than once Chantal complained about Holden and his ubiquitous sunglasses, playfully flicking at the lenses, demanding he let everyone see his gorgeous baby-blue eyes. Max would always flinch at the compliments and flirtations she sprayed at Holden, and they made Holden's stomach churn because he hated knowing that, with every word of praise Chantal heaped on him, he went down in Max's book as a rival, when all he wanted—all any of them wanted, of course—was love.

———

It happened on a sharp night when they were on the cusp of eighteen, one of those October days where the sky smells of dried corn, fallen leaves, and wood smoke, fireplaces lit for the first time in months, flues expelling all their gunk into the sky. A day when desperate barbecue freaks fired up their grills one last time and the maples and larches and bald cypress flashed red and yellow, the privets and dogwood turning gangly. They'd caught wind of a rager being held in a ramshackle barn owned by the parents of the starting tight end for the football team. Max pilfered one of his mother's boxes of Franzia from the storehouse she kept in the basement closet. He'd started drinking on his own, when his parents left for some fancy ten-course dinner at a new French restaurant where a reservation had to be booked three weeks in advance and not a single dish was larger than a soup ladle.

"I'd much rather be with you guys," he said, tongue sloshing over the words as he spilled into the passenger seat of Chantal's car. Holden liked drunk Max; something about intoxication made him more handsome, as though the loosening of his tensed musculature revealed some deeper beauty, adding a grace and depth to his dark eyes, his mouth falling open in a warm O.

The party was down a rural route without any streetlights; Chantal missed the turn, hidden away behind tufts of overgrown scutch grass, twice. The barn was half-collapsed, as though a bomb had gone off and blown out its rear wall and part of the roof. But the interior, minus its missing rear wall, through which whooshed chilled autumn air, was cozy. Wing-backed chairs with torn leather arms sat around towering heat lamps, and a mahogany bar was strung with paper Chinese lanterns whose light twinkled against the glass bottles. Someone had painted the three standing walls a warm cream color and erected larger versions of the same paper lights in the barn's corners. The space smelled of pumpkin, apple, and cinnamon. Teenagers were clustered in small circles throughout the barn.

"Let's get something to drink," Chantal said. She took Holden's hand, pulling him along as she skipped like a gazelle toward the bar.

They drank for what felt like an eternity. Holden, with each slurp of the strong rummy concoction Chantal produced, felt his body stippling with sweat. They managed to snag seats at an aloof cluster of chairs, the frayed leather broiled to a soft warmth thanks to a nearby heater. Chantal sat between Holden and Max and kept adding more rum to their cups from a bottle she'd pilfered from the unwatched bar. With each pour, the liquid Holden slurped became more fiery, and he resisted the urge to sputter and cough every time he drank.

An hour later, Chantal declared her intentions to dance. Max was quick to rise in agreement but Holden begged off, shaking his head, the dim world around him spangling. "I think if I do that I might puke," he said. Chantal blinked at Holden but said nothing, and off they went. Holden set his cup down and leaned back, waiting for his friends to return.

Twenty minutes passed. He needed to pee. Holden slipped out the gash at the back of the barn and relieved himself, leaning his head against the rough-hewn side of the building. Somewhere in the field behind him a cluster of kids laughed at something. He zipped up quickly.

He found Chantal in the middle of the throng, cocking her hips as she filled her cup. Holden asked where Max had gone.

They scrambled out of the party to look for him, passing kids smeared with sweat and smelling of Bacardi. Holden could see bangles holding last breaths dangling precipitously on drunk wrists. One girl who kept hers in a small vial stored in a satchel she wore constantly thrown over her left shoulder was grinding her pelvis against the crotch of the captain of the football team, who was known to stuff the tiny Tupperware container holding his in it into his letterman jacket's left front pocket.

The wind had picked up speed, cutting across Holden's face and drawing wet, hard tears from his eyes. He couldn't see Max anywhere. The field between the barn and the highway was dotted with cars and small groups of partiers, their hands fisted around cups, heads tilted in toward one another. On the hood of a Honda Civic a couple was making out, a belt buckle clanging as it was unhooked. Two girls were spinning in the high grass, their arms wide like propellers. They knocked into each other and fell down, screeching with drunken joy.

When Holden called out for Max, there came no response.

All of a sudden the night exploded with light and noise: a burst of police siren, then the political blue and red of swirling, erratic light. At first, Holden thought the cops were en route to kill the party, but then he heard the distinct whine of an ambulance.

Chantal's breath caught. Emergency vehicles shot past the gravel drive leading to the barn and then slowed less than a quarter mile down the highway, their fearsome light leaking through the gaps between trees, shimmering and rocketing like an alien signal.

———

Holden didn't burst past the EMTs and firefighters and police officers. He didn't cradle Max's broken body, hit by a car when he stumbled into the road at the exact moment a Volvo came around a tight curve and slammed into him. He didn't look Max in the eye and will him to life. This was not a movie, nor was Holden a star.

But he did manage to shriek out the location of Max's last breath. Holden had to yell several times before he got someone's attention. The medics were already sidling Max onto a stretcher, his neck wrapped in a bulbous stabilizing brace. As he shrieked

233

about Max's car keys, Chantal blubbering next to him, he watched the EMTs stop. Holden gestured toward Max's pocket.

They found the keys. Holden watched as they aimed the pepper spray toward Max's mouth and pushed the trigger. At first, nothing appeared to happen, but then Max's body shook. His eyes opened; in the gleam of the emergency lights, Holden could see how wide and wild they were. Chantal's grip on his arm tightened. Holden felt stars flood his vision, but he stood strong. His eyes locked with Max's, which then slid toward Chantal. She loosened her grip on Holden and waved at him, Max's right hand giving the same feeble gesture in return.

They dashed to the hospital, one of the EMTs spitting out their destination before climbing into the ambulance's cab. Chantal drove down the highway, boozy vision be damned, and seared into the emergency room lot.

They waited and waited.

Chantal's face was streaky with tears as she tapped one foot on the puke-green linoleum.

What a terrible color for a hospital, Holden thought. Better than red, he supposed.

"I never knew," she said.

"What?"

She looked at him. "I never knew you felt that way about him."

She reached out and grabbed his hand. Her fingertips were cold. "You don't need to lie, Holden." He could hear the desperation in her voice. "Or pretend. Please don't pretend. Not now. You can tell me the truth."

Holden looked down at Chantal's wrist. It was delicate and thin, the bones poking out on either side like tiny wing nuts.

"How could you tell?" he said.

"Oh, it was easy. When you were screaming, I could tell."

Holden reached up toward his throat with his free hand. He was proud of his throat, its length, the graceful, lean muscles there.

"How?"

She leaned over and engulfed him in a snug embrace. "Oh, Holden. Because you yelled for Max exactly how I would yell for you."

2

Five years later: college graduation on the horizon, a harsh January that dumped twelve inches of snow on the hard Missouri ground, cars drizzling down streets at the slowest of speeds, suburbanites not bothering to traipse out to shovel their driveways out of fear of twisted ankles, bruised knees, broken hips. Holden was off in Champaign, Illinois, finishing up his English degree while Chantal and Max had stuck around at University of Missouri–St. Louis and Saint Louis University, respectively. They were freshly engaged. Holden was happy for them, though he felt a sharp point of suspicion: he'd never told Max how he felt, and Chantal had promised, at the hospital, that she would never say a word. After the accident, she started to siphon her attention away from him, pouring it into Max, who, after having to waste his last breath so young, became cautious and brooding.

Chantal lived on a side street off Cherokee. The string lights from a corner restaurant twinkled through the blizzard that was cooking itself into a frenzy as Holden mushed his way through the accumulation to a latched gate camouflaged in a wooden fence. Chantal's apartment was on the second floor of a converted house, accessed by a slick iron stairwell that curled up to a side door. Holden gripped the rail as he made the narrow ascent, convinced with every step that he was going to take a murderous tumble backward and break his neck.

The door opened as he was about to knock and Chantal stood before him, armed with a glass of wine.

"Your hair," he said.

"You like?" She pawed at the dark mane that had, as long as he remembered, been wheaty and light. Chantal was wearing a loose pink blouse, low cut so that the Burt's Bees tin shined against her sternum.

"It's different," Holden said.

She frowned. "I'm going to take that as a compliment. Now come inside. And drink this." She handed him the glass and closed the door behind him. Holden was dumped into a narrow galley kitchen, the appliances new but the countertops old stained laminate. Several corked bottles of wine were gathered behind a cutting board where three blocks of cheese—Havarti, Gruyère, La Tur—were still half-ensconced in their shrink wrap. Somewhere, a scented candle gave off the aroma of lilacs.

"The celebration is underway?"

"Well," Chantal said. "We started two hours ago."

"The weather slowed me down."

She leaned in to peck his cheek. "Of course. Safety first, as we all know." She gave his fanny pack a rap. Holden had gotten in the habit of keeping it tucked against his left hip instead of centered beneath his belly button. "You haven't changed at all, have you?"

He poked at the Burt's Bee's tin. "Speak for yourself."

"At least mine is stylish. Mum and pop still antiresurrection?"

"Pure as ever."

She rolled her eyes. "After all that's happened."

Two years ago, Holden's father had been in a car accident, T-boned at a slick intersection at the top of a hill by an F-150. The truck had slammed into the driver's side, fracturing his father's skull and breaking several ribs. He was nonresponsive when EMTs and firefighters carved him out of the swirled wreckage, and they barely managed to resuscitate him the old-fashioned way. He'd lost a bit of mobility in his left arm but was otherwise all right after a long bout of physical therapy.

"Please," Holden said. "They view it as a sign that they're doing things the right way. The natural way."

"Natural, huh?" She smirked and looked him over. "Interesting. Follow me."

The kitchen opened into a combination living room and dining room that was tiny but cozy thanks to the decor and furniture that Chantal had chosen: a single sectional sofa, fuzzy brown microfiber, that was curled around a circular, glass-topped table on which a trio of electric candles gave off warm light that one might find in a romantic French or Italian restaurant. The walls were covered in framed art, and the single window was dressed with purple drapes, nearly transparent in their wispiness. A single bookshelf held thick novels, classics like *The Grapes of Wrath* and *David Copperfield*, a smattering of knickknacks—a carved wooden elephant, a jewelry box, an unlit Chinese lantern— serving as bookends. A hallway led, he assumed, to a bedroom and bathroom.

Five other people were crammed onto the couch, including Max, who stood and gobbled Holden in a bear hug.

Over the years, Holden's feelings toward Max had waned. The night of the accident, something had broken in Holden when he thought, despite his last breath, that Max might die. In a quick snap of a moment, his desire for his best friend had suddenly fizzled from a hot spike down to a low simmer, and each time they'd seen each other over the past half decade—mostly brief sojourns during the summer or holiday season—a little bit of the bubbling water of desire had boiled off into vapor. Now, it barely registered in the back of Holden's throat, something ghostly and gone even though Max, despite coming so close, was not.

"It's good to see you," Max said when they separated. His eyes were shiny, but Holden couldn't tell if that was thanks to too much wine or the dim lights. "How was the drive?"

"Harrowing," Holden said.

Max smiled. "Of course you'd say it that way." He turned to the four strangers on the couch. "We have an English major in our midst. Watch your subject-verb agreement."

Titters of lazy laughter came from mouths drizzled in darkness.

"Here," Max said. "Sit. I'll introduce you."

Names washed over Holden in a quick waterfall of sound. Chantal appeared with a bottle that she sent around the group, everyone taking a refill.

"So," one of the friends—Paddy—said when their glasses were full and sloshy. "You're the one with the fanny pack."

Holden looked down.

Chantal was crammed onto the end of the couch, balancing on the armrest, her legs sprung out so they sat on Max's lap. "I've always told Holden he should have gone for something more stylish." She tapped on the tin.

"I like it," Paddy said. He was leaned back languorously on the sofa, his legs bunched in the space between couch and table. His hair was curly at the ends, licking around his ears. Holden liked the acid green of his eyes. Paddy stood and excused himself to use the restroom. Holden caught sight of a flash at his ankle where his pants rode up: a little bracelet with a small vial attached, banging against his sock. He saw Holden staring and offered a friendly smile, revealing crooked but blazingly white teeth.

Chantal turned back to Holden and asked about Illinois. "Seeing anyone?"

Holden blinked at her. She took a sip of wine and blinked back. "Not at the moment."

"The ever-bachelor, huh?" Max said.

When Paddy returned, his little vial clanged against his ankle when he vaulted over the table. As he settled back in his place, popping a throw pillow in his lap and balancing his dwindling store of wine atop it, he seemed to be staring with failing surreptitiousness at Holden. He was good looking, as tall as Holden but a little wider in the shoulders. His nose was a straight downward arc, ending in the slightest of hooks angled floorward, but this was a feature on his face somehow rather than a flaw. His eyes were wide and deep. When he caught Holden giving his appraisal, he licked his lips.

"Who needs more wine?" Chantal said. She removed her legs from Max's lap and passed around the bottle.

"Don't worry," she said. "There's more where that came from! Hope no one plans to drive tonight!"

She disappeared into the kitchen, and as they listened to the shifting of bottles on the counter, they heard her crash to the floor.

———

The diagnosis was an embolism caused by a blood clot.

The hospital was dank and quiet, the floors in the waiting room slick with dragged-in slush. The ride to the hospital had been silent and tense, filled with alcohol-tinged breathing and the swish of coats rubbing against one another in the back seat. In the waiting room, Max paced, unable to sit still.

"Thank goodness for the breath," the doctor said when he appeared in the lobby. He tapped at his sternum. "We administered it, and she should be okay. She'll need to see her physician about warning signs and lifestyle changes to hopefully cut down future risks."

Max nodded dumbly, then said, "She's only twenty-two."

The doctor offered a grim smile. "I know."

"We're getting married."

"Congratulations. You'll get to do that still."

Holden closed his eyes. He didn't like hospitals, with their overly cheerful smells vomited out from wall plug-ins and Pine-Sol and steel canisters, as if potpourri and sanitizer-laced water could subdue the odors of death and gore and illness.

Chantal was led out by a nurse who kept one hand on her shoulder until Chantal was safely in Max's arms. She was dressed in the same blouse, and seeing her bare sternum was a harsh punch in Holden's stomach. Their other friends surrounded her, but Holden remained seated, listening to their comforting whispers. She nodded through their consolations, clearly only half listening. Eventually she looked past their heads to Holden. He smiled, but he could feel the falseness, how desperately covered in hopelessness and fear his grin was. Holden remembered the last time they were all crammed into an emergency room, waiting for Max to pull through. How so much had spilled out of him then. This time, he felt dry already, used up, his ability to feel sorrow and salvation an empty well. He thought of his father, life teetering on the precipice in the absence of a second-chance salve, how that harrowing moment had felt so displacing and discombobulating. Holden shivered. Paddy, sitting next to him, patted his arm, squeezing the bones. He smiled, and Holden felt the slightest stir of warmth.

3

"We're seeing good improvement in language, but we still need to work on her social skills. The bathroom is still an issue."

Holden nodded and shifted in his seat. The social worker's office was tiny, he and Paddy hemmed in by bookshelves. The room smelled like cabbage and tuna fish. The social worker placed her hands on her desk, pushing them down on Mona's file.

"I know it's hard," she said. "But you really have done well. We're seeing progress. There shouldn't be any significant barriers to permanent adoption."

Holden felt a tingling between his ears and could hear Paddy exhale. Between their chairs, their hands found one another.

"Now," she said, "there's one other matter that I know we wanted to discuss."

"Her last breath," Holden said.

The social worker, Donna, was an older woman, in her fifties probably, but her job and its ravages had set her looks forward at least ten years. Crow's-feet ate at the edges of her eyes and lips, and her neck was wattled. The backs of her hands were arched with veins and liver spots. She wore a pair of reading glasses when she reviewed Mona's file; they otherwise hung from a chain, nestled at her sternum like Chantal's Burt's Bees tin. When Holden scanned her, he wasn't sure where, if anywhere, her last breath hid. Maybe she'd used it. Maybe she'd never been given it.

Donna cleared her throat. "As with most children in the system, her parents didn't bother having the procedure done when she was born. Mona is young enough that it won't be invasive, but the state still considers it nonessential."

"So we would pay for it," Paddy said.

"That's right."

"We want to do it." Holden glanced at Paddy, who nodded. They had discussed this the night before, after Mona finally fell asleep, following a rigmarole of three bedtime stories plus a bit of playacting with her favorite pair of stuffed monkeys, Oot-Oot and Minkey. Paddy had been the one to bring it up when they slid into bed, the sole of his foot pressing against Holden's calf as it did every night. The vial, still carefully snugged against Paddy's ankle, brushed against Holden's skin. His fanny pack was snaked on the nightstand next to his alarm clock. When Holden was on the cusp of sleep, Paddy said, "We should ask about her breath."

"Yes."

"I think she should have it."

"I do, too."

And then they'd slept until about four, when Mona's howls woke them. She'd wet the bed again, a problem she'd suffered ever since she was a toddler—she was now five and a half—when her birth parents regularly left her locked in a bedroom for eight, ten, twelve hours at a time with no way to relieve herself without wallowing in her own excrement.

Donna smiled but crossed her arms. "Okay," she said. "We'll only have to wait until the final adoption hearing. Technically, until you're her permanent legal guardians, we can't grant you the authority to make that decision."

"Three months," Paddy said unnecessarily. The date was circled on the wall calendar in Holden's office, and the notice was held up on their refrigerator by a magnet, the date in thick, bold letters, underlined thrice in red pen.

"I'm sorry this is such a long process," Donna said. "But it is what it is."

They stood and shook her hand. Her skin and bones felt brittle, but her grip was hard. She reminded them of the date of their next appointment, one week before the final adoption hearing. "Just to get our ducks in a row."

"Quack, quack," Paddy said. Donna cupped her hands at her waist, a series of charms clacking together. Holden wondered whether maybe one of them held the power to bring her back to life.

"Jesus," Paddy said in the car. He rubbed his temples with his index fingers.

"The headache still?"

"Yeah." Paddy reached into a coat pocket and pulled out a travel-size bottle of ibuprofen and uncapped it, swallowing down half a dozen pills dry. "I've never had one like this before."

Holden felt both hot and cold. He drove straight to Mona's school, he and Paddy having agreed they would take her out early today. The adoption process was atrocious, so many complications and fences and stoppages. First, the Catholic agency that they'd heard good things about was cagey; they didn't say so out loud, but Holden could tell it had to do with two men wanting to raise a child together. Then they were stuck with a social worker who wanted them to take on a sibling pair, an idea that actually made Holden ill. He suffered a bout of severe heartburn; it was so bad he had to go to the hospital with constant chest pains. Paddy requested a new caseworker, and thus they landed Donna, who worked some kind of magic to plop Mona in their arms for a six-month fostering period filled with weekly check-ins and a bevy of paperwork.

The school was a long, squat building, all brick and opaque windows. Holden had to be buzzed in by an administrative assistant. He waited while Mona was called down. When she appeared, the assistant handed Holden a clipboard with a form to sign. She asked to see his ID, smiling as if to say, "I know, I know, but protocol." Then she waved at Mona as Holden took her hand and led her outside.

Paddy was lurched out the passenger's-side door. Holden froze when he saw the puddle of runny vomit on the asphalt. He picked up Mona and held her so she wouldn't see, then he ran to the car, her body thumping against his, her loose foot kicking at his fanny pack.

Sometimes he wondered whether his parents weren't right about letting go. Having watched Max and Chantal teeter on the brink and return, Holden felt like he was living through a melodrama, a breakneck script written by someone who thought action equaled substance. Death had become cool and distant, on the other side of a wall. But he still felt spikes of fear every time, the chill of its umbrella blocking out the sun.

Paddy's foot felt different against Holden's leg with the vial gone, his ankle cool and bare, a little spike that dug into Holden's calf with pleasant pressure. But each touch brought back the fiasco that was chemotherapy and radiation.

"A last resort," the oncologist had said of Paddy's last breath.

"This sure seems like last-resort territory," Holden said at the end of one of Paddy's sessions. Paddy's hair had fallen out; he'd lost weight. His shoulders were slumped, his eyes funneled by dark shadows.

But the chemo didn't work; the mass in Paddy's chest didn't get smaller. The doctors opted for an immunotherapy treatment that required him to stay in the hospital for three weeks. His thighs withered away. He complained of pains in his lower back. He missed going running. He had managed to get to Mona's final adoption hearing, which had gone as smoothly as possible, neither of the birth parents showing up unexpectedly to make a last-minute claim to parenthood. The judge had granted the order, and the few strangers in the courtroom had clapped. Holden and Paddy, who managed to hide the difficulty with which he had to walk and stand, shook Donna's hand, and they walked out a family.

Holden brought Mona to visit the hospital, when they were allowed. They had to wear little face masks and wash their hands until they chapped and cracked.

And in the end, the doctors still had to administer Paddy's last breath.

"We can't guarantee remission with this," the oncologist said.

"I know," Holden said. Paddy nodded. Mona hid behind one of the visitors' chairs. "But what else can we do?" He took Paddy's hand, ran his fingers over the ridge of his knuckles. He knew his whole body, front, back, top, bottom. He knew where calluses formed on the pads of his feet when he went hiking, how his palms, just beneath his fingers, were hardened and blistered from years of lifting weights to create the arms and hips that Holden relished still, every day.

And so Paddy was saved. Every three months he was subject to blood tests and a chest X-ray. The first was tense and terrifying. Holden's heart pounded with such pace he thought he might pass out. But the doctor said everything looked good. Then at six months, the same. And now, at nine months, another appointment cleared, celebrated by shipping Mona off to Holden's parents for a night, which Holden and Paddy—who had finally recovered his body and his hair—spent going nowhere except to bed.

4

Holden's father died of a heart attack, gasping for the air as his mouth pulsed and his vision spangled; at least, that's how Holden imagined it the day of the funeral. His mother peeled away the single tear that rolled down her cheek. She gripped his thigh and smiled at him when he stood to give a eulogy that, afterward, he could not remember a single syllable of. It felt strange to Holden, experiencing real, unalterable grief for the first time.

The years flushed quickly after that, Mona sprouting from five to ten and then fifteen, her own last breath, eventually excised quickly and painlessly, kept in her own little silver tin, gifted by Chantal and Max upon Mona's adoption, flashing in the sun when she ran on the soccer field she fell in love with. And then she was, like a sucker punch, packing off to University of North Carolina to play midfielder. Paddy's cancer never returned; he suffered a stroke at fifty-three. Holden was desperate to unzip his fanny pack and dump the breath within down Paddy's throat even though he knew that was not how it worked. He hated the feeling of loss that cascaded over him, the absences that he experienced one after another, his empty house surprising him over and over again in the days, weeks, months after that.

People asked him his secret to seemingly eternal youth as his friends and family fell off one after the other. Chantal: sixty, another embolism, this one taking her down during high tea with other members of the women's auxiliary where she was president; Max: a descending spiral into alcoholism after her death, his liver overwhelmed and seared by cirrhosis when he couldn't manage his own loneliness; Holden's mother, quietly in the dead of night, discovered by Holden when he came over the next day for their regularly scheduled Friday lunch and a sour, cloying smell had filled the house, emanating from the master bedroom. He saw her, prone on the bed, still tucked into the quilted comforter. Holden didn't bother trying to revive her. He called 911 and shook his head when the EMT asked about a last breath. Again he thought about his own, still slung dutifully on his hip, because who doesn't want their mother back?

And in what seemed like only a passing moment, he himself was old, his fingers achy with rheumatism, his lungs working too hard to produce too little oxygen; his nose itched from the cannula shoved up his nostrils all the time. He blinked around rooms that suddenly felt foreign even though he recognized them. Holden wondered about dementia, but his mind was fine. His body, like all bodies, was simply refusing to keep cooperating.

Mona brought home boyfriends, then a few girlfriends, and then a boy who became her husband; he kept his last breath in an empty vodka bottle, the kind they serve on airplanes, always tucked in the front left pocket of his pants, affixed on a small chain that he hooked to the closest belt loop. Holden joked about what it would smell like when the breath was administered; would Mona's husband come back eternally drunk? Mona gave him tolerating smiles when he said these things.

Holden's doctor made a house call near the end, which felt antiquarian but kind of him. He told Holden that there was no particular diagnosis for his creakiness, his exhaustion.

"You're advanced in age."

"A kind way of calling me old."

"The term is technically *geriatric*."

"That sounds so sterile."

The doctor smiled and patted Holden's shoulder.

He could feel it coming, days later. A fit of coughing wracked his chest. Mona ran in from the living room; she'd been sleeping in the guest bedroom, refusing to leave him alone.

"Dad," she said. Her voice was buttery. She'd never smoked a single cigarette as a teenager, and Holden thought of this as one of his and Paddy's greatest victories.

"Sweetheart." His breathing was shallow. He could feel his pulse in his throat, hard, fast, fading.

"Is it time?" she said. Her eyes rolled to the nightstand, where his dutiful fanny pack lay. Its black top layer had long flaked off, revealing a knitted white pattern beneath. It reminded Holden of a mangy dog. The zipper, he suspected, was welded shut after so many years.

"It is," he said, but as she reached for it, he added, "though I'm not sure for what."

"What do you mean? You want me to use it, don't you? Tell me what you want me to do. Please."

He smiled at her. He thought of Max, the night of the party. Of Chantal. Paddy embroiled in IVs and heart rate monitors. Of all the mothers and fathers he knew who had been on the precipice of leaving but came back, only to go again. His own life was filled with lives and people he knew and loved and wanted and needed, lives he'd seen returned only to have them dragged away again.

Holden rolled his neck, turned his head toward his daughter, and told her what to do.

ACKNOWLEDGMENTS

First, I owe a huge debt to my incredible editor Marisa Siegel, who not only saw the promise of the stories in this collection but guided this book into its final iteration with kindness, grace, and dedication—this project feels as much yours as it does mine, and I am forever in your grateful debt for the work you put into getting this manuscript out into the world.

Further thanks to the many editors of the many journals and anthologies who gave homes to versions of many of these stories before they came together in this collection:

"The Vanisher" *Packingtown Review*

"Veneration" *Bookends Review*

"The Night of Missing Children" *Released*

"Vernix" *Mud Season Review*

"The Time You Give and the Time You Take"
Hashtag Queer

"Lockstep" (as "There's a Lock on the Door and a Key in Your Throat") *Steam Ticket*

"Monarch"   *Superstition Review*

"Three Strikes"   *Oyster River Pages*

"There Is Love Under This Mountain"   *Spire Light Magazine*

"A Tough Man to Love"   *Westerly Journal*

"Gethsemane"   *Eleven Eleven*

"Shrinking"   *The Radvocate*

"Glass Hammers"   *Defunkt Magazine*

"We Are Rendered Silent"   *Reed Magazine*

There is, of course, also a massive village that stands behind me, bolstering me and my work. I have a deeply supportive (if hilariously annoying) family in my mom, dad, sisters, and nieces. My colleagues have been my friends and supporters for years, and I am endlessly grateful for that continued and continuous backing.

And finally, as I mentioned in my dedication, all of the teachers whom I have had throughout the years—you planted creative seeds that have blossomed and (I hope) will continue to do so. Thank you for sowing those in me. What I have reaped is as much yours as mine.